The Highland Witch

KAREN J

D1670606

ISBN: 9781519141811

Author's Note

While this is indeed a work of fiction, it is based in historical fact. In 1296 Scots King, John Balliol, yielded the crown of Scotland to Edward I of England, Edward Longshanks. During the years of 1297 and 1298, William Wallace encouraged resistance to the English rule and defeated Edward at Stirling Castle. After living in hiding for eight years, Wallace was executed. Scotland continued to be a land at war until 1314, when Robert the Bruce defeated the English at the Battle of Bannockburn. Our story begins here.

As for the setting, Castle Lochalsh does not exist, but Loch Alsh does. The areas mentioned such as Cassley Waterfall, Carn Ban (ancient burial site), Corrieshalloch Gorge, Fionn Ben (mountain), Dornoch (a town residing near the Moray Firth on the east coast of Scotland) do exist. In addition, Falls of Shin are quite real as is the Dalchork Wood, and all are wonderful places to visit.

Thomas the Rhymer was born in 1220 and lived for almost 80 years, a great age in that time. The appellation "True Thomas" resulted from his prediction of the death of Alexander III and the Scots victory at the Battle of Bannockburn.

Scottish terms of note are thus:

dirk - a small sharp knife
trews - trousers
leine - linen knee-length tunic with belt
clarsach- small Celtic harp
burn - fast-running stream
haggis - pudding of sheep liver, heart, and lungs
mead - alcoholic drink of fermented honey and water
keek-stane - a scrying surface like a crystal ball, a divination device

... A wall of stone is a gift well said. But within its heart is a depth of dread. With a hunter's speed there comes the song: To claim the gift is to right the wrong...

....Evil in those walls will dwell, Beside the waters Alsh knows well. The red-haired one is hunted then. Beware the circle comes again.

Prologue

THE HIGHLAND MIST swirled as Silobah crept silently through the forest, one hand grasping the reins that pulled her horse uphill behind her, the other tightly clutching her skirts. A golden eagle circled high in the grey skies, its piercing cry slicing the stillness. Lifting her head to catch sight of the bird, she stumbled. With a painful thud her knees hit the ground and she paused for a moment, too weary to move, too tired to gather the reins back into her sore hands. The horse pushed his nose against her shoulder and she shoved back, irritable, feeling every one of her forty years.

The three-day journey had been grueling. She wanted nothing more than to return to sea air and the soft greens of Lochalsh, leaving these jagged peaks, this unforgiving cold, grey land far behind. When she looked up again, the eagle was gone. All that was left were the dark great-limbed pines and spidery wych elms silently standing guard, watching. With a shudder, Silobah got to her feet and wished herself back home, not here, not climbing to find the great Falls of Measach and the sacred Corrieshalloch Gorge, doing Lady Stannard's bidding.

The roar of falling water reached her ears. With a small surge of relief, she hurried forward. Pushing through the trees she froze, staring at Corrieshalloch. The sacred gorge at last. She sent a silent prayer of thanks to the goddess. Holding her breath and holding even tighter to the trees, she gazed down into the vast Falls of Measach, its sheer blue-black rock plunging deep into the earth. Ferns, moss, and sorrel clung to its dripping sides. How could anything live in the cracks of these cold rocks jutting into thin air? A gust of wind blew into the chasm and mist from the falls moved up and toward her as if to draw her closer the edge. Quickly she stepped back.

The branches closed around keeping her safe but there was no soothing her heart. There was no choice, no way out. Lady Stannard would go to any lengths to hide what she had done. It was a horror. A mistake from the start. Silobah had counseled against it to no avail, trying to fulfill the oath she had once sworn to True Thomas. But the strong-headed arrogant Englishwoman had had her way, and a devastating nightmare, a blood-ridden disaster was the result. And now the bairn was to be taken to the high forest and abandoned. The message was clear. Silobah would do as commanded or die. And no matter her choice, it would be death for the days-old child anyway. The least she could do was send it on its way with the goddess watching over its spirit.

The angry caw of ravens snapped Silobah out of her reverie. Looking up for the birds she noted the sky. It would snow tomorrow. If the bairn did not die of the cold overnight then the soft snow would indeed bring its own brand of death. Slowly walking to the horse, emptying her mind of all thought, she reached into the basket and withdrew the bundle. Holding it tightly against her breast she paused, exhaled her grief, then turned toward the falls. Gently she placed her burden on the ground then stood straight and began her prayer to the goddess of the sacred gorge.

A thin wail drifted from the folds of cloth. Silobah trembled, a small rift of fear traveled up her spine. Surely the trees, the very sky heard the cry, boar witness to her actions. The crying became louder and Silobah backed away one step then another, the palms of her hands rubbed down the front of her cloak. Suddenly silence. Silobah paused, and held her breath, staring at the bundle. A tiny hand lifted and batted the air. At the same moment the eagle returned, crying high in the heavens. Terrified, Silobah wheeled about and, gasping for breath, ran to the horse.

Grabbing the reins she fled, stumbling down the hill pulling the horse behind her. Moments later, a small silent figure moved toward the babe.

Chapter 1

1314 Cassley Waterfall, Scottish Highlands

COLIN OF DUNROBIN rode through the forest on his colossal black horse. Silently following on his own huge mount, Arden watched his best friend's straight back. He knew what the set of those broad shoulders meant and he knew well when to hold his tongue, so he contented himself with looking at the terrain. Rugged barren rock, rushing clear-water burns tumbling down mountains and lush green grass made the highlands the only place worth living. Arden shifted in his saddle, tired from the long hours. At least there was a rejoicing in this trip. No bloody Englishman would bother them. Arden fingered the hilt of his sword. But then maybe it would be a pleasure if one did.

His soul still itched for English blood, but for the moment he'd have to be content with the victory at Bannockburn. He and Colin had been instrumental in helping Robert the Bruce chase the English back to the southern border. Exactly where they belonged. The dark-haired Arden gave a grim smile. Hell was where they belonged but no matter.

What mattered now was that Colin had been given the stronghold of Lochalsh as a reward and should be happy. Lochalsh was a beautiful keep. Solid and formidable it faced the great Inner Sound of the western sea; the blue-black waters of the great inland lake, Loch Alsh sat to its back. Built eighteen years ago in 1296 by the English Lord Stannard, it had been part of bloody Edward the First's ravaging of Scotland.

Arden gave another grim smile. The worm had turned, as the old ones say. And now Lochalsh was in Scottish hands, Colin's hands to be exact, and thus the problem. Glancing up he once again considered his friend's straight back. Both Lord and Lady Stannard had died when the castle had been taken. Rumor held that it was the clansmen of Loch Alsh who helped fate along with an arrow to the Lord's heart and a push down stone steps for My Lady. No surprise there. The Lord and his Lady had been greatly hated. But their daughter was spared. And thus, Colin's stiffly held back. It was to this daughter Colin was to be wed. A gesture of kindness, for whom in Scotland would have her. She was lucky indeed to marry the blond-haired warrior with the slicing blue eyes. But kindness aside, it was also a gesture of triumph showing the Scots domination over the English.

"Halt," Colin whispered and raised his hand.

Arden snapped back to the present, tightening his legs to rein in his horse and still its prancing. Colin turned his head back to his friend and quietly spoke, "Someone is hunting."

Arden gave a shrug. Someone could be hunting indeed. These were free forests, unlike those of the English where a man could be killed for trying to feed his family. Silently Colin slid from his horse and covered its muzzle with his hand. Leading his horse forward he beckoned Arden to follow. Sighing, Arden complied. On second thought, it probably wasn't anyone at all. More likely it was a fox or a boar. The faint roar of a waterfall came to his ears. Who in their right mind would climb these rocks to chase a large, angry animal? Arden quieted his thoughts and concentrated on sounds and smells.

"It's ahead. I think it's a boar." Colin's urgent whisper flew back to Arden who arched one eyebrow. Both men reached for their bows. Holding their weapons with one hand they quietly looped their mounts' reins over a pine bough and stalked their prey. A twig snapped. A boar for sure with that kind of weight. Colin and Arden eased up the side of the ridge toward the falls.

A louder snap, then a scrabble of rocks. The animal broke cover, scrambling up the ridge, racing away. Colin gave a shout and charged in pursuit with Arden hard on his heels, up the ridge, slipping on slick pine needles, jumping a fast-racing burn. The rushing water briefly drowned sounds of the animal's escape.

Over the rocks, higher and higher Arden followed Colin, panting, wishing his friend hadn't chosen this way to work off his anger about the marriage. After all, he reasoned while he ran, having to marry wasn't the end of.... he slammed into Colin's back, his thoughts scattering. Stumbling backward he caught his balance and raised his bow, ready to shoot. Colin's back was in the way. Why didn't the man move? He was as still as a stone. Arden yanked his head to the side to see the prey and froze as well.

There, at the edge of the cliff, back to the waterfall, stood a young woman poised for flight. Knees slightly bent, sharp dirk grasped in her hand, leather boots laced up to her knees, trews of dark wool tightly fitting her slender legs. It could have been a boy except for the long red hair escaping its ties, flaming around her fine-boned face.

The threesome stood silent, waiting, watching. Without warning, the lass whirled and darted to the side, skimming the edge of the cliff as she raced downward and away. Colin and Arden watched in disbelief as she disappeared from view.

Colin turned his gaze to his friend, his voice quiet, "Did you see her?"

Arden nodded. Of course he had, but that wasn't what Colin was asking. "Aye, like the lights in the north sky. Here then gone."

Colin snapped his head around, "North lights? Are you mocking that old druid we visited last night?"

"Dinna get angry at me because he told you what you did na want to hear." Arden continued, turning his voice into a mocking whine, "But I want to be a warrior not a laird. I dinna want to marry that wretched lass."

Colin's mouth tightened as he glared at his friend. Arden grinned back, "North lights just came into my head. It means nothing."

Slowly Colin nodded, but his mind was elsewhere. "Did you see her?" he questioned again, "She was like a vision. What was she doing out in these woods?"

"And wearing men's trews," Arden added.

"We could give chase," Colin grinned. Arden shook his head. "We should get back on our horses and be on our way. We are a day late as it is."

Silently the two friends turned and made their way back down the slope to their mounts. Each lost in his thoughts, they continued the journey to Castle Lochalsh.

Chapter 2

ELDEN OPENED HIS eyes and stared into the dark night. The dream was the same as always. He had seen the movements of the woman, how she placed the child beside the sacred gorge, how she wiped her hands as if ridding herself of the deed, how she turned and ran. He sat up. The ropes of the bed rasped with his movement.

"Elden?" A low feminine voice called from the other side of the room. "Elden?"

"Hush lass. It's nothing."

"Another vision?"

"Aye. Another vision," he had no intention of telling her it was a memory dream. "One that shows you too tired to hunt to-morrow if you dinna sleep."

Rowan smiled and snuggled underneath the furs, pulling them up to her nose. Hearing Elden rise from his pallet and add some peat to the fire she burrowed deeply into the pelts. He was up and about. She was safe. With a deep sigh she sank back into sleep.

Elden heard the sigh and smiled himself. Aye she was safe, secure. He would guard her with his life. A frown darkened his brow. Thoughts of guarding her, defending her, saving her had been coming to him more and more of late. He tossed another chunk of peat into the fire then sat beside it, the light playing on his craggy face. A face that matched his body, hard, heavily built, and tough. A body at odds with the man who lived inside of it. A man of visions and dreams. A man who had raised a lass from a bairn to a young woman. And it was this young woman who now worried him. Shifting uneasily, he stared into the fire's glow. It meant something, these thoughts that would not go away. He had

5

lived with his visions and their truths too many years to ignore their appearance now.

Rowan turned over and snuffled in her sleep. A glint of laughter danced in Elden's eyes. Glancing across the room he watched her hair gleam in the firelight. Red. Bright, fierce red. The kind of hair that made no apologies for its color and dared someone to dislike it. Fierce, just like the lass who wore it. He closed his eyes and in the warmth of the room, another woman with hair just as red came into his thoughts. Drawing his knees to his chest, Elden wrapped his arms about them and sat quietly letting the image of his mother come into his mind, wondering if she was there simply as a memory, a warning, or one of his visions.

He frowned. Again, he sensed danger. Staring into the fire's glow he tried to open his mind. Sweat from the effort formed on his forehead but nothing happened. He couldn't make it come to him. He had always been at the mercy of his visions knowing they would arrive when they wanted and leave of their own accord. He could never call them to come. Only his mother had been able to do that. Lifting his hand, he wiped his brow and let his thoughts flow. Fiona, his mother, the highland witch. As he stared into the fire her face formed fully in his mind. He gave a thin smile. Finally, there she was and she wasn't going to leave him alone this night. He settled more comfortably beside the fire. The smoke drifted up through the center hole in the roof, and his mind drifted with it.

***

Cold air made its way past Rowan's nose and crept into the covers bringing her slowly awake. Pulling the furs up higher she let her eyes adjust to the dim light. Dawn. Her favorite time of day. Lifting her head, she saw Elden seated beside the fire, eyes closed, arms around his knees, head bent and resting. So, it had been another night of visions for him. She moved quietly, pulling the furs away. Reaching for her leine, she yanked it over her head. So, what if she wore it shortened to mid-thigh as only men did? She had her leg-hugging wool trews for modesty and besides, she had never worn anything else. The idea of a leine trailing at her feet and fancy leather lacing at her waist filled her with contempt. Holding her boots in one hand and a pelt in the other, she walked softly toward the sleeping man. Stooping, she covered him with the fur then added peat to the fire. At the door she laced her boots and pulled on the heavy wool outer jacket she used when hunting. It would be cold and damp this morning but with any luck she would bring back a hare, a fox. If the gods were with her, perhaps a small deer.

Adjusting the dirk at the top of her right boot she pulled the quiver and bow over her shoulder and started for the woods, her long-legged stride quickly eating up the ground. At the edge of the clearing she stood for a moment, sniffing the air. Anyone seeing her would think she was going to hunt by scent alone, so primitive was the gesture. At least that's what they might think if they could get past the picture of her lit by the morning sun and framed against the black woods. She appeared almost a boy; long slender legs encased tightly in her trews, the heavy jacket enhancing her shoulders, her hair bound behind her. It would only be on close inspection that the viewer might change his mind. Instead of a first growth of fuzz on the chin he would see clear, milk-white skin; instead of heavy hands he would see long elegant fingers more suited for playing the clarsach harp than pulling taut a bow. If the hair were unbound it would cascade down her back in a bright shock of curling red. No. This was no boy, but a female, sixteen years of age on the verge of womanhood, unconscious of her beauty, knowing only that she belonged to Dalchork Wood and to Elden, the brother of her heart.

Rowan tilted her head and listened. The usual sounds of a sleeping forest wakening to a new day were muted. It was unlike the woods to be so silent this time of morning. A ray of sunshine glinted in her eyes. Instinctively she stepped away from the light into the darkness and continued to listen for familiar sounds; a black-throated diver chattering, a red squirrel burrowing under leaves for nuts, a grey fox rustling in the juniper bushes. Nothing. Silently she eased into the woods keeping her slender form in the shadow of birch and pine trees, stepping only where the patchy snow would not show her passing. The deeper she went into the forest, the quieter it became. Bending over, she slid the dirk from her boot and held it in her hand, the bone handle fitting nicely in her palm.

Suddenly she turned her head and took a hard sniff of the air. Smoke. Shrinking instinctively behind a large pine, she sniffed again. The smell was coming from the direction of a fast-moving burn that tumbled down the mountain like a miniature waterfall; one of her favorite places in Dalchork Wood. The sound never failed to sooth her, but today it wasn't the sound that drew her. Moving stealthily, she followed the scent, more angry than afraid. Who was it that dared hunt in her woods, who dared invade the land of Elden the Seer? Her ice-green eyes sharpened and the line of her jaw became firm, masculine, and ready for challenge. It seemed absurd; a young woman ready to threaten hunters with only a knife in her hand and her fierce temper, but Rowan knew no other way. She belonged to the deep woods. After all, hadn't Elden told her that he had found her only days old beside the sacred gorge? When she questioned him about her parents, he said he simply didn't know, and so she grew up believing that somehow, in some magical way, she was a child of Dalchork Wood. And now this child of the woods moved forward on silent feet, ready to defend her home.

The smell of smoke increased and Rowan slowed her pace. Cautiously she approached the clearing and stood, listening for movement. The deep silence of the woods met her ears again. Surely hunters wouldn't still be sleeping. Peering around the tree she scanned the space. It was empty save for a smoldering fire. Looking carefully in all directions and satisfied that no one lingered, she moved forward scuffing at the hard dirt with her boots. Here was where one had made his bed, and another. Moving to the fire she kicked aside the embers, scattering them, watching them flare briefly before death. So, this was the reason for the early morning quiet. The creatures of the forest were no more used to visitors than was Rowan herself. Squinting her eyes, she gazed at the three makeshift beds in the dirt, then moved her glance to the evidence of horses. Uneasiness crept up her spine.

Highland hunters did so on foot. It was unusual to see horses used for hunting this far north. Indeed, the last time she had seen a horse was a year ago, when she had been on a three-day hunt near Cassley Waterfall. Scowling, she remembered the men; the tall fair one who had led the way and the powerful dark-haired one who had followed close on his heels. Was this camp theirs? Could they have ventured this far up into the highlands? The satisfaction that usually came from her morning hunt faded away as she gazed at the clearing, searching for answers. There were none.

Checking that the fire was dead, she eased the dirk back into the top of her boot and went deeper into the woods. Visions of dark figures silhouetted against a gleaming campfire skittered through her mind as she pushed her way through the forest. She rubbed her forehead. The hunt would clear her thoughts. Besides, there was nothing she could do about the intruders now.

Shaking away the feeling of unease, she concentrated on the day's task. Elden would have need of meat. His visions always left him weak and ravenous. The farther she moved away from the campsite, the noisier the birds became. She gave a little smile. Whoever had made camp had not ventured here; had most likely been too scared to go any farther into the deep woods. Unconsciously her shoulders straightened and her chin lifted into the air. She was one of the few who had the courage to travel deeply into Dalchork Wood, a place known for its darkness, its unaccountable happenings, and strange occurrences. After all, she was a child of these woods, was she not?

A sudden rustling in the bushes caught her ear. Freezing into place she became as still as the trees that surrounded her. Listening intently, she eased the bow from her shoulder, then slowly pulled an arrow from the quiver. Quietly she stepped forward, then paused, frowning. An animal would have sensed movement no matter how slight, and either frozen silently into place or run. The bushes continued to rustle. Carefully, Rowan reached out with the tip of her bow and parted the branches. Her mouth turned down in anger. There on the ground, trembling, trying to bite the arrow from its side was a fox, eyes mad with fear and pain. Quickly Rowan moved forward pinning the fox's head to the ground with the end of her bow. Swiftly kneeling she pulled the dirk from her boot and in one sharp movement slit the animal's throat. The fox stiffened, then sagged. Rowan watched the blood pour from him, rage churning deeply inside of her. So, the men who had made the fire were indeed hunters - of a sort. Leaning over the fox she yanked the arrow from its side, giving it a close look. She would remember these men as those who lacked the courage to track their game into the deep woods, preferring to let the animal die a lingering and painful death. Thinking of the two men at Cassley Waterfall, she gathered the fox and bound its paws together. She would take nothing more from the woods that day. The fox was enough. It would feed Elden and not be wasted. She placed the arrow back into the quiver and rose to her feet and slinging the fox over her shoulder and headed back.

Chapter 3

Lochalsh Castle, western coast of Scotland

NAY MY LADY, let me." Silobah raised her hand to take the brush from Gwynneth but was met with an angry twist of the shoulders. Seeing her mistress' eyes harden, the serving woman dropped her hand and edged away. My Lady was no one to tangle with when she was in a temper. Walking over to the bed, she concentrated on arranging the leine Gwynneth would wear for the day watching out of the corner of her eye.

Gwynneth pulled the brush irritably through her hair. Frowning into the mirror, she focused on her reflection. Hard black eyes stared back at her and she narrowed them, concentrating. Her long face tightened, the thin mouth turning down. He had stayed away from her again last night. Not, she shuddered, that she wanted to bed him. Colin, the new Laird of Lochalsh was, after all, a Scot and for that she hated him. She had learned well at her mother's knee about this wild and wretched race; the lowest manner of peasants, living in smoky crofts, eating animal bowels, believing that spirits stalked every inch of the land. Unable to hold onto that land, they were enraged when the English had taken it. But their unbelievable ferocity had won it back, and in the process her parents had died. Murdered, is what she believed in her heart. And then, to her fury, she had been forced to marry Colin of Dunrobin.

Her arm moved faster, catching the brush in her long black hair. Yanking it free, she threw it to the floor. Jumping up she moved swiftly to the window, her gaunt body as full of edges as her thoughts. It wasn't a view of the sea she wanted. It was movement, for movement's sake, and her nightclothes swished against the stone floor.

Thoughts of revenge glowed deeply in her breast, but how could she have it if she couldn't get Colin in her bed? She needed him to come to her, lay with her, get her with a son who would rule Lochalsh. Yes, the babe would be half Scots but also half English. She had no doubt that the superior Stannard blood would triumph. After all, she herself had been born here, raised here, with the Scots influence everywhere and look at her! Her mother had made certain that she had not been tainted and remained true to her English blood. From birth, Gwynneth had seen her mother use the clansmen when she needed to learn about herbs and medicines, had listened as her parents spoke with distain about the villagers, had watched her mother grow stronger, more domineering as her father grew increasingly fond of his wine. Soon, like her mother, she would be the stronger one, and her parents' blood would again rule Lochalsh. All she had to do was get the seed of a son firmly planted in her belly. And then the Laird of Lochalsh could conveniently die.

"Would My Lady like to be dressed?" Silobah quietly questioned.

Gwynneth's jaw hardened, "No. My Lady would like to be left alone. Now."

Silobah moved out of Gwynneth's path, stepped over the brush on the floor, walked to the door and closed it quietly behind her. Standing in the hall, she shook her head at the lass bringing in water.

"Did not come again last night, now did he?" The scullery maid gave Silobah a wink.

"I wouldna know and you know better than to prattle on about such matters. Go on now with your business."

The maid tilted her chin and knocked on the door. Silobah gave a tight smile and walked away. The lass would soon be slinking about, her tail between her legs like a whipped hunting hound. Hounds. Her thoughts went back to Gwynneth and her ill temper. Would the laird use the fact of his favorite bitch whelping at midnight as the excuse for avoiding her bed this time? Silobah gave a small wince, envisioning how Gwynneth would receive that particular news. Behind her came the sound of a crash and the maid's shriek of dismay. Silobah hastened away from the noise. She knew all too well when to stay out of Gwynneth's sight. Hurrying down the long hall she found the back passage to the kitchens and continued her flight down the stone steps, her mind still on Lady Gwynneth. She was becoming the image of her mother.

Silobah's feet paused as her mind envisioned Lady Stannard during that one unspeakable night sixteen years ago. She shut her eyes as if she could banish the image of the witch with hair the color of fire, the sounds of pain and the blood. Shaking the thoughts from her mind she continued down the tight circular steps to the great kitchen.

In the huge stone fireplace, a fire burned brightly under an enormous boiling pot. Hanging above the slops sluice, cleverly fashioned to send kitchen waste sliding down the castle walls, were newly slaughtered doves from the dovecot, heads removed and nicely draining. A chopping table was covered with onions, herbs, toasted oatmeal, minced sheep's lung, and liver ready to be stuffed into a sheep's stomach bag for boiling. Usually, her mouth watered at the thought of a good haggis, but not today.

"And just how is 'Our Lady' this morning?" Sly words came from the corner where Ewan of the Little Head lounged in his chair, tilting back, whittling a piece of wood. The name was a good fit. His unnaturally small head sat atop his thick neck, giving the appearance of a melon picked too soon. Silobah would have nothing to do with him and indeed would like to have him banned from Lochalsh, but he had been a favorite of My Lady since she was a child and was thus untouchable.

Silobah looked sharply at the man and he grinned back at her. "Sorry. How is 'My Lady' after the laird was up all night helping that new bitch with her pups?"

Folding her lips into a straight line, she busied herself arranging the morning tray of bread, cheese and morat, Gwynneth's favorite drink of mulberries and honey. Wisely she refused to be drawn into a discussion of the lady and laird's bedroom habits. She had felt My Lady's wrath more than once, more than twice, and she knew the steward would quote her as soon as her back was turned.

"Here," she said turning and thrusting the tray out to the startled Ewan, "if you're so interested in knowing about Lady Gwynneth you can take this tray to her."

The chair crashed to the floor as Ewan jumped to his feet, holding his hands behind his back. "No." Sidestepping behind the chair he began to slip through the small door leading to the courtyard when the cook walked into the room. The steward paused as Silobah met her old friend's eyes. This cook ruled his kitchen with a heavy hand. A good Master of Food was almost impossible to come by and greatly valued.

Moving to the chopping table, the cook picked up a cleaver and ran his thumb across the edge, testing it for sharpness. "Do as Silobah says." The words were quiet but effective. The cook didn't raise his eyes. He didn't have to.

Glaring at Silobah, Ewan pushed himself away from the doorway. Yanking the tray from her hands, he turned and stalked toward the stairs. Silobah gave a thankful look to the cook and he smiled back at her.

"No day to be going to that room, eh?"

Silobah shook her head no and the cook nodded to himself. It was no great secret. The state of the marriage between the laird and lady was fodder for castle gossip and had been so since Colin had arrived to marry the surly young woman almost a year ago. The sound of a sigh broke into the cook's thoughts. Looking over at Silobah he saw that her round face was unusually pale and lined. Eyes closed, she leaned against the table as if for support. The cook studied her more carefully. Her hair, once so shining and brown had turned almost completely white. Her shoulders had begun to curve to the front as if she were protecting herself. Today she looked much older than her years.

"Silobah?" The cook spoke gently, "I'll make sure Lady Gwynneth's needs are tended to. Why don't you go and rest?"

Silobah looked at him, nodded and smiled. Rest. That's what she needed. It had been weeks since she had gotten through one night without Lady Gwynneth calling her, wanting Silobah to brush her hair, open a window, find the laird. "May the goddess bless you, my friend." she said, and left the kitchen.

Out in the courtyard she slowly placed one foot in front of the other, moving down the dark stone path that crossed the interior square of the castle. Her skirts moved past the flowerbeds, bright bluebells swaying in the air. Primroses, every shade of red and yellow, bobbed their heads. Among the lavender, weeds pushed up towards sunlight. The sea air of Lochalsh was as good for weeds as it was for flowers. The beds, for all of their color, appeared untended. She moved through the herb gardens that she shared with the cook and paused briefly. It was bursting with mint for savories, garlic, and chives for seasoning. Her plants included lady's slipper for calming the nerves and goldenseal to ease pain. She glanced at the adjoining plot belonging to Gwynneth. It too was dotted with weeds. She made a mental note to speak with the weeder women. It would not do for My Lady to see weeds crowding out her figwort. Silobah wondered if the castle women knew that this plant, so valued by Gwynneth, was an aphrodisiac. Most likely they did, and this fueling the gossip surrounding Colin and his bride.

Hearing the cry of a gannet, Silobah looked up past the encircling stone walls. Tall and severe, Lochalsh castle was built for defense, for guarding Loch Alsh and Loch Carron, a critical water passageways leading into the interior of the highlands. This was exactly why the English Lord Stannard had built Castle Lochalsh in 1296 and exactly why it was captured by the Scots eighteen years later. The castle's grey stones gleamed in the morning mist and Silobah let her eyes scan the changing colors. Ignoring the bustle of activity around her she gathered in the warmth of the strengthening sun. "Whoa there. Hold now," the cry came from the stables.

Smiling faintly, she knew a groom was most likely trying to control Colin's huge black war mount. She pulled her skirts aside as two tire-women bustled across the courtyard, linens in their arms, heading for the vast stone laundering tubs. The clang of metal against stone came from the blacksmiths. All seemed as it should be. But Silobah knew differently. Wrapping her arms around herself she continued across the courtyard through a heavy wooden door and entered her rooms.

Lying on the bed, she pulled the wool blanket up to her chin. Thoughts from this morning flew through her head as she drifted off. Silobah wished that Lady Gwynneth did not share the traits of her mother, Lady Stannard of the black hair, the black moods. She twisted to her other side and opened her eyes. The sunlight made patterns on the ceiling as it began to cross the sky and Silobah thought of the old prophecy 'Beware the circle comes again.' Her thoughts flashed back seventeen years to the night Lady Stannard had sent for the witch.

***

"…. I tell you this is what I want," the words were as cold as ice, as cold as the air swirling through the window and circling the room, "and besides, there is no other way. Not one of the clansmen will help me. And that seer, Gylys, is never anywhere to be found."

From her place beside the fire Silobah spoke "My Lady, it is not right."

Lady Stannard glared back, eyes black as coals, steady, unwavering. "And why not?" The tall thin woman fixed her eyes on Silobah, who shrank closer to the flames under that dark hard gaze. *"You think it wrong for me to do?"*

Silobah nodded her head.

Lady Stannard clenched her jaw, the muscles underneath the delicate skin bunched and knotted. Silobah watched the woman as one would a poisonous snake and continued to listen.

"It will cause no harm. I will simply learn from this woman they call a witch and then send her back. And besides, a spell from her will help me bear a male heir. All the gods know the lord is not fit to govern." Lady Stannard continued to justify her desires; *"I do it for all of us. We need protection from these barbaric people. Living in crofts. Wild is what they are."* Silobah shook her head. She was one of these barbarians, and as far as she could see, Lady Stannard was more primitive in her soul than any Scot. Seeing the movement out of the corner of her eye, Lady Stannard's mouth twisted down in a smile. *"Oh, and are we so delicate about all of this? That's not what I have heard. It is said that you know well the ways of Thomas the Rhymer."*

The fire snapped as the wind howled outside of the castle, whipping the stones in its fury. Inside the quiet room Silobah paused. Aye, she knew Thomas, had been one of the young acolytes who served him. Before his death as a very old man, he had called her to his side, speaking of the coming invasion of the English and of the war that would ensue until Robert the Bruce declared victory. He spoke also of a castle that would be built by the English on the inner sound of the western sea near Loch Alsh.

Evil in those walls will dwell,
Beside the waters Alsh knows well.
The red-haired one is hunted then.
Beware the circle comes again.

And so, at the age of twenty, after swearing an oath to True Thomas to avert the prophecy, Silobah was sent to the people of Clan Loch Alsh to live with them as a respected healer and wise

woman and to serve the village seer, Gylys. When Thomas' fore-
telling proved true and the English indeed built castle Lochalsh,
Silobah offered her services there hoping to forestall what
Thomas had predicted. Her thoughts returned to the present and
she answered, "It is true, My Lady, that I knew True Thomas but
only as a friend. I was quite young."

"Old enough to learn his secrets I'll vow," her eyes took on
a greedy glow. "Tell me, how did he foretell the death of your
King Alexander III? How did he know the king would fall from
his horse?"

Silobah kept her eyes on those of the woman, "It is a gift,
these seeings. It is nae learned."

"Do not tell me you learned nothing! I have seen you tend
the herb garden. I know what grows there – lowbush blueberry
to send even a saint into madness and enough bignonia to put
the most stalwart enemy to sleep forever."

"That I learned indeed." Silobah snapped, her voice rising,
"Anyone can discover those things, but to have the green eyes,
the visions, one must be born to it." She bit her lower lip. Too
late. These were the words Lady Stannard wanted to hear.

Harsh laughter erupted. The lady approached and put a long
thin finger under Silobah's chin. Lifting the serving woman's
head, she looked into her eyes. "Yes. Exactly. Born to it. That
was very good. Now let me tell you a thing or two. Thomas the
Rhymer may be dead by many years, but there are others who
not only see the future but can bend it to their will." Silobah sat
as still as a hunted hare.

"Do not give me that look. I want the one they tell tales
about. The one who lives high in the mountains. The one with
the green eyes who is 'born to it'," her voice hardened, "go now
and bring me the captain of the guards."

Silobah stood to speak then bit her lip. There was nothing
she could do but send word to the clan. And even then, who knew
exactly which woman My Lady had heard about and would be

hunting. There were so many who claimed the magic arts and so few who possessed the actual power. The best she could do was wait and watch. Bowing her head, she walked to the door. Lady Stannard walked to the window, smiling into the cold night..."

***

As Silobah dreamed her troubled memories, Gwynneth once again read the words in the leather-bound journal. Clear bold lines of black-inked words slashed across the page of her mother's diary. Shifting in the chair she tucked her feet under her and concentrated... *"I have heard that there is a powerful witch living in the highlands. One who knows of the dark arts. One who can teach me..."* Gwynneth's finger moved as she read the lines. *"...They say she can seed the womb and turn the child from female to male, if need be, that she knows how to divide the night and the day. Many know about her tho' the people of the village refuse to speak of her. But I am decided I will send for this witch..."*

Gwynneth closed her eyes for a moment. Finding the diary after her mother's death had been a gift from the gods. The young woman smiled. Her mother had not sat back and cried at fate. Her mother had not waited patiently. No. Her mother had taken matters into her own hands and had twisted fate to her bidding. And Gwynneth was happily following in her mother's footsteps. Recalling how her trembling maid servant had scoured the village for rumors of seers and witches, and then her midnight meeting with the three rogue hunters Ewan had found, she knew her coins would be well spent her desires met. The men would bring her exactly what she needed. Smiling again, Gwynneth turned the page and continued to read as the castle went about its busy day, noisy villagers coming to and fro. She heard not a sound. Her thoughts were far away with Lady Stannard and the highland witch.

***

"Silobah. Silobah! Wake up!" Yanked gratefully from her dreams and twisted blankets, she heard a fist pounding on the door. "Silobah. Open the door!" The pounding increased. Throwing aside the covers she stumbled to the door and drew the bolt.

The young maid burst into the room and ran into the middle of the floor frantically turning left then right. Abruptly she went as still as a hunted deer, her hands at her face. Shoving the door closed Silobah went to the lass, reached up and pulled her hands away. The old woman gave a gasp then folded her lips together. Holding the maid's trembling hands in hers, Silobah spoke quietly, "Who did this?"

Sobbing, the girl raised her eyes to Silobah's, "All I did was drop the bowl. I did nae mean to, I swear it, but she said I meant to but I did nae." The last words were lost in a wail, but Silobah didn't notice, she was concentrating on the red mark running across the side of the girl's face. Blood trickled from the corner of her nose where the large ring had torn the tender flesh. Silobah's lips tightened in disgust. Tenderly she reached out her hand and touched the maid's nose. There was a yelp of pain.

"Hush. Be still now." Softly Silobah pressed with her finger trying to move the nose back and forth. The girl squirmed and Silobah let go of her hand and grabbed her shoulder, holding her steady. The old woman pressed again. There was no movement. "You can thank the gods your nose isn't broken." The maid's breathing slowed but still she shivered. Feeling the tremble, Silobah softened her voice, "There lass. You are a lucky one but here, she held the shaking girl at arm's length, "Why did you nae come to me directly?"

The girl answered timidly, "She made me stay to clean the chamber."

Silobah gave her a gentle smile and led her across the room, sitting her on the bed. The old woman turned to her healing box. Sorting through the many small pots she found the right ones; goldthread for swelling, pyrola to ward off the putrid drip and woody nightshade to make it smell of power and magic. Mixing a modest amount in a small wooden bowl, she dipped her finger in the mixture and lightly rubbed the honey-colored paste on the maid's face. She spoke as she worked. "Put this on in the morning and before you go to bed at night. Take care to wipe it from your fingers. It is nae friend to the eyes or mouth, but it will keep you from becoming marked."

Under Silobah's gentle hands, the girl ceased her trembling and only the occasional shudder passed through now. One of the shudders turned into a stiffening of the spine, a rising of the chin. Silobah smiled to herself. Here it comes. Putting the pots back into the box she turned to the maid and crossed her arms over her breast ready to listen.

"I did nae wrong. It was an accident." Indignation rang in the words and Silobah nodded sympathetically, letting her tell her tale of injustice in safety. For the words could not be said outside of this room.

"Aye, lass. I warned you before you went prancing into the room." The maid began to sputter again, but Silobah held up her hand for silence. "It is nae secret about Lady Gwynneth. You have lived in the castle long enough to know how she is." Silobah stopped there and carefully chose her next words. "When you serve a laird and his lady you know they are to be obeyed completely. Anything that looks like disobedience, even if it is an accident, can be taken the wrong way and is cause for punishment." The girl tried to speak and Silobah shook her head. "This is the way of it," she looked meaningfully into the maid's eyes, "and I dinna see it changing." That was as close as she would come to speaking against Gwynneth.

The young maid gave Silobah a reluctant nod then stood. The old woman followed her to the door. "If you are wise you willna speak of this and let others think what they will." The girl nodded again and left the room. Silobah shut the door and drew the bolt. Tiredly she walked back to her bed and silently sat, staring into the distance.

Chapter 4

Dalchork Wood

SO, IT'S FOX for dinner this time?"

Rowan looked up from the rock where the animal was stretched, gutted, and skinned. Elden stood over her looking down, smiling. Standing this way was the only chance he had to see the top of her head. Rowan had grown like a young sapling during the past two years and had drawn interested looks at the last clan gathering. It was this height, topping his by several inches that made him smile. For all of his breadth and powerful muscles he was not a tall man. His was an unremarkable presence with his plain brown hair and ordinary craggy face. It wasn't until you looked into his tawny eyes that you became aware that here was much more than a simple ordinary man.

Glancing up Rowan studied his face for signs of last night's visions and saw lines of fatigue. She gave him a quick smile then looked down and continued butchering the fox. Elden stood quietly watching, admiring how deftly she wielded the dirk, how truly capable she was of survival. Once again, unbidden, came the dark thoughts. He shook his head trying to clear it of last night's visions but still they danced in his mind. Determined to ignore them he hunkered down beside Rowan. Watching her blade flash through the air he noticed the dirk cutting with a bit too much force. Glancing over at her face he saw her jaw set in hard lines.

"What was it you found in the woods besides this fox?"

Rowan jerked back and glared at him. How dare he use his vision on her? Opening her mouth to tell him to save his powers for the common folk, she stopped as Elden gave a low chuckle, "Nae, not a vision. I did nae see you hunting today I merely saw how you were slashing at our dinner." Gently he reached out and chucked her under the chin.

Rowan gave him a thin smile and sat back on her heels, tossing the dirk point-down in the grass over and over. Elden waited.

"There were hunters in the woods today."

The smile left Elden's face and he studied her carefully. Last night's thoughts flared in his head. As she spoke, he watched the set of her chin, the lines that appeared on her face. Those told him more than her words did. He might be the one who had visions, but Rowan had a powerful intuition. It was apparent from her demeanor that she was deeply disturbed by those who had intruded into her woods.

"I need to find out who they are." Rowan's words startled Elden. "Can you make the vision come tonight? Can you help?"

Elden needed no forthcoming vision. Briefly he closed his eyes knowing that life had indeed turned back upon itself with a sudden swiftness. Old patterns were closing in and he was once again caught. Sadness ached at the back of his throat. There was no time to prepare her. There was barely time for him to take in that hunters were so close. He had always hoped she would remain safe. But it was not to be.

Steeling himself, choosing his words carefully he replied, "The vision has already come."

Rowan paused, her hand in the air holding the dirk she had been tossing into the soil. She exhaled impatiently. Elden shifted uncomfortably under her gaze. The vision had been a powerful one indeed. Their mother, Fiona had stood in front of him and talked with him as if she were in the same room. He recalled how she had looked; her long red hair, her intense green eyes, her body swathed in wool for she disdained fur, pelts, and leather unless the temperature was bitterly cold.

Rowan watched the small sad smile creep across Elden's face and wondered at it. There was no doubt that his vision last night had been a strong one. She had seen for herself his exhaustion as he dozed beside the fire this morning. But usually when he told her of powerful visions, they were ones of warnings, danger, and impending tragedy. They never brought a smile, even a sad one, to his face. She pulled her eyes from him and again tossed the dirk into the ground, waiting for his answer.

"I had a vision of the hunters."

"You knew about the hunters?" her voice rose in the morning air. Elden held up his hand and cautioned her to silence. Angrily she held her tongue and glared at him. He knew her ways well and should have wakened to tell her. Her green eyes began to snap fire but Elden again moved his hand in the air and she kept a firm hold of her tongue. Slowly he stood up and eased his legs while he spoke.

"I did nae see them clearly, but I know it was last night they were in the woods. They were indeed hunters but it was nae game they were seeking."

"But there was an arrow in the fox."

"Aye. But that was a matter of food."

Rowan gave an exasperated sigh and looked up at him, "Well what exactly were they hunting for?"

Elden took a deep breath, "You."

The air exploded out of Rowan's lungs and she sat still as a stone, her eyes asking a thousand questions. Her mouth opened once, twice. Elden held up his hand for her to keep quiet. It was an unnecessary gesture.

"You. They were hunting you." Elden stood for a moment and watched the words sink in. He saw the long, elegant fingers twitch then curl around the dirk and he shifted uneasily. Moving his gaze to her face he saw her eyes begin to snap, locking on to his.

"Why?"

Elden began to answer. She interrupted him, "Tell me all of it. Now. If I am being hunted, I need to know so I can protect myself."

The last word held a slight quiver and Elden relaxed. She was angry but also scared. Good. That would make her easier to deal with. He spoke, "Some I know from tales I grew up with and some I know from visits to the clan. And I will tell you this, the vision was a warning."

Rowan's eyes narrowed. Silently she held his gaze as if she could draw out information with the intensity of her glare. Elden paused and looked down at the ground, thinking. He didn't want to tell her the entire story now. Aye, she knew he had rescued her from the falls as a bairn, but she believed herself to be an orphan. As for the rest, a half-truth would have to be good enough to convince her she was in danger. He wasn't ready to tell her about the mother they shared and the Englishwoman who had destroyed her. He pushed aside the thought of the weak, wine-muddled English lord who had sired his fiery-haired half-sister. Rowan's true protection was not the truth told coldly in a rushed manner. It was her firm belief that she was a child of the woods.

Elden was not only a seer of visions. He a student of human nature and knew that if someone thought something was keeping them safe, then indeed it did. Rowan's belief that she was a child of the forest gave her confidence, helped her hunt, gave her an unshakable belief in who she was. Elden saw no reason to take this away from her. He knew in the days to come she would have need of this inner strength, this sureness of self, and he wanted it left intact. The words about Fiona, the beautiful highland witch who had been their mother slid to the back of his throat and he began to weave his tale of half-truth.

"They are hunting you because of me."

Rowan gave him a warning glance to hurry the tale. Elden rushed to speak, "Aye. You see they have heard of me, my visions."

Impatiently Rowan interrupted him as she jumped to her feet, her hands braced on her hips, "But why hunt me? It's you who has the dreams, it is you people come to for your visions."

26

Elden shook his head. "That may be true, but these powers are stronger in a woman than in a man. People at the clan gatherings believe us to be brother and sister. Tales travel."

"But we aren't brother and sister and even if we were, I have never had a vision in my life." Rowan pushed her dreams far back into the recesses of her mind. "Nae person has reason to think I can do the things you do."

Elden shook his head and pointed to her hand. "Tales of us being brother and sister aside, here is all the evidence they need."

Rowan snatched her hand from sight and held it behind her back. Smiling, Elden reached over and gently grabbed her elbow. Reluctantly, she let him pull her arm forward. Elden placed her long fingers on the palm of his hand and smoothed them out. Delicately he ran his index finger over the smallest one, the sixth finger on her left hand, "You know well this is the mark of a true witch. Tell me honestly, have you had visions?"

Indignantly Rowan snatched her hand away. She began playing with the dirk again. "I dinna have visions. I hunt." The words were arrogant, hard, and finally, defensive.

Elden smiled. So, visions were for sissies, eh? He looked at Rowan and grinned. She sniffed at his look and pointed her nose in the air, studiously ignoring him. He relaxed now that the tension had been broken. Rowan turned serious with her next question.

"And just who is it that wants me so badly?"

"Gwynneth, Lady Lochalsh. She seethes with revenge for the recent murder of her parents when castle Lochalsh was given to Colin of Dunrobin."

"Why doesn't she kill him?"

"She is surrounded by his loyal Scots and wisely does nae want to follow her parents into early death. She plots and stews. A witch to help her is what she desires."

"She is a fool to be taken in with wild tales and dry pine cones tossed into the fire for magic." Rowan said dismissively.

"Have you been in the woods too long?" Elden said, "Is your brain addled? If these men have been told to bring you back, they will do just that."

"So, I will go. And when Lady Lochalsh finds out that I have nae powers, I will come back here." She wiped the dirk on her woolen leggings. Elden reached out and grabbed her by the arm. Roughly pulling her toward him, he spoke fiercely into her face.

"You willna do such thing. Do you understand?" He emphasized his question by yanking her arm and drawing her even nearer. Rowan shrank before his fury. She had never seen him like this. Angrily, she tried to pull away, but he tightened his grip and his words were harsh, clear. "They kill witches at Lochalsh. The last witch brought to that castle is dead."

Rowan stopped struggling and her eyes searched Elden's. He kept a firm grip on her arm and continued, "Aye dead. It was Gwynneth's mother, Lady Stannard who had the witch captured and brought before her. And when that witch could nae do what the lady wanted, she was killed. Do you hear me?" He increased the pressure of his hand on her arm for emphasis then flung it away.

Rowan stumbled back and gave him a stunned look, startled by the violence of his words and his actions. Elden stood in front of her breathing hard, watching her rub her arm where he had gripped her, watching her look at him with new eyes, watching fear come over her face as his words sank in. Good. She was too arrogant by far. Mayhap he had done his job raising her too well. Confidence was necessary, but hers was over weaning and she needed to be scared in order to be alert, careful.

Elden tried to soften his voice, "We canna let them find you. We must leave here. Now. Finish with the fox. I will pack."

Rowan kept her eyes on him and slowly nodded her head. Satisfied that she understood, saddened that harshness was necessary, he slowly turned and walked into the croft.

Chapter 5

Lochalsh Castle

THE WOLFHOUND WHINED and lifted her head, begging for more. Her master's hand that had been stroking her wiry fur was now still. Restlessly, the bitch pushed her cold nose against his hand and whined again, the sound deep in her throat. Looking down, Colin smiled at the hound and absently began scratching her behind the ears. The animal gave a soft groan of pleasure and closed her eyes. Colin grinned, "Aye, aren't you so easily pleased?" The last two words echoed in his head; easily pleased. With a sudden frown he rose abruptly, brushing his hands on the sides of his legs. Restless he moved away from the dog and her new litter and walked to the stable window looking out, seeing nothing.

Easily pleased. He gave a bitter inward laugh. There was none of that with Gwynneth. At the thought of his wife, another involuntary grimace crossed the laird's face. He leaned against the window breathing in the air, willing himself to push her from his mind, but it was no use. Gwynneth was a fact. There was no escaping her. He was trapped here as surely as any fox that had taken the bait.

The wind shifted and smells of the sea drifted into the stable. Colin smiled and this time breathed in more deeply letting the scent remind him of his home far away. A place much like this with the sea at its door. But here the sun set in the sea, while at his home the sea began each day as if the sun was from its depths. Here the sea was angry and rough, at home the sea was gentle. He let his thoughts drift to the eastern shore of the highlands and Dunrobin Castle. Set high on the raised beach overlooking Dornoch Firth, its pale sandstone walls stood proudly. He thought of the long shoals and banks at low tide; remembered trailing behind his two older brothers to hunt for clams, crabs, and eels. His sturdy legs had to pump hard to keep up, but keep up he did, eventually surpassing them both in height and skill with the sword. But to the eldest went the Lairdship and Dunrobin Castle, to the next son, lands lying to the south. Colin, as the third son, had turned to war and Robert the Bruce to earn his fortune.

His mind drifted back to those battles, the fighting, and the results. It had been victory for Scotland and honor for him, but at a price. Taking Gwynneth as his wife had been a matter of duty, obedience, and in the end, no choice at all. And so, he had become Laird of Lochalsh. His eyes traveled up the stone walls of the castle to the large square tower. The cawing of gannets pierced the air accompanied by the sound of the sea and the common folk moving back and forth through the castle gates; some bent on errands others merely passing the time. He envied them their simple lives, their plain thatched crofts, their allegiance to clan and family. His ice blue eyes stared into the distance. Anyone walking by the stable would not have recognized him. Yes, they'd have seen his six-foot plus height, his broad shoulders and yellow hair, but it was his stance - usually straight enough to imply arrogance, that was so different. At the moment it was the stance of defeat. Colin continued to stare out of the window, not hearing the approach.

"A fine litter it is."

Startled, he turned, then smiled as Arden knelt roughing the wolfhound's head, carefully avoiding touching the pups. Watching his friend gently cuff the hound, Colin gave a sigh of thanks that here, at least, was one who knew him, had fought battles with him, one who understood the situation exactly.

Arden heard the sigh and shook his head. The castle was abuzz with talk of the laird once again spending the night with his hounds instead of Lady Gwynneth. He laughed to himself; indeed, his laird had chosen the better bitch. The hound whined and licked Arden's hand. He gave a smile of affection. She was a good dog, loyal, faithful, and kind. The last thought brought him back to the problem at hand. Lady Gwynneth was once again in an evil mood, but then wasn't she ever thus? Arden raised his eyes and watched Colin stare moodily out of the stable window. He wished his friend would realize that it would be to everyone's advantage if he began spending nights in her bed, getting her with child, and hopefully changing her foul humor.

Feeling Arden's eyes on him Colin looked down, "I know what you are about to say."

Arden pushed the hound to the side and rose, dusting his hands on his trews, "If you think I am going to give you one more lecture about where it is you should spend your nights, you are wrong. I came to tell you that Gwynneth is in an evil mood." Colin raised an eyebrow as if to question why Arden would mention something that was taken as a matter of course.

"It is worse than usual, Colin. The talk is this morning she marked the face of the serving maid. Her ring tore the lass' nose. It is an evil wound. Silobah tended it so the maid won't be permanently marked."

Colin's mouth turned down. Arden continued. "Silobah is keeping to her room." Arden watched as this information registered with the laird. Seeing Colin's face change slightly. There. Let him chew on that. Silobah had been with Gwynneth from the moment she was placed in the cradle. The old woman was tireless in her care of Lady Gwynneth and unceasing in her watchfulness. Arden knew that many assumed Silobah, never having had a bairn, looked on Gwynneth as her own flesh and blood. But Arden thought differently. There was something else that kept Silobah at Gwynneth's side. The old woman had been handmaiden to Gwynneth's mother and, as tales in the village had it, had been sent to live at castle Lochalsh by one who had the second sight. Stories were also told about Lady Stannard and her terrible secrets. Exactly how terrible and precisely what secrets remained vague; the stuff of conjecture, insinuation, and stories filtered through mead beside smoky peat fires.

Colin knew Arden spoke the truth whether or not he wanted to hear it. So Silobah was withdrawing. On one hand it astonished him, knowing the old woman's devotion to Gwynneth, but at the same time it didn't surprise him at all. Gwynneth had been full of wrath when he had claimed the castle, and rightfully so. Her parents had died in the confusion of battle; Lord Stannard slain by an arrow and Lady Stannard tripping on her gown, tumbling down the long stone stairs as she ran to his side. It was fate, or so it was said. But it was also whispered that fate had had a helping hand, and this tale Gwynneth firmly believed. Colin had hoped he could make her see reason, but there were no English warriors left to tell the truth of the deaths. All had been slain by the Scots fighters, a fact Gwynneth pointed out whenever Colin spoke of the deaths being an accident. Her disposition had not lightened during this first year of marriage, and Colin knew in her heart she believed it had been murder and betrayal. But no matter what she believed it was no excuse for ripping the serving lass' face. He was honoring his oath of marriage, but it was a hard thing. Much more difficult than he had expected, and he had expected the worst.

Briac had warned him. Colin and Arden had visited the ancient seer in his cave beside the Falls of Shin on their way to take possession of Lochalsh. It was a familiar place. A place to where Colin and the steward's son Arden had escaped as boys, throwing off the constraints of the castle hierarchy, playing as equals and learning the ways of the woods.

"You dinna know the value of the gift you have been given!" Briac thundered in response to Colin's complaints of having to wed Gwynneth. *"Lochalsh is a gift indeed,"* Colin swiftly replied, *"but I hear the lass is ill-humored and hates Scots."*

"Stone towers and women. This is nae what I speak of you arrogant young hound! The gift is a chance to right a wrong, but

it will flicker away as quickly as the north lights in the sky if you dinna pay heed!"

Arden sat well back from the fire, leaning against the cave walls watching, heartily glad it was Colin on the receiving end of Briac's ire. Irritably the old man pointed to a small wooden box, dark and worn with age, that rested near the back of the cave. Silently Arden rose and fetched it. Laying it at Briac's feet he moved quickly back to his seat. The old man raised the lid and reaching in, lifted the keek-stane from its dark bed. Arden tried to shrink into the cave walls. He held no belief in witching stones such as these. Practical and grounded in common sense, he believed a keek-stane was but trickery to be used on the everyday folk. But the hair rising on the back of his neck deemed it safer to keep his distance.

Firelight danced on the black stone, highlighting the rounded side, and deepening the shadows in its hollow. Colin stared at it. He was a warrior, aye. He believed in his sword and his horse and his men, but he was also enough of a Scot to recognize when powers other than those he could see were at work.

The old man gazed at the stone. The fire cracked and danced. The keek-stane began to glow. Arden shifted uneasily. Colin leaned forward. Briac spoke, "A wall of stone is a gift well said. But within its heart is a depth of dread. With a hunter's speed there comes the song: To claim the gift is to right the wrong..."

The hound whined once again and Colin snapped back to the present. Involuntarily he folded his arms across his chest as if in protection. Turning, he saw Arden watching him, thoughtfully. His friend quoted quietly, "To claim the gift is to right the wrong."

Colin stared at him, not knowing if he teased. Arden spoke again "This is about more than you think."

"You dinna believe in witching stones and Briac's predictions. You never did."

Arden answered sharply, "That may be true, but I know when to believe that which is under my nose." Irritated, he turned and stalked out of the stable. Colin moved back to the window, his thoughts far away.

Chapter 6

Loch Shin

ROWAN LEANED AGAINST the tree, panting, her head tilted back, neck arched, gasping for air. Elden panted just as deeply trying to quiet his rattled breathing. For a moment, all was silent. Then, piercing the air like a shot, a branch snapped. Rowan's eyes met Elden's. The noise of men pushing their way through dense brush became louder. Rowan moved away from the tree. She paused for a moment to listen, then motioned. Elden nodded. Placing his feet carefully in her tracks, he followed.

They had fled the croft with very few moments to lose and were now on the move with only a little food and a few possessions in the packs on their backs. Elden shifted his bundle and watched as Rowan moved silently through the woods. It may have been his vision that warned them, but it was his half-sister's instincts that were keeping them safe from the hunters so far. The bright red hair tied with a leather strap swung from side to side as her long legs moved through the brush. Watching her he was again amazed that she blended into the woods so well, knew just where to go, which path to take. He knew that if he were in the woods alone the hunters would have caught him in the first hour.

Two hours later, Rowan paused and lifted her hand, motioning him to stop. Gratefully he slid the pack off of his back and leaned against a tree. Rowan slung her pack silently to the ground and with a graceful leap, grabbed a low-hanging branch and swung herself up. He watched as she stepped delicately from branch to branch, sensing rather than seeing where she next needed to put her foot, gaining a viewpoint. Feeling his eyes on her she looked down, and grinning, dropped from the tree like a stone. Landing lightly on her feet she walked over to him and spoke softly. "We are far enough away." Rowan eyed the packs. Elden smiled, knowing her ferocious appetite. Opening the pack Rowan pulled out some dried deer meat, offered some to Elden, then sat back on her haunches, chewing.

"Why did they burn our home? We were already gone, so why do it?"

Elden understood that however wise as she was in the ways of the woods, Rowan knew little of her fellow man. It was time for a lesson, "They burned the croft as a message to us."

Rowan gave him a perplexed look. Elden nodded to her, "They intend to hunt us until they find us, they willna give up and they're letting us know we willna need a home to return to."

Rowan silently chewed on the meat and thought about Elden's words. So, they were determined to catch her, were they? Well, they weren't going to succeed. Rising to her feet, still chewing, she walked silently away from his knowing eyes. Only then did she let herself feel the fear that had been lying in wait. The fear that had flashed through her like a knife as she and Elden watched their home burn. When Elden had told her about the hunters, she had realized instinctively that these men truly meant to destroy her. Taking another bite of the meat, Rowan leaned against a large pine, thinking about what Elden had told her while they fled. Lady Gwynneth. So, she craved revenge for what she believed had been the murder of her parents and her forced marriage to Colin of Dunrobin. Rowan silently agreed with her about the forced marriage. Surely this Colin of Dunrobin was a ham-handed brutish warrior with a mouth full of greasy meat and his hand groping his lady's buttocks. Rowan gave a shudder. Not for her. Never for her. She would never be with a man. The woods were her home. Elden was her family. That was enough. As for the Lady Gwynneth, she must believe everything she hears. It was easy for almost anyone to gain a reputation as a witch, a seer of visions in a land where almost every stream had its spirit, every tree, its ghost. The only true seer she had ever known was Elden. So great was his reputation that people ventured to the vast Dalchork Wood seeking his wisdom. In return they brought salt from the sea, oil for the lamps, cheese, and dried fruit. Her thoughts turned to their present flight.

"Exactly what is it that I am supposed to do for Lady Gwynneth?"

Surprised, Elden choked on the last bit of meat and swallowed hard. Rowan sat down beside him. Elden threw her a keen look. "She wants revenge, so she most likely wants you to cast a spell so she can have it."

"And precisely how am I supposed to do that? Build a big fire, dance around, throw pine knots in it so there are bursts of noise and flame?"

Elden smiled at her words, remembering the times they had seen others who claimed to have powers do exactly that. "I have nae idea. The visions dinna give instructions you know."

Rowan smiled back at him, then suddenly without warning she leaped to her feet. Tilting her head to the side she stood still for a second then quickly turned to Elden. "Go." Without another word they grabbed their packs, Elden stepping to the side letting her take the lead. Moving through the trees they swiftly made their way deeper into the woods, hoping that the silence, the darkness of the forest would unnerve the hunters and make them turn away. What they didn't know was that the leader of the hunters feared Gwynneth much more than he could ever fear the woods.

Lifting her head Rowan gave a great sniff and smiled. Turning, she quickly made her way to the stream. Pausing at the edge she unlaced her boots and shoved them in her pack. Elden did the same. Arms waving for balance they eased their feet into the icy water. Carefully picking their way through the cold slippery rocks they moved upstream.

The hunters would track them to the stream. Half would go upstream and half downstream, searching for where she and Elden left the water and their trail resumed. Rowan kept to the center, making sure not to step on a dry stone and show their path. Her eyes scanned each tree they passed. She was looking for one that had a low hanging branch and grew close to the others. If they could swing themselves out of the stream, climb into the tree and make their way through several other trees before dropping to the ground, they stood a good chance of eluding the lady's men. The fact that the hunters wouldn't give up the chase until she was caught didn't cross her mind. She was thinking like a hunter of animals, not a hunter of men.

Elden looked at a branch hanging over the stream and gave an inward sigh. Rowan was the one with the ability to leap and run, not he. Rowan looked back at him and with a nod of her head, yanked off her pack and tossed it to him. Bracing himself he caught it, swaying only once. Rowan turned her back on him, lifted her arms, crouched then jumped, grabbing the low-hanging branch. Pausing to exhale, she stilled her body, then swung it up and onto the branch. Shifting her weight, she locked her legs around the limb and motioned for the pack. With a sigh Elden moved under the branch and lifted it to her. Giving him a grin, Rowan climbed to the trunk of the tree and secured the pack. Turning around she looked at Elden and lifted her hands as if in question.

Pulling off his pack, he wobbled as a stone underfoot shifted. Silently cursing, he flailed at the air with his arms swaying right, then left, then right again and back to the center. Leaning over he rested his hands on his thighs, catching his breath. A faint clapping sound came from the center of the tree. Clenching his teeth Elden raised his head and gripping the pack, threw it up to Rowan. Deftly, she caught it. With a quick prayer to the gods he jumped, grabbing the limb. Slowly he hauled himself up and over the branch, resting on his stomach, teetering back and forth.

Rowan crammed a fist into her mouth, snorting. Elden gave her a glare that should have turned her to stone. Struggling to right himself, he tested his balance and carefully crawled to the center of the tree.

"You have the grace of a young fawn." Rowan whispered and pointed to the next tree. Pulling her pack from the crook of the branch she tugged it onto her shoulders and stepped lightly from one branch to the other, heading away from the hunters.

Chapter 7

Castle Lochalsh

COLIN SAT IN THE chair beside the fire. Alone and grateful for the silence, he eased his long legs toward the warmth and closed his eyes. Firelight danced across the tapestries hanging on the stone walls and highlighted the outline of the great bed. It had been an exhausting day. A frown appeared as he recalled the sight of the serving lass' face. He hoped Silobah would indeed be able to heal it so there would be no mark. Silobah. When he had gone in search of her today, wanting to hear about the damage Gwynneth had inflicted, he had found the old woman sitting in her room, silently staring out of the window. She had answered his questions briefly but offered no comment on Gwynneth's actions.

Colin raised his hand and rubbed his face thanking the gods that it was the end of this day and that he was quietly in his room. He knew he should have gone down at sunset and joined in the day's final meal, but the thought turned his stomach. Over Arden's protests he had ordered a light repast of bread and Cock-a-leekie stew be brought to him, sending a message by that creature of Gwynneth's - the one with the head like a small gourd - that he was tired from being up all night and would retire early. He winced, thinking how the news would be received by the court and Lady Lochalsh. The court he could well imagine. There would be smiles and nods.

A knock came on the door. "Enter." Turning, the laird gave a start of surprise. Gwynneth entered his chambers carrying his evening meal. Colin narrowed his eyes as she set the tray on a side table. She never entered his rooms. It was well known that no one entered his rooms save Arden and his personal servant. Remaining beside the fire he waited.

"Since you were too tired to come down and we could not eat together, I thought I would bring your meal." Gwynneth stood beside the table and gave Colin a brittle smile. The laird briefly closed his eyes imagining the scene in the kitchen. Since there were no reports of mangled faces, he supposed she had sent Ewan to get the tray for her. He chastened himself. Opening his eyes, he gave a sigh.

"Thank you, Gwynneth. It was kind of you to bring the tray up so we could spend some moments together." Hoping she noticed his use of the word 'moments' He watched her face. He had no intention of having her in his room any longer than was necessary.

The corners of her mouth tightened and Colin knew the word had been noted. Stretching her smile even wider, Gwynneth took the cloth that lay beside the tray and shook it out. "Here, My Laird. Come and eat. I know you are tired from the long hours you spent with your hound last night. This food will do you good."

Rising from the chair Colin walked toward her, and it was only then that he noticed her clothing. Trying not to close his eyes in exasperation and weariness, he realized that Gwynneth had dressed for the occasion. Not for the meal, but for the occasion she obviously hoped would follow. In Colin's sight it was anything but enticing. The bright red gown glared against Gwynneth's pallid skin, drawing the color from her face, leaving it pale and bloodless. The bodice of the gown was deeply cut, exposing all but the tips of her breasts, pressed together and pushed up painfully high.

Avoiding her eyes, Colin took his seat. Quickly, before he could protest, she pulled a chair up beside him. Placing herself so his eyes would fall naturally on the bodice of her gown, she proceeded to make conversation. "How many pups were there? I have heard no one say."

Between chewing Colin answered shortly, "Five."

"And they are all well?"

"Aye."

"I am so glad. I know how much you have worried about them." Gwynneth continued to make light, breathless conversation and Colin continued to pay close attention to his food. As he listened to her honey-coated voice speaking gaily about castle matters and making small jokes, he thought of the serving lass, her ripped nose and the tender flesh of her cheek swollen and bruised by the force of the blow. His eyes shifted from his plate to the bodice of Gwynneth's gown then flicked away, unmoved. Stabbing the meat forcefully with his knife he sent it flying through the air. Cursing, Colin threw the knife down and pushed back his chair, rising to his feet. "I'm nae hungry."

The abrupt icy words hung in the air, cutting Gwynneth off in mid-sentence. Startled, she looked up at him. The cold hard planes of his face were tight, his mouth firmly closed. She shifted in her seat watching the handsome face grow even harder.

"Why did you hit the lass?"

Gwynneth opened her eyes wide and looked startled, "What?"

Colin took a step toward her and she shrank back into her chair. "You hit the serving lass. Her face is badly cut. She may be marked."

Gwynneth quickly began her defense. She needed Colin in her bed and this insignificant matter must not be allowed to delay it. "It was a terrible thing, My Laird. I scolded her for breaking a bowl and she lost all control. She frightened me. I will swear to you right now that I thought she was going to strike me." Gwynneth raised her hand to clutch at her throat and Colin narrowed his eyes. She continued, "I ran toward the bed to get away and she kept coming I turned around and hit at her. I didn't mean to mark her." Lowering her head, Gwynneth widened her eyes so the air would dry them, causing tears to flow. A few seconds passed until she could look up at Colin pleadingly with wet cheeks.

"The slap seemed to bring her to her senses. She turned and ran from the room before I could stop her."

"You did nae call Silobah?"

"No," timidly, "I just wanted to be alone." Letting her lip tremble, she forced another tear from her eye. Willing it to trickle down her cheek she took a quivering breath, "I did not wish for anyone to know. The girl has always served me well and I thought perhaps given time I could find the reason for her sudden madness and help her."

Colin cocked his eyebrow and then gave a quick, false smile. "I commend you on your tender feelings. Have you spoken with her and told her these things?"

Gwynneth shook her head no.

"Well, there is nae time like the present." Gently grasping Gwynneth's shoulders, he pulled her up from the chair. Placing his hand on her waist, he walked her to the door and opened it before she could protest. "Seeing how much you want to help the lass; I shall relinquish my demands on you this night and let you attend to your duty." Moving her out into the hall Colin smiled at her. "Good night." Closing the door in her face he turned and walked back to his food. Gwynneth stared at the closed door. Seething, she turned and stalked down the stone corridor to her room. Flinging open the door she startled a maid who was turning down her bed. Frightened out of her wits, the young woman stood like rooted tree. Gwynneth motioned with her head toward the door. The maid circled the bed making sure to keep far away from Lady Lochalsh's reach and ran to freedom. Swiftly Gwynneth followed her slamming the door and almost catching the maid's leg in the closing. Grabbing the heavy bolt, she pushed it through the notch and leaned her head against the thick wood. Her fingernails dug into the palm of her hand as she pounded slowly and with deliberation. Hearing movement in the hall she held still. Realizing anyone passing could hear her she quickly stepped away from the door. She needed no servant carrying tales about her. They were all too eager to do so. Her mother had complained that the servants concocted wild tales about her simple herbal practices. Untutored was what they were, she had said. They imagined all sorts of evil from her simple mixing of herbs, from her questioning about kelpies, spirits, and the old practices.

Gwynneth hugged herself. Walking to the bed she stood, pushing her forehead against the post. The tales had swirled for as long as she could remember. When the castle had first been built, Gylys the clan seer, the reader of Loch Alsh's keek-stane, had cautioned the villagers to plant a rowan tree beside each dwelling to ward off evil and witchcraft. As the years passed the servants had increasingly avoided her mother. The number of young girls in the castle had slowly dwindled to almost nothing, until Silobah was finally the only female who attended Lady Stannard. The people of the Clan Loch Alsh came to the castle only when necessary, and Gwynneth had felt uneasy whenever she and her mother ventured into the village. Her mother was contemptuous; pointing out that the Scots had no intelligence, no perspective, no true understanding of the world.

Gwynneth had grown up believing this to be true. And now she was married to one of them. She thought back to her wedding night. She had expected Colin of Dunrobin to behave as a barbarian; throwing her roughly on the bed, pushing brutally into her and leaving when finished. She had steeled herself for the ordeal. She had no choice and had hardened herself with thoughts of revenge. Surprisingly, she found him courteous, although remote, performing his marital duty in a polite perfunctory manner before leaving. And now it seemed he was never coming back. She banged her fist on the post. She had to get him back into her bed. She had to have a child. Only then could her parent's blood rule the castle they had built, only then could her laird conveniently die.

A knock sounded. Irritated, Gwynneth swept from the bed to the door and yanked back the bolt. Angrily she pulled open the heavy door and found herself looking at Arden.

"What is it you want?" her words were harsh and to the point. She had no love for this one. If not for him she felt sure the laird would be in her bed. In her heart she knew Arden was whispering evil things into Colin's ears about her. He was ever in the village, eating bread and cheese with the clansmen, entertaining them of an evening with stories of Dunrobin Castle and Briac of Shin. Her eyes narrowed to slits.

Arden spoke, "I have been in the village." Gwynneth kept silent. "There are tales."

"And?" the word cut through the air.

Arden looked down at her, his eyes unblinking, his manner undisturbed, knowing that even if she was as bad as that evil mother of hers, she was lacking one important thing. Lady Stannard had ruled Lord Stannard. Lady Lochalsh had no such control over Colin. Giving Gwynneth a hard look he brought his attention back to the matter at hand.

"It is said that Ewan of the Little Head brought hunters to the castle some days ago."

Gwynneth shrugged her shoulders. "What has that to do with me?"

"Everything, if the tales are true. We all know Ewan is your creature. What need have you of these men?"

Gwynneth gave Arden a hard smile. "What makes you think I have to answer you? I am Lady Lochalsh. I may do as I wish." Backing into the room she began to push the door shut when Arden grabbed its edge and held it still.

"Listen to me well, Gwynneth. Your power as My Lady means nothing. We both know that you were wed from charity and duty. And while it is true that you dinna have to answer to me, I dinna like the smell of this. I ask one more time. What use did you have for these men?"

Gwynneth yanked the door from his grasp. Smiling, she slowly pushed it shut in his face.

Arden stood in the hall, lost in thought and fuming. He didn't want to go to Colin with this. The laird disliked his wife badly enough as it was. But this thing with the men, it was too close to tales told around village fires about her mother. That one had used men too, supposedly sending them out hunting for things other than game. And then there were the whispers of unjust death. Were those tales true or only the rumblings of the clansmen against the hated English on their soil? Deep in thought, Arden turned and made his way down the hall.

Chapter 8

Cassley Waterfall

ELDEN SHIFTED UNCOMFORTABLY on the skins serving as his bed, their meagerness unable to protect him from the cold stony floor of the cave. Turning over, he opened his eyes and saw Rowan sitting near the opening of their hiding place, her arms clasped around her knees, her profile lit by the moon. The soft light outlined the troubled set of her chin.

"Rowan. Why are you nae sleeping? You need to be fresh. Tomorrow will come soon enough." He paused to look at her, squinting his eyes with the effort then continued, "but you already know that. What is it?"

Rowan turned her head away from him and continued staring out of the mouth of the cave. "Nothing."

Elden gave a low snort, "It is me you are talking to."

A faint smile crossed her face and she turned back to him. "All right. It's nae use trying to hide anything from you anyway," pausing and taking a deep breath she continued, "I am thinking about what will happen if we get caught." Elden raised himself up to a sitting position trying to read her expression more carefully. Slowly he nodded his head for her to continue. She did. "I've been thinking about what you said," Elden arched an eyebrow in question and she kept on, "about my finger."

Glancing down he saw her rubbing the delicate sixth finger of her left hand. The witch's finger. Rowan's words broke into his thoughts.

"I am supposed to have certain powers because of this, aye?" Elden nodded his head. She continued, "You named me for the sacred rowan tree that wards off witchcraft to balance the power of this witch's mark." Rowan took a deep breath, "It did nae work."

The man's mouth dropped open with astonishment. He had known her since she was a bairn, had guided her and raised her and thought that there was nothing he did not know about her. He crawled over to her, looking carefully at her face. Rowan gave a tired smile at his approach.

"Look as closely as you want. I dinna think it shows, but it is true. I dream things," she continued, "I dinna really see the future like you do and I canna make the visions appear like they say some can, but things come to me."

"What are these things like?"

Rowan shifted her position, easing out her legs. "Oh, they are misty and nae very clear and they more bring feelings than they tell me things."

"Like?" he gently prodded her.

"Well, like I knew that something bad was going to happen."

"Explain."

"Last week I dreamed I was being chased through the woods. I thought it meant I would wound an animal and it would turn and chase me." She gave him a tired smile, "I have been extra careful with my hunting, but it was about this wasn't it?"

Elden nodded his head at her and she gave a sigh. Reaching over, he put his arm around her and she snuggled into his shoulder the way she used to when she was little. Elden felt her relax and, bending over, kissed the top of her head. For all of her prowess as a hunter, for all of her boyish climbing of trees and fording streams, she was shy about her feelings, almost timid. His arm tightened around her protectively as an image of her being captured rose in his mind. Rowan snuggled even closer into his chest. The fierce protectiveness that had risen in him when he witnessed the capture of their mother Fiona now rose up in him and consumed every other feeling. He couldn't bear to think about what would happen if the hunters caught them. His mind turned again to the past, to that other capture. The heel of his hand ground into his eyes as if to shut out the memories but they forced their way into his mind's eye.

Lady Stannard. The name came to him rising out of his consciousness as black as night, as cold as death. His blood turned to ice at the thought of her. Even dead, she could still affect him. Tall, black hair, black eyes, with skin deathly pale, she had drifted through the castle wielding her power, destroying anyone and anything that got in the way of her pleasure, her will. His forehead wrinkled as if in pain. Feeling his unease, Rowan looked up at him. He smiled down, giving her a squeeze.

"Here, you had better get some sleep now." Giving her a gentle shove toward the back of the cave he motioned to the pile of skins. "Sleep. We are safe for now. Tomorrow you need to be fresh so you can torture me with more tree climbing." Rowan smiled. Moving to the back of the cave she gratefully stretched out and pulled the furs up, closing her eyes.

Elden turned from her and looked out into the shadowy night, his thoughts again on Lady Stannard. If he concentrated, he could feel her beside him still. His thoughts embraced the past despite himself, and he recalled the first time he had seen her face. He had been standing beside his mother, his hands balled into fists, stomach quivering. Lady Stannard had been sitting in the great hall looking at them, her eyes fixed on Fiona.

"And so you are the highland witch?"

Fiona stared at the Lady without expression.

"Answer me."

Still Fiona stared straight ahead. She sensed the evil in this one, felt it miles before they reached the castle. She had also heard tales in the highlands; tales of Lady Stannard's will, her control over her husband, her search for the dark forces of power. Fiona watched as black and red, the colors of death and anger swirled around the woman. Fiona lowered her eyes not wanting Lady Stannard to see her revulsion.

"So you choose not to answer me?"

Fiona kept her head lowered. Abruptly Elden was jerked from her side. Fiona's body screamed to grab him back but every fiber of her being concentrated on keeping her hands at her sides. Her instinct was to kill the man who held her son, then slit Lady Stannard's throat until the stone floor ran bright with blood, but she held herself back. This one had absolute power in the castle and she ruled by fear. No one dared cross her. All who knew her lived in terror of her wrath. Slowly, deliberately, Fiona raised her head and stood silently waiting.

"I'll have him gutted if you do not answer. You are the highland witch, are you not?"

Struggling to hide her rage, Fiona quietly answered, "Aye, they call me so."

"And what have you done to earn the name?"

Fiona kept her eyes away from her son and concentrated on Lady Stannard. Choosing her words carefully, hoping to convince this evil one that her power was a fraud, a useless thing, she answered, "It is easy enough to convince the simple folk."

"But they say you can read thoughts."

Fiona showed a slight smile. "It is nae thoughts that I read; it is faces."

Lady Stannard sat back and looked at the witch. "Read mine."

Fiona shivered and searched the woman's face. Words came to her but they were not ones this twisted woman would want to hear. She could utter words of flattery but they would not be believed. Fiona gathered her strength and sent her power out toward the woman; hoping to indeed read her mind and find words she could safely use. Suddenly she gave an uncontrollable start. She connected more quickly than she wanted. Desire for dark power and hatred of the Scots surged forth. Rapidly Fiona tried to pull back, but the powerful emotions continued to reach out and trap her with their strength. She trembled, struggling to be free. Suddenly her head snapped up and words flew out of her mouth, *"It is the dark power that draws you, and lust for a male bairn."*

Lady Stannard jerked back sharply, drawing in her breath. "Yes." She let the word out in a long hiss. Fiona closed her eyes. She had been unable to control her speech and now this evil one knew she could enter minds. Lady Stannard's hands clasped and unclasped on the arms of her chair; her eyes locked on the witch.

"So, you do read minds."

Fiona shook her head no. "It is known that you are interested in the highland ways, the sprites, the brownies, and kelpies. And you only have one babe and that a lass. Using information is how I trick the common folk."

Lady Stannard sat thinking. Yes, the want of a male heir could be reasoned and many knew of her quest for magical knowledge. But what they didn't know was her deep desire to learn and practice the true dark powers. She had always hidden her interest under the guise of questions concerning herbal remedies and superstitions, hoping to ferret out other more useful things. But this one, this witch from the highlands had seen those innermost thoughts. Lady Stannard slit her eyelids and studied Fiona for a moment. Silence filled the air. The men who had captured the witch shifted uneasily from one foot to the other. Lady Stannard pursed her thin lips; this red-haired one had power indeed. Fiona gave a shiver of apprehension.

"Take both of them to the tower. Lock them up." Two men began pulling Elden away. The others hesitated at approaching Fiona and stopped a few steps away. Lady Stannard gave a deep laugh.

"Yes. It is a good thing that you are scared of her. But you would do well to be more scared of me." The men looked from the witch to Lady Stannard. It was a simple choice after all. Grabbing Fiona by her arms they began dragging her from the hall.

"Wait!" the word burst from Fiona. It was more a command than a request. Lady Stannard widened her eyes. After a moment she nodded her head and Fiona spoke.

"It is me you want, nae my son. I will do as you wish. You dinna have need for him. Let him go." Fiona plunged ahead making it up as she went along. "He is just a plain boy with nae power. It is I who have the power. When I carried him as a bairn the power made him simple in the head. He can do you nae harm and he is of little use. I ask you, let him go and I will come quietly."

Lady Stannard leaned back in her chair and gave Fiona a smile. "He may be of no use to you but he is of great use to me. Of course you will go with my men quietly. You will also obey my commands. And your son will stay here to make sure that you do."

Rising from her chair Lady Stannard stood still for a moment, her eyes sweeping the room freezing everyone into place. A look of complacency crossed her face as she turned and silently swept from the room. Fiona stood still, staring after her until the men jerked her arms and led her away..."

A noise startled Elden from his memories. Tilting his head he stared into the darkness, listening. The wind picked up and the sound came again. Leaves against dry ground. Exhaling, he shifted his position then gave a soft groan. Rowan had been hard on him today. Stretching his neck, he tried to ease the pain in his shoulders. He hadn't climbed trees like that since he was a boy. The thought led him back to his memories of the great hall of Lochalsh castle. He could still hear his mother proclaim to one and all that he was simple in the head.

He gave a sad smile. How furious he had been to hear those words come out of her mouth, but at the same time how proud he had been of her cleverness. It had been in vain. Lady Stannard had used him like a whip over Fiona, trying to make the highland witch teach her the ways of the dark power. It hadn't worked. Fiona had died. Elden had lived.

Rowan gave a soft moan. Elden crawled to the back of the cave and pulled the skins up over her exposed shoulders. He looked down at her with love. She was all he had that was left of their mother. How much like Fiona she was with her beauty, her flashing green eyes and her long red hair. And how unlike Fiona in other ways. If Rowan indeed had power, she didn't like it. Elden was sure she would never try to use it. His eyes fell on the sixth finger so similar to Fiona's. He looked down at his own hands thankful the telltale sign had not fastened itself onto him. He had enough trouble with people expecting him to produce miracles when all he could do was see into the future, and even then, it was often vague, never truly clear. Elden watched Rowan sleep, wondering if a true dream was drifting through her head and if so, what it meant. He saw a frown cross her face and he turned his eyes to the night.

Chapter 9

Lochalsh Castle

"ENTER." COLIN CALLED the word carelessly over his shoulder keeping his back turned to the door. Pulling his foot out of the dark leather boot he gave a harsh smile. It certainly wouldn't be Gwynneth coming back for another try. He recalled the look of fury on her face as he had eased her out into the hall. Thank the gods she had gone without a fight, too surprised at his quick thinking to out maneuver him.

Hearing the door open he paused in his reach for the other boot and gave a scowl at the thought of her staying the night. His hand hovered over the boot as he imagined her in his bed. Quickly closing his eyes, he tried not to see those bouncing bosoms and frantic movements meant to drive him to passion. Tiredly he grabbed the other boot and began to tug at it. He wished he could like Gwynneth, he wished he could stand to be in the same room with her, but it seemed as if the kinder he tried to be, the more bitter she became. Oh, she tried to hide it, but the deep anger showed on her face and in her actions. He wasn't fooled for a moment.

"Colin"

The laird turned around hopping, still trying to pull off the boot. Arden stalked into the room shoving the door shut behind him and leaned against it, frowning.

"That's a pleasant face to see last thing at night." Colin said, catching his balance on the back of a chair and succeeding with the boot. Straightening up he gave Arden a smile. It was not returned. Arden walked over to the fire and sat down. Colin watched him. So, this was going to be friend to friend and not warrior to laird. Colin arranged his face to be carefully neutral, waiting to hear what Arden had to say.

Arden watched the fire, keeping his eyes away from Colin. He let the silence linger while he tried to choose the best words. But it was useless. The truth was the truth and a guess was a guess and he may as well plunge ahead. Taking a deep breath, he told his friend what he had found out while drinking mead in the village.

"Gwynneth wanted hunters?"

Arden nodded to him. Colin looked bewildered. "Why?"

"I asked her and she reminded me that she was Lady Lochalsh and did nae have to answer to me."

Colin nodded, of course.

"I dinna like the smell of this, Colin."

The laird focused his eyes sharply on his friend. It was more his tone of voice than the words he used. Arden was serious about this then. "Go on."

Arden paused and let the silence emphasize his next words. "It smells of her mother."

Colin gave him a look and Arden nodded back. "There are tales told about Lady Stannard doing the same."

"Doing what?"

"Using hunters."

"For what?"

"She sent them to bring back a witch from the highlands."

Colin looked at Arden, "She sent hunters after a witch?"

"Aye. You've never heard that, have you?"

Colin shook his head. Arden continued, "Well you don't drink with the people in the village but I do. It is one of the tales they tell."

"Village tales." Colin began but his friend interrupted.

"Village tales might grow and stretch with the telling but use that thick head of yours. Do you remember how it was when we first arrived here? Or were you too upset at having to marry Gwynneth to notice?"

Colin opened his mouth, but Arden plunged on. "Remember the lack of serving women? Remember how the clan's people avoided the castle?"

"Of course. I'm nae simple. They did so because some of them probably killed Lord and Lady Stannard. Oh, I know it is said that their deaths were a result of the battle and I've tried to make Gwynneth believe it, but that's something even I question. The village folk were avoiding the castle, lying low making sure no one blamed them. As if anyone would blame them for killing an Englishman."

"You're wrong. It was nae retribution they were afraid of; they had been avoiding the castle for years."

Colin sighed, "Of course they avoided the castle. It was ruled by the English and from all accounts, nasty ones at that. And anyway, what does that have to do with Gwynneth sending for hunters?"

"It has everything to do with it. Nae," Arden held up his hand as Colin attempted to dismiss him, then pointed to a chair beside the fire, "sit and listen."

Eyebrows raised at the command; Colin decided to humor his friend. He eased into the chair and stretched his feet to the fire. Folding his hands under his chin, he rested his elbows on the arms of his chair and waited.

Acknowledging the pose with a brief smile, Arden began. "Tales from the village have it," he strengthened his voice as Colin again arched his eyebrows, "that Lady Stannard was interested in witchcraft."

"Half of Scotland is interested in witchcraft," Colin interrupted, "there is a spell and fairy for every bush, and people plant rowan trees beside each village gate."

Arden ignored him. "Lady Stannard was interested in the dark powers. Evil. She tried to make it appear as though her interest was innocent and she was only curious about savory herbs, potions for healing and calming the nerves. But she underestimated the village folk. They knew it was true power that she was after. The kind that comes from the dark arts."

"Why?"

"Who knows why people turn to the dark ways. They say that she hated the Scots, hated being here and despised the clansmen. It's well known that she completely ruled her husband, that drunken sot Stannard, as she ruled the castle; with a strong hand and an iron will. They also say that she wanted a son to rule in her husband's place but her womb would not give her one. When she heard tales of the Druids, the old ones, the vision seekers, she became relentless in her quest."

"And so, she sought a witch?"

"Aye. And she had to go to the highlands to get one. None of the clansmen would help her even with the simplest spells. And there is another thing."

Colin turned his hands palms up in question. Arden pretended not to notice the sarcasm, "The tale here is vague but from what I can gather, the witch disappeared into the castle never to be seen or heard from again. There are mutterings about a death. Some months later Gylys, seer of the clan, left the village claiming great evil was afoot."

Colin rose, stretched, and walked to the window opening. Turning, he leaned against the stones of the wall and studied his friend's face. "Briac has spoken of Gylys and his wise ways."

Arden nodded his head, keeping silent.

Colin mused, "And you think Gwynneth is following in her footsteps?"

"Of course! Who raised her? What lessons do you think Gwynneth learned at her mother's knee? Dinna tell me that Lady Stannard conducted her spells in secrecy. If half of the village knew what she was up to then surely a child who had the run of the castle did. And I am telling you this; if she indeed follows her mother's footsteps then she herself is hunting a witch."

"If that is true, then why?"

Arden closed his eyes in frustration. Opening them he said in a tired voice, "Have you nae brain, Colin? Have you nae seen how she is? Dinna you know that she hates the Scots the same as her mother? Do you think she would have wed you if there had been any other choice? Think of the death of her parents as the castle fell. It's a wonder she hasn't plunged a knife in your breast while you've slept!"

The truth of these words was something Colin had side-stepped since he claimed the castle. Yes, he knew Gwynneth hated the Scots and yes, he understood her rage at her parents' deaths. But he had pushed this information aside, busy with his efforts to secure the castle, trying to gain the support of the clansmen and take the seat of power he had been given. And after things had calmed, after the castle was running in its routine, ignoring Gwynneth had become an easy habit. It was only the occasional outburst and her attempts to bed him that he had to deal with. He stared off into space as he thought. But now here was something he could not ignore, could not comfortably push aside, and let settle itself. Sending for a witch? It defied reason. A witch to help with what? He spoke out loud, "Revenge."

Arden nodded in agreement, then pulling his eyes from his friend's face, looked into the fire, "What will you do?"

Colin rubbed his face with his hands and walked to the window looking at nothing. Arden's voice came from behind his back…. *"A wall of stone is a gift well said. But within its heart is a depth of dread. With a hunter's speed there comes the song: To claim the gift is to right the wrong…"*

Turning, Colin looked at Arden. "You think this, with the mother and now the daughter, has something to do with what Briac said?"

"It would pay to ask."

Colin nodded briefly, then turned back to the night.

Chapter 10

Cassley Waterfall

IN THE FAINT light of dawn, three men crept toward the mouth of the cave. For a moment they paused, waiting for the sun to illuminate the way. If they were right, this was the seer and his sister. If they were right, Lady Gwynneth would be generous with their reward. Softly they made their approach.

Elden wrestled in uneasy sleep. A muffled sound drifted into his dreams then suddenly a foot slammed onto his back, pushing him viciously face down in the dirt. Jolted awake he found himself pinned to the ground. Quickly curling his body, he tried to flip over. He heard swearing, then was jerked straight. Once again, he curled then arched his back trying to unbalance whoever held him. Brutal hands grabbed him and held him still. For a moment all was quiet. Then again came the muffled sound. This time he was awake. It was Rowan. Snapping his head around he saw her standing propped against the wall of the cave, hands tied behind her back, ankles lashed together. A rag filled her mouth and her green eyes flashed a hard and angry light. Elden gave a groan of despair as one of the men grabbed his arms and harshly tied a rope around his wrists. The hunters had found their quarry. One of the men roughly turned him over.

"Aye. It is Elden the Seer, look at those yellow eyes," the man glanced over at Rowan, "and this must be his witch sister."

Angrily Rowan shook her head no and the muffled words behind the gag rose in volume. The men laughed at her and turned back to Elden, yanking him to his feet. He closed his eyes briefly. So, the fates would have their way after all, returning him to the castle where it had started. His mind worked quickly to push away the fear and devise a way out. It would be best if they did not fight these men. It would be best to make friends with them. He and Rowan must use the coming days of travel to conserve what energy they had in order to remain calm and strong.

His eyes turned to Rowan. She was definitely not of the same mind. Pushing away from the side of the cave, she launched herself at one of her captors. Losing her balance, she tumbled to the ground striking it hard. Rolling over she slowly pulled herself to her knees shaking her head back and forth. Elden watched, telling her with his eyes to keep quiet. The three men stood looking down at her. It was plain they didn't want to deal with a fighting captive for the rest of the trip and Elden knew what they were thinking. A beating would keep her quiet.

"Let me talk to her. I am sure I can get her to stop fighting. I'll make her see that you are just doing your duty."

One of the men nodded abruptly and pushed Elden toward the lass. Carefully kneeling Elden lowered his head to Rowan's ear and rapidly whispered. Rowan shook her head no and a small moan escaped her lips at the movement. Elden's whispering became more vehement, "You canna fight them. They have caught you. Go past it. It is over and done. What is important now is to conserve our strength. They will beat you bloody if you cause them trouble."

Rowan lifted her head and Elden nodded solemnly. She knew he was right, but still it burned inside knowing that she had been caught, trapped like the dumbest of creatures. Grudgingly she gave a brief nod in return. Elden smiled faintly and slowly pulling himself upright, looked at the men. "She will behave. We willna cause you difficulty."

The leader grunted in response and gestured to the other men. Roughly he grabbed Rowan and yanked the gag from her mouth. With her brother awake there was no need for it now. She could yell all she wanted to. Maybe it would wear her out faster. Untying her ankles, he pulled her to her feet, spun her around and pushed her out of the cave. Spitting, she missed his boot by an inch. The man jumped back with a curse. Hearing a harsh cough from Elden she glanced at him catching his frown. Folding her lips, she nodded to him. Aye. She would do better. Quietly she walked from the cave and approached the horses.

Suddenly the man's hands were on her body. Picking her up, he threw her face down over the back of a horse. The air slammed out of her in a rush and spots of black and white danced in front of her eyes. Rough laughter quickly dissolved the spots, replacing them with clear vision fueled by anger and hate. Struggling, Rowan arched her back, lifted her chest, and swung her body long-ways on the horse. Swinging her legs forward she pulled herself up, sitting astride. Hands tied behind her back, shaking the long red hair away from her face she tried to keep her seat as the horse pranced. Furious she yelled at the men.

"Here. You." Her voice cracked through the air. The men paused and stared up at her. She continued, "Untie my hands."

The men looked at each other and laughed. Ignoring her request, they turned back to preparing their own horses. Furious, Rowan twisted around to yell again and saw Elden sitting on the ground, his head resting on his knees. The horse shifted and Rowan moved her body to its rhythm, trying not to fall. So, he had another night of visions and would be in no shape to travel. Staring at him she willed him to lift his head. Feeling her gaze, he did just that. His face was completely white, his eyebrows making a black slash across his forehead. He looked like a captured deer, with the blood drained out of it. She had been too intent on her anger earlier to see, but there was no denying it now. Raising her eyebrows in question he only shook his head in reply then lowered it again to his knees. Rowan turned her attention to the men saddling their horses.

There were three of them all wearing the garb of hunters, trews of wool and leather-laced hunting boots. Their brats, long lengths of heavy wool cloth, were worn like cloaks, each fastened at the shoulder by a simple ring brooch. These were harsh men. There could be no trickery with such as these. They would do their job efficiently, mercilessly if they had to. A sudden movement from the horse interrupted her thoughts and she turned her concentration to the task of staying on the back of the restless animal.

Elden heard the sounds of the men readying their horses and shuddered. Soon they would pull him to his feet. He kept his eyes closed fighting the pain that followed his visions. Last night it had been Fiona again, her red hair flowing down her back, her green eyes flashing, her long slender hands outstretched, imploring him to run away, to take Rowan ever northwards, to the tip of Dunnet Head and then across to the Orkneys where they would be safe.

"Get up." The words were abrupt. Elden raised his head and a bright hot pain pierced him. "Now."

Slowly Elden rose to his feet and tried to will the pain away. "Give me your hands." Roughly the man turned Elden around and untied the ropes. Elden's fingers tingled as blood rushed back into them. Flexing them slowly he hoped this particular pain would take his mind off of the one in his head. The hunter grabbed his hands and pulled them in front of him, tying them together once again.

"There. You will be able to sit your horse, but dinna think of running off."

Elden nodded his head and the man was satisfied. It was unlikely this one would abandon the lass. He could be trusted to ride with his hands in front. The hunter swore under his breath as he thought of the lass. She was the one to watch. He thanked the gods they had been able to get that dirk away from her before she had a chance to use it. He turned a wary eye on Rowan who glared back. If he had his way, he would have trussed her like a pig and tied her to the back of the horse. Thank the gods that Lady Gwynneth had given them horses for the captives. He would have hated to have her ride behind him. Tied or no, she would probably have bitten his ear off. He looked at her again sitting straight and tall on the restless animal; chin in the air, eyes snapping, her arms tied behind her back. And that's exactly where they were going to stay. He would lead her horse. If she became unbalanced and took a tumble, well it was no more than she deserved. He looked down at his boot and rubbed it against the ground but stopped when he saw Rowan watching.

Scowling, he turned and walked over to his horse. Pulling himself up into the saddle the hunter reined his horse in a circle, checking the area once more. He watched as Elden pulled himself awkwardly into the saddle. He knew the sickness that accompanied visions. His grandmother had been plagued with the "sight" and had suffered the same after-sickness. Hopefully the man wouldn't hold them up. The tracker decided they would ride until dark or until the man could no longer stay in the saddle, which ever came first. Yanking at the bit he walked the horse over to Rowan. Leaning down he grabbed the reins and held them firmly in his hand.

"So, you dinna trust me?" The words were mocking and the man ignored her. She continued, forgetting Elden's cautious words. "You are worried that a lass like me could outrun you, out-ride you? A strapping big man as yourself?"

The tracker yanked the rein and Rowan's horse danced sideways. Desperately trying to keep her seat Rowan bit back the rest of her words. Looking back, the hunter chuckled. She glared. Kicking his horse, the man led the group toward Lochalsh.

Chapter 11

Lochalsh Castle

STANDING BY THE window, Gwynneth looked toward the waters of Loch Alsh. A sudden movement in the morning light caught her attention. Leaning out of the stone casing she narrowed her eyes, recognizing the large black war-horse and rider. So, Colin was headed away from the castle. Again. Her hands tightened against the stones as if she would tear them from the wall. Abruptly turning, she walked back to the mirror and stood looking at her reflection. What she saw pleased her. The fine planes of her face, the dark straight hair, the delicately arched nose. Her eyes drifted down to her neck then lower. Turning to the side she looked at her profile. Surely these breasts would entice any man. Facing the mirror once again she looked past her reflection and into the rest of the room. Silobah. Where was she? It wasn't like the old woman to leave her alone so long. Striding to the door she yanked it open and looked down the hall. No servants in sight. Frowning, she walked down the hall to the top of the servant's stairs. Starting down the tightly winding stone steps, she paused as the words drifted up.

"Gone again. And if he has his way he won't be back for days." Laughter greeted the statement. Gwynneth shrank back against the stone walls. The voice continued, "That's what I heard. First it was that bitch hound of his and now I suppose he will make an excuse to be tending something else." The laughter increased. Another voice chimed in, "For certain he won't be tending the bitch upstairs."

Holding her skirts close to her body, Gwynneth silently backed up the stairs. At the top she whirled and ran to her rooms, swinging the door shut behind her. Damnable Scots. They hated her. Well, that made them even. Barbarians. Killers. Her mother had been right. They are less than human. And that bitch dog! How dare he put a hound above his wife and give the servants reason to laugh? The door to her room opened interrupting her thoughts.

"My Lady?" It was Silobah.

Gwynneth narrowed her eyes, "Where have you been?" The words were sharp, cutting.

Silobah shut the heavy door behind her and walked to the fireplace. Bending over she picked up a log and placed it onto the fire, ignoring the question.

"I said where have you been?" Gwynneth's voice raised an octave as she whipped across the room reaching out to grab the old woman by the shoulder. Silobah wrenched herself free and spun around with unusual defiance.

"I have been checking on the face of the maid."

Startled at the tone, Gwynneth looked at Silobah carefully then gathered her composure. Turning her head, she walked to her favorite chair. Dropping into it she straightened her long tunic and complacently picked at the edging of the belled sleeves. "And that takes precedence over serving me?"

"It does when I am trying to undo what you have done."

Choosing to ignore her, Gwynneth rose from her chair and restlessly paced the room, changing the subject to one that mattered. "He has gone again." Angrily she threw her hand out in the direction of the window. "I saw him riding to the woods. He did not tell me that he was going. Or where he was going. Or how long he will be there." Her voice hardened with each sentence.

Silobah watched the young woman's back. That Gwynneth could so easily dismiss what she had done to the maid, that she could care so little for the result of her temper and be concerned only for her immediate needs, cast Silobah further into a deep gloom. She had prayed to all of her gods that marriage would change Gwynneth, would ease the hate she felt, would guide her away from a path taught so early to her; the path that was surely turning her into her mother.

Watching Lady Lochalsh pace around the room, Silobah prayed for patience. She knew the lass as well as she knew herself. Hadn't she swaddled her, raised her, watched her every move? Aye, she had known the malformed seeds were there, planted by simply being the child of Lady Stannard. She had hoped those seeds would not grow. But they had, nurtured by what Gwynneth had learned watching her mother. When Silobah learned that Colin was the one to be given Lochalsh and marry Gwynneth, her hopes had flown to the skies. Everyone knew of this warrior from tales told of the fighting. Colin of Dunrobin was a man of the finest bravery and honor. He was a good man, a seasoned man a few years older than Gwynneth but not too many to matter, and a man not given easily to impulse. If anyone could keep the circle from coming again as Thomas the Rhymer had said it would, it was such a man. It was tragic that he now felt as he did about Gwynneth. Silobah would give anything, practice any charm, pray to any gods to get Colin to love the young woman, ease her heart and give her a bairn.

"I am going after him." Gwynneth swiftly moved to the heavy wooden chest reaching for her cloak and riding whip.

"Nae My Lady, not while you are in such a temper." Silobah's words hung in the air as she watched Gwynneth stalk through the door. Left standing in the middle of the silent room, Silobah's shoulders sagged, helpless to stop the circle's return.

***

Colin rode quickly away from Lochalsh choosing a path on the north side of the loch. Beautiful and inviting, the dark blue water slapped against the pebbled shore, hiding a deadly cold embrace. The deep greens of oak trees contrasted with the pale willows clustered near the water. A peregrine falcon sliced across the sky intent on the hunt. Lost in his thoughts Colin saw none of this. It was three- days ride to the Falls of Shin, and he was concentrating on what he would say to Briac. Surely the old man would tell him if Arden's tale and Gwynneth's sending for hunters had to do with the wrong needing to be righted. And if not, then at least he would have words of wisdom and advice about Gwynneth. Perhaps Briac knew of some herb or plant that would drain her of her bitterness before it festered into madness. If the tales of the village were even half true, then things were very much awry.

A faint breath of sea air made its way inland and brought with it once again memories of Dunrobin Castle. A pain shot through his heart and he gave a half-smile. He was pining for his home like a lovesick lass. Arden would have given him fits. But his old friend wasn't here right now, so Colin closed his eyes and let the sun play over his face. As if sensing his master's mood, Colin's horse slowed down then stopped, lowering his head to graze. The laird sat quietly for a few minutes, the peacefulness surrounding him, filling him with comfort. The sun streamed down on his handsome face; a face showing his twenty-four years and a bit extra for the battles he had fought.

A cloud passed over the sun and the mood broke. Leaning forward he reached for the reins when a sound made him stop. Hoof beats. Swiftly and from long practice he gathered up the reins putting his hand to his sword and whirled his horse around to meet the rider. His steed danced sideways and Colin narrowed his eyes. His face tightened. It was Gwynneth. Settling the horse, releasing his grip on the sword, he sat waiting her approach. His mount moved restlessly in response to the tense pressure of the laird's legs. He quieted the horse and took several deep breaths.

Gwynneth's temper quickened as she spotted Colin waiting at the edge of the loch. Digging her heels into the sides of her horse she hurried her pace. She didn't want him leaving. She needed him in her bed. Pulling near she summoned a smile and a pleasant tone. "Where are you going?"

"I am going for a ride in the woods."

"Will you be gone long?"

Colin sat back on his horse and took her measure. Slowly he answered, "I will be gone as long as I see fit."

The words bit into her. How dare he speak that way? She was daughter of Lord and Lady Stannard and an Englishwoman by blood. He was nothing, a Scots warrior. Laird of Lochalsh only because her parents were dead. Her hand tightened on the riding whip and her chin went square. "I said how long do you plan to be gone?"

Colin noticed her hand tightening over the whip and it pricked him. Who did she think she was? English, that's what, and a worse thing to be he could not imagine. He had agreed to the marriage. He had seen it as both a duty and a price to be paid for having Lochalsh. Knowing Gwynneth would be unhappy with the marriage and in pain from the deaths of her parents he had tried to be gentle with her, had tried to make every excuse for her, but she had repaid him with endearments that rang false and abused helpless servants. And now this rumor of hunters. He was a man, a warrior. It was not his job to placate his wife. Her situation was not the best, but neither was his and you didn't see him whipping his hounds. Colin's thoughts churned. She had no right to question him. He had answered to few in his life and he certainly wasn't about to answer to her. Deepening his voice, he carefully spaced his words, as if speaking to a dim-witted child.

"I said that I was going for a ride in the woods. I have nae intention of telling you how long I will be gone. I have nae need to answer to you."

Anger exploded in Gwynneth's head. Swiftly and without thinking, her hand tightened on her riding crop. Swinging it above her head, she hacked down toward Colin's face. Grabbing her wrist, Colin held it steady, his fingers tightening and bruising her flesh. The horses shifted, bumped together then danced, trying to move apart. Controlling his mount with his knees Colin continued to hold Gwynneth's arm. Again, the horses swung around uneasily. She glared into his eyes, her own glittering and filled with fury. Struggling to pull free she felt his fingers tighten even more.

"Drop the crop." His words were deathly cold and beyond fury.

Gwynneth tightened her fingers around the whip's handle. Feeling the movement, Colin increased the strength of his grip. Biting her lip, she held the whip in place. Colin gave her a thin smile. Shifting his horse even closer to her mount, he began to push Gwynneth's arm away from his face, out from her body and behind it. Slowly he increased the pressure, knowing if she did not surrender, her shoulder would pull from its socket.

Pain deadened her fury and brought her to her senses. Her mind began to turn and calculate. He was deeply angry and this would get her nowhere. Slowly Colin continued to push her arm. Gwynneth gave a small cry from her throat. Slumping forward she pretended extreme pain, dropped the whip, and slid into a half faint. Startled, Colin released her arm and pulled her to him. Limp and feigning a swoon, Gwynneth lay in his arms. This was better. Let him get the feel of her. Moaning, she shifted so his hand would cover her breast. She breathed deeply. Let him get a taste of that and surely he'd come back quick enough from his ride.

Looking at the woman who was his wife, Colin remembered how Arden had compared her to Lady Stannard. "Your breathing is better, My Lady." The formal words broke the moment and Colin pushed Gwynneth from his arms and helped her sit upright on her horse.

"You will need to retrieve your crop." His sarcastic tone was not lost on her. Watching his face Gwynneth saw anger, determination. He spoke once more. "I am going riding in the forest. I dinna know when I will return." The words were without emotion and tone. Quickly reining his horse, he turned toward the woods and with a kick to his mount slowly trotted away from her.

Gwynneth sat on her horse watching him leave. That he had grabbed her arm, bent it back, had intended to hurt her mattered not. At least she had roused some emotion in him. That meant there was hope. Hearing a sharp cry Gwynneth raised her eyes to the sky. A falcon was riding the thermal winds high above her head, hunting. A smile crossed her face. Surely by now the hunters had found the seer and his witch sister and were on their way back. Sliding from the horse she retrieved the whip then mounted, gathered the reins, and pulled her horse around, pointing him in the direction of the castle. There were things to do, the tower room to make ready. Kicking her horse into a trot, she smiled.

***

Silobah stood staring out into the courtyard, her eyes seeing days gone by, her vision turned inward. It was going to happen again. Even though she had no proof, as surely as she stood in this room, it was going to happen once again and there seemed to be nothing she could do about it. She felt old, tired, and beaten down. The years of service to Lady Stannard in hope of averting disaster had taken their toll. Silobah gave a shudder and tried to close her mind to the past.

A knock came at the door and she was grateful to leave her thoughts. Opening it, she stepped back in pleased surprise. Arden. The laird's man. Gesturing for him to enter, she stood silently waiting. Arden closed the door tightly behind him. Silobah raised an eyebrow. Arden answered, "I dinna want to be overheard."

Silobah kept her eyebrow arched and Arden gave a laugh. "Actually, Silobah, I wanted to keep the others from hearing our passion cries." The old woman broke into a genuine chuckle. She liked Arden, had liked him from the moment he had entered the keep on Colin's heels. Here was a true black Scot; brawny, good-hearted, loyal, and handsome enough to turn heads. Arden moved to the chair and Silobah nodded her head. Sitting down, he waited as she sat in the chair opposite. For a moment they sat in silence, both looking out of the window, neither wanting to begin. Arden cleared his throat. Silobah turned her eyes toward him then closed them quickly, having read his thoughts. Go away, she said to herself. Opening her eyes, she saw him still there and gave a sigh. He began to speak.

"It is about Gwynneth."

"It is ever about Gwynneth."

Arden peered carefully at her, wondering just how he should begin. This old one had served Lady Stannard, had raised Gwynneth. She knew everything there was to know. That was exactly why he was in this room. He shifted uncomfortably in his chair, weighing the words he could use. He could pretend concern for Lady Lochalsh. He could say that he was here by Colin's request. He could say any number of things, but what he decided on, what he was always best at, was the truth. In his usual fashion it came out bluntly.

"I am uneasy about something Lady Lochalsh has done."

Silobah looked at him unwilling to hear. Ignoring her silence, he plunged ahead. "It is said that she has called for hunters."

Silobah gave Arden a blank look.

"Damn it woman. Did you nae know?" Arden's voice was angry, harsh.

Silobah's eyes were old and dark, older than time. Her voice was flat. "Nae I did na know but it is no surprise and I know what it means." Standing, she walked to the window and looked

71

out. Arden began to speak but seeing her take a deep breath he held his peace, waiting. The woman turned to him and leaned back against the stone walls as if for support. "I know what is going to happen. You dinna have to be a seer to know that it is beginning again." Arden shifted in his chair and watched her face intently. She spoke, "It will be the same as with Lady Stannard."

"Tell me now."

"I have been here many years for a reason. I failed the first time. I canna fail again." Silobah looked at him and gave a faint smile. He was so determined, so strong and blunt. What a good man he was with his raven black hair, his snapping black eyes, broad chest, and wide shoulders. Would he be strong enough to face this? She wasn't. She knew it and so did her gods. Old and tired, she could feel the weight of the years, the knowledge, the secrets dragging her down. Her voice cracked as she spoke. "First, you tell me what you have heard."

"She has called out hunters to search for a witch if you can fathom that. It seems she has heard of a man who lives in the highlands, a seer of sorts."

"Gwynneth wants the seer to find a witch for her?"

"No. Gwynneth wants his sister."

The old woman stopped breathing. It did not seem like she could live. Could it be possible? Could the young boy whose escape she had so carefully feigned and then hidden so he could be near his mother be the one Gwynneth sought? But that was nonsense, it couldn't be him; her thoughts stumbled over each other in their haste. She had sent him on his way the day after the bairn had been born, telling him that his mother and her babe were dead and there was no need for him to stay in the castle. She had seen him leave. Indeed, she had waited until he did so he would not see her leave with the bairn. And all the gods knew the bairn certainly did not live. It couldn't have. The wind had been bitter and the snow ready to fall. Surely the goddess of the sacred gorge had seen to her death.

Silobah sat in her chair as if stunned from a great fall. Arden leaned back, his thoughts churning. If this old one was scared then things were worse than the village rumors held, and they had been bad enough. It seemed that Gwynneth was bringing this poor lass here as surely as Lady Stannard was said to have brought her own witch to the castle seventeen years before. He took a deep breath. "This must nae be."

"Aye but how will you stop it?

"For one thing, I have told Colin the story."

"The story?"

"Aye. I told him the village tales about Lady Stannard and the highland witch."

Silobah's eyes widened and Arden nodded his head. The old woman turned her face from him and blindly looked out of the window. Thank the gods, she thought, now he finally knows. "If he knows then what is he going to do?"

"He did nae say. But he has gone to visit Briac and that means he is seeking wise counsel." Arden placed his hands on his thighs and stood as Silobah spoke.

"Let us hope that the counsel is indeed wise and that it is in time. We need nae more death here, and none of the other." Arden's eyes questioned and Silobah gave a thin smile. "I see the village tales were lacking. Did they tell you also of the rape?" Arden stared at her. Silobah motioned again to the chair. "Sit. And listen well."

Chapter 12

Corrieshalloch Gorge

COLIN EASED HIS shoulders as he rode through the evening, tired but pleased with the progress made in his second day of travel. Yesterday, once away from Gwynneth, he had made good time. He worried that in his hurry to get away from Gwynneth he forfeited the opportunity to question her about calling for the hunters, but consoled himself that he truly did need Briac's advice before approaching that coil. Looking up at the sky he thanked the gods that the weather had held, unusual for Scotland. Last night he had camped at the foot of Fionn Ben; the hump-backed mountain of bare, grey rock had thrust itself up into the pale night sky, and Colin had rested easy in its shadow.

Now approaching the sacred gorge, he visualized another night of peace. Pulling his cloak tighter, he rode through the cool air as the first stars began to appear against the deepening blue. Small sounds of the twilight forest surrounded him as he rode; the nestling of red squirrels in birch branches, the rustle of large wood grouse as they pushed through juniper. Spotting a break in the trees, he rode forward and found a clearing to his liking. Dismounting, he tethered the horse to a pine and lifted the saddle from its back. Colin had hunted earlier in the day and a fine grey hare would soon be sizzling over the flames.

As he searched for firewood, the sound of cascading water beckoned him. A view of the falls, pale against the night sky would be a fine thing. Setting the wood aside, he climbed in the direction of the crest taking care not to slip on the slick, grey rocks. Brushing past wych elm and birch trees, stepping over crawling ferns and guelder roses, he gazed at the great Falls of Measach as it tumbled into Corrieshalloch Gorge. Grey-white water plunged down hundreds of feet into the rocky canyon where fat trout swam in the cold water. Sheer rock sides festooned with ferns, mosses, and sorrel offered perches for ravens beginning to nest for the night. He let the fine mist swirl around his face as he breathed in the icy air. It was no wonder this place was worshipped, revered, believed to house sprites, brownies, and all manner of mysterious, secret things. A memory flashed into his head; a different waterfall, Cassely, where a young woman in leather boots and tightly fitting trews had stood poised for flight, her long red hair flaming. It had been only a year ago but seemed much longer. He hadn't thought of her since. No, that wasn't true, but he had always pushed the memory aside when it surfaced, relegating it to the category of dreams. For a moment the spell of the falls held him. Again, breathing in deeply he let his mind linger on the memory. He could still see the dirk grasped in her hand, her sudden stillness, the fine white planes of her face. The angry call of ravens fighting for space on the rocks broke the spell. Pausing for a final moment, he let the magic of the falls seep into his soul before he turned to practical things. Smiling faintly, he made his way back to camp.

The hare consumed, his horse grazed and hobbled for the night, Colin fed branches into the fire, watching as the flames danced. The forest was finally quiet. Only the roar of the falls broke the stillness. And then a footfall shattered the peace. Jumping to his feet, Colin grabbed his sword. Stepping to the side of the fire he adjusted his eyes. "Who goes there?"

The shadow gently moved into the light and Colin loosened his grip on the sword and grinned. "Briac!"

The old man smiled and endured his friend's hearty embrace. "But I was on my way to see you!"

Briac nodded, "Aye. I know."

Colin gave him a look. "So, you decided to meet me halfway because you are fond of leaving that cave of yours and venturing out into the cold night air?"

Briac acknowledged the jest then turned serious, "I dinna travel for my health, that is true." A soft nicker and a responding welcoming snort from his own horse confirmed that Briac indeed had hurried to meet him, traveling on horseback, something the old man avoided at all costs. The fact that Briac knew his friend was on his way didn't seem odd to Colin. He had seen stranger things happen with this one.

"You should have waited for me in that nice warm cave of yours. I was on my way."

"That was nae possible."

Colin took Briac's arm and led him to the fire, giving his old friend a keen look. He appeared rested despite the fact he had traveled a good distance over rough terrain, but then his lean form rarely showed exhaustion. The light from the fire glinted on the white hair flowing back from Briac's high forehead and accentuated his arched nose. His face, creased by wrinkles, held an aura of unease that contrasted with his usual peaceful countenance. Colin gave the old seer a worried look as he helped him sit. Briac reached out a gnarled hand and placed it on Colin's shoulder.

"There are things you must hear."

Colin looked at Briac and spoke, "And there are things I must ask. It appears that Gwynneth has called for hunters."

"Aye, but there is more you need to know."

Colin nodded his head, settled himself by the fire and listened. Briac spoke.

"This is about a circle repeating itself until it is broken. One has already failed at the task. It is now up to you."

Colin kept his silence. Briac smiled at him and gazed into the fire, gathering strength, and resumed. "The circle was foretold by Thomas the Rhymer." Briac looked a question and Colin nodded his head, remembering the tales Briac had told of this one. Briac continued. "He knew of course that King Alexander would be killed in a fall from his horse and Scotland would collapse into disarray. He also predicted the victory of Robert the Bruce."

"Aye. These things are well known."

"What is nae so well known is that before his death, he foresaw a pattern that if left unchanged, would circle back and destroy lives once, twice, many times until stopped." Briac looked up from the fire emphasizing his next words. "During his last days, as Thomas drifted in and out of the shadow world, he made sure those who tended him remembered this verse:

Evil in those walls will dwell. Beside the waters Alsh knows well. The red-haired one is hunted then. Beware the circle comes again.

"Alsh?" Colin asked. "Lochalsh."

A horse nickered in the night, the branches cracked and popped in the fire. Colin rubbed his forehead under the pale night sky gleaming with stars. This was why he had ridden to see Briac. He fixed his eyes on his old friend. "The rest please."

Briac nodded. "One of True Thomas' acolytes was chosen to live with the clan of Loch Alsh to stop the circle. She did as he bade, living in the village until she went into service at the castle as maid to Lady Stannard."

"Silobah."

"Aye."

"And the circle?"

"It is believed to have had its beginnings when the castle at Lochalsh was built. The site was a sacred one containing the ruins of an ancient place of worship."

"The old religion?"

"Aye. The stones were pushed aside by the English to build Castle Lochalsh. Perhaps the old gods were angry and cursed the site. Perhaps Lady Stannard called evil powers in her twisted desire to master the dark arts. Perhaps a combination of both." Briac shifted to ease his sore bones. Colin reached over and lifted another small log onto the fire. Sparks flew into the night air. Briac resumed.

"Whatever the cause, the result was the same. The circle was begun and it is now beginning its second cycle."

"And I am to stop it."

"Aye."

"So, I will."

Briac smiled. "Your confidence smacks of arrogance but you were ever thus. Listen to me. This is different from other battles you have fought. This is about forces you canna slay with that sword of yours. This one will take strength of a different sort."

Colin tilted his head. Briac continued. "Lady Stannard despised living in Lochalsh. In truth, there couldn't have been a worse pair to send to Scotland than those two. She thought Scotland primitive and our people barbaric. There were few court fripperies to take up her time and few women she considered worthy of her friendship. The dark arts fascinated her and seemed to exert a heavy pull. In addition, she had given birth to only one child, a daughter,"

"Gwynneth."

"Aye. And Lady Stannard wanted a son to inherit and start an English dynasty in Scotland. As much as she scorned the country, she still wanted to have her heirs rule it. Thinking our people dimwitted because they lived in crofts, she began asking about the ways of herbs and healing. No one was fooled. Her questions were designed to lead to other answers. The people of Loch Alsh would have nothing to do with her and pretended ignorance of mystical things. She tried to command Gylys the seer to attend her but somehow, he was always out of the village." Briac smiled faintly at this, then continued. "She became obsessed with the dark arts and with no one to turn to, she finally decided to get a witch to help her."

Here Briac stood up, stretched, then made his way to his horse. After fumbling in his pack for a moment he withdrew the small wooden box, dark and worn with age. Walking back to the fire he again settled himself, then opened the lid. Reaching in, he lifted the keek-stane from its dark bed and held the black stone in his palm.

"This will tell the tale," he said handing the seeing stone to Colin. The warrior shrank as the stone touched the palm of his hand. Briac gave a sharp bark of laughter. Colin eyed the keek-stane warily.

"Clear your mind and look into the stone."

Colin took a deep breath. Briac watched intently. Seeing the young man's eyes widen, the old seer nodded to himself and again shifted to a comfortable position, prepared to wait.

The black stone glimmered and danced in the firelight. Colin looked deeply into its depths but could see nothing. Trying to clear his mind he concentrated, letting his eyes glaze over, letting the surface of the stone become dim and distant. And then she was there. The lass with the dirk in her hand, poised to run. Colin sat completely still, afraid to move and break the stone's spell. The lass dissolved into the mist and then reappeared. Wait. It wasn't her, but someone much like her on horseback with her hands tied. Riding behind her on the same horse was a small boy, dark and sturdy, fear on his face and anger lighting his yellow eyes.

The keek-stane glowed brightly for a second and the scene shifted. The red-haired one stood in a stone chamber with a look of contempt on her face. In front of her stood a woman with a remarkable resemblance to Gwynneth, tall, angular, pale with black flowing hair. Surely this was Lady Stannard. The Englishwoman raised her hand and hit the red-haired one in the face knocking her to her knees.

The black stone flared and the red-haired woman was running down tightly winding steps, her pale bare feet barely touching the stones. Reaching an opening she looked about, frantic in her haste to escape. Flying down one corridor then another, she screamed as a hand sprang from the dark recesses of an open door. Yanked into a shadowy room she struggled to breathe as a large hand clapped over her mouth. Twisting and trying to bite she was spun around to face her captor. A fist landed in her stomach. Doubling over, she gagged as the man dragged her to his bed, roughly pushed up her shift, settled himself between her legs and thrust.

Trapped by the stone's spell, Colin tried to wrench himself away but failed. He gave a low growl as he saw the man finish his battering, settle his clothing and weave drunkenly from the room, ignoring Lady Stannard who had watched from the hall.

A flicker from the keek-stane, the scene shifted and Colin saw the red-haired one lying on a pallet of straw. The stone chamber was the same except for the blood. It sheathed her from waist to feet, curdling in pools on the floor. The woman's face held signs of having been ravaged by ferocious pain. The side of her head showed blood and bruising. But she was somehow now strangely at peace. Another woman stood holding a small bundle of rags, her head bent, listening to Lady Stannard's apparent rage.

One last flare from the stone showed the other woman again, a younger Silobah beside the Corrieshalloch Gorge placing the small bundle of rags on the earth.

The stone went dull and dark. Colin sat silently holding it in his hand, seeing nothing. A small breeze swept through the trees and their branches rustled adding to the muted sounds of the fire and the faint roar of the falls. Rousing himself he turned to Briac.

"The red-haired woman?"

"Her name was Fiona. She was known as the highland witch."

"The boy?"

"Her son, Elden. What else did you see?" Briac questioned.

Colin looked back at the stone as he spoke. "I saw the red-haired one on a horse with her son. Then she was in a stone room, the tower room at Lochalsh and Lady Stannard hit her. I saw her try to escape. She was raped," Colin's voice went flat with disgust and anger. "Next I saw her in a pool of blood and then saw Silobah here at Corrieshalloch." He stopped speaking and looked up at Briac.

The old one nodded "The highland witch was captured by Lady Stannard and brought to the castle. In this, the village tale is true. When Fiona refused to help the lady learn the dark arts she was beaten. The rape was an unplanned bonus for Lady Stannard; she knew the witch had one son and hoped she would bear another from the rape who could be passed off as her own."

"And Silobah simply sat by and let this happen?"

"She tried to stop the circle by helping Fiona escape. But it was not to be. Lord Stannard grabbed her up as you saw. Aye the circle is strong indeed. But she did manage to get the boy Elden safely away from the castle and she dealt with the bairn as best she could."

"And where is the bairn now?"

Briac reached out his hand for the keek-stane. Colin gratefully gave it back rubbing his hands unconsciously on his thighs. Briac spoke, "Silobah placed the bairn beside these falls so she could send it on its way with the goddess watching over its spirit."

"She's alive." Colin's voice held a strange note.

"You saw this in the stone?"

Colin shook his head "No. Arden and I saw her at the Cassley Falls. We were on our way to Lochalsh. It was the day after we left you."

"Tell me." It was a command.

Colin complied and Briac sat back, listening until the tale was done. "The boy must have followed and found the bairn." He gave a tired sigh. "And so the circle indeed comes around again as True Thomas foretold," he paused and looked at Colin. "You now know why Gwynneth called the hunters and who she hunts." It was a statement, not a question but Colin had one of his own.

"Does Gwynneth know the lass is her half-sister?"

"Nae, I canna think she does. Why would she know about the rape? She was just a bairn herself at the time. Nae, she hunts the lass because she is sister to Elden the seer from the highlands. Women in the family of seers are supposed to have great powers. Who better to help Gwynneth achieve her revenge?" Swiftly the old one held up his hand forestalling the next obvious question "It is the circle returning," his eyes locked on Colin's. "Your duty is clear."

"I am to stop the circle by stopping Gwynneth."

"No easy task."

"I canna change her heart. It is too bitter and filled with hate."

"Aye but stop her you must. Another must nae die at Lochalsh."

Colin nodded his head and turned his gaze to the fire.

***

Cairn Ban

The same pale night sky that arched over Corrieshalloch Gorge sheltering Colin and Briac, glowed its dim light above the figures camped beside Cairn Ban. Rowan sat with Elden beside the fire. The seer had his head lowered and was dozing fitfully while Rowan gazed at the ancient burial site. The mound of rocks had long ago caved in, sealing the passageway that burrowed down into the earth, leading to the remains of the old ones. Strips of stone set flat into the ground radiated out from the mound to the standing stones encircling the site. Silent, keeping their own memories, the stones stood outlined against the night. Rising from the ground, Rowan walked closer to the nearest stone. Covered with the ancient symbols of cup and ring, the stone stood almost as high as her head. Bending forward, her hands still tied, she tried to make out the inscriptions.

"Here. Get away from that," the leader of her captors called to her. Rowan turned, glaring. He began to rise to his feet and she turned around. It was not worth the fight. They were letting her sit beside Elden and she shouldn't antagonize the hunters if she didn't have to. Walking back to the fire she awkwardly lowered herself to her knees, then dropped sideways settling herself. She gave Elden a worried look. She had heard the sounds coming from him again last night disturbing his rest, turning him haggard and old beyond his years. Leaning her head to the side, she nuzzled his shoulder in comfort. The touch startled him awake. Their eyes met and affection sparked from her eyes to his. For a brief moment they were not captives, were not exhausted and fearful.

Looking at her, Elden acknowledged the decision that had been building within. She needed to know the truth. Even if it shook her confidence, even if it removed the edge she so needed, there were things she had to know to protect herself, and this might be the last time they were left alone together. He frowned as he gathered his thoughts, then spoke, "I need you to listen."

Rowan saw the seriousness of his request and she nodded her head. He continued, "We share the same mother; Fiona was our mother."

Rowan jerked back in surprise. Elden kept his eyes locked on hers, holding her gaze. "We are brother and sister." Rowan caught her breath. Mother. The word was alien to her. She had never had a mother. Her mind tried to make sense of Elden's words. Brother and sister? Ever since she was a child, she had fiercely pushed away any thoughts of her birth, instinctively knowing that acknowledging the fact that she had been abandoned and left to die would hold too much horror. In their place she constructed the myth that she was born of the woods. After all, hadn't Elden's visions led him to find her? In her wildest fantasies she never imagined he was her brother.

Elden waited. Gazing into his eyes, Rowan saw the truth of his words. It was time she grew up and left childish fantasies behind. She knew that no one was truly born of the woods. She was flesh and blood as surely as the man beside her, and so indeed she had a mother and father. The image of herself as a bairn wrapped in a blanket beside the gorge rose in front of her, and the pain she would not let herself feel as a child now rose and clutched at her throat. Tears of pain began to fill her eyes but were immediately overcome by flashing lights of anger. Her words cut through the air. "She kept you and threw me out to die?"

Elden rushed forward with his own words. "Nae. Our mother did na throw you out. She would never have done so."

Rowan fixed him with her eyes. He took a deep breath knowing there was no way to soften the reality. "She saw you once. That was all. She died right after you were born."

Rowan turned away "Then who placed me by the gorge to die? Our father?" Her voice cracked at the last word and Elden studied her back, concentrating. He had not only shattered her myth of belonging to the forest but was forcing her to face the truth that she had been tossed aside like so much unwanted cloth. He saw her take a deep breath, straighten her shoulders, and turn back to face him. She was strong in so many ways, but he wondered if she could bear knowing the entire story.

"We share only our mother. If your father knew of you, he did nothing to stop what happened. Our mother was kept hidden away from him."

Rowan closed her eyes refusing to hear the words. She had always known she was unwanted. Why else had she chosen to live her life as a hunter, spending most of her time with the sky, the animals, and trees? These were comforting things, always staying the same. These things never disowned her and only changed in ways that had a rhythm, ways that could be foreseen. She only came in contact with Elden's clan once a year at the gatherings, and when others came to Elden for his visions, she slipped silently away into the forest. Elden was the only human with whom she was close, and even with him she had kept her distance; being tender only when he was asleep, covering him up with extra blankets, making the fire hotter so he could be soothed in the deep slumber after his visions. She loved this man but crept around the outside of her love like a wild animal, attracted to the warmth of the fire but fearful of being burned.

Elden watched the emotions play across her face. He listened to the thump of his exhausted heart, its once steady beat now fitful and occasionally pounding. Soon he would not be beside her as her guide. Even if he regained his strength, there was no guarantee they would be together once they reached their destination. He scowled remembering his last time at the castle. He and Fiona had been separated and he had no reason to believe it would be any different this time.

A small smile crept over Rowan's lips and Elden peered closely into her face. What on earth did she find to smile about?

"So, you are my flesh and blood, if only by our mother."

Elden returned her smile, "Aye. We belong together."

"Then you did not just stumble over me."

"Indeed. I waited and followed the woman when she left the castle with you."

Rowan looked at him, confused. Elden opened his mouth to explain when the leader of the hunters walked up to them, "We start well before dawn. We need sleep." Elden shot the man a look that begged for a few minutes more. Why hadn't he told Rowan sooner? Quickly he leaned toward her and whispered, "Our mother, she," his words were cut short as the hunter grabbed Rowan and pulled her to her feet, dragging her away to be tied securely for the night. Elden watched her go, willing his words to cross the very air between them, to leap from his mind to hers. She needed to know how their mother died. She had to be prepared. Silently he cursed his visions and the exhaustion that had caused him to sleep when he should have been telling her the truth. Lowering his head in defeat, he closed his eyes and begged forgiveness from the highland witch.

Chapter 13

THE FOLLOWING EVENING, Colin reined his horse to a stop. He had traveled a good distance back toward Castle Lochalsh from where he had sat with Briac. Dismounting, he led the horse to a rushing burn for a drink. The streaming water beckoned him to strip his clothes and bathe but he knew its frigid temperature was no friend to the skin. Looking up he could see Fionn Ben looming in the distance. A few more miles and he could stop and camp once again in the shadow of the massive stone mountain. Starting to mount his horse, Colin paused for a moment and rested his hands on the saddle, tired. He was astonished at the weariness he felt. He had fought battles for days, slept on the rocky ground, gone weeks on poor food and little sleep and had not felt like this. Briac's tale had taken its toll. He thought about his old friend. After a morning meal of bread and hardened cheese, Briac had prayed to the gods of the sacred gorge, asking for their help. Then placing his hands on Colin's shoulders, he had blessed him, embraced him with affection, gingerly mounted his horse and had ridden away. For a moment Colin had stood, watching the old man depart. He wished he could follow Briac back to the days of his boyhood. Days when he and Arden had splashed in the falls, fishing for fat trout. Those simple days of shouting with laughter as they played a trick on Briac, falling exhausted, into sleep, safe and secure, all knowledge of death, war, blood, and betrayal a thing of the future.

The horse turned its head and tried to nip his master. Quickly sidestepping, Colin reached out and shoved the beast's head away. Putting his foot in the stirrup he mounted then turned his horse in the direction of Fionn Ben. The stillness of the country-side unexpectedly erupted when he heard the sound of approaching horses. Colin pulled back on the reins. His horse snorted with impatience. Tightening his legs around the animal in reprimand,

Colin tilted his head to the side and sat listening. The sounds were coming from deep in the woods to the north, some distance away. Backing his mount into the trees he waited, wanting to see who they were before he decided to show himself. Perhaps they were the hunters whom Gwynneth sent to find that poor lass. He fingered the hilt of his sword and silently backed even farther into the juniper bushes. He placed his hand on the animal's neck keeping him quiet.

***

The captors made plenty of noise as they headed back to Lochalsh. After all they were no longer hunting. They had captured what they had been sent after and were relieved to be one day's ride away from ending the matter. The leader eased his shoulders, loosening the tension. He would be more than happy to hand over the lass. Looking back, he caught her eye and was rewarded with a scowl. He turned his eyes back to the front with disgust. She had been trouble the entire trip. It was a good thing they had taken her brother captive, too. He seemed to be the only reason she hadn't tried to escape. And she had wanted desperately to do so. He had seen it in her eyes; the way she measured how they let the reins of their horses loose when giving them water, watched how they went about building their camps for the night. He envisioned her plotting a way to get a large branch and smash it on his head. Aye, he would be handing her over and he was glad of that, but he wished it would be to someone other than Lady Lochalsh. Determinedly, he pulled his thoughts away from the picture of Gwynneth with the lass. It was not his problem. He had been sent to capture her and he had. And he would be glad when it was over; he would have his money and could leave.

The two other hunters would be glad as well. They were tired of maintaining a close watch on their prisoners and longed for the comfort of a roof over their heads, a warm bed, a soft woman, and plenty of mead. Knowing they were but one day away from home, the two had become laxer than the leader. Having been convinced by her actions and devotion, they believed Rowan would never leave her brother. Complacent, they released the binding that had held her arms behind her back and tied her wrists in front of her, draping the reins over her mount's neck. Instead of one man riding between the two captives, the two hunters rode together behind the group, talking and softly laughing while the leader pushed ahead.

Rowan lifted her eyes. The deepening color of the sky outlined the large stone mountain that dominated the horizon. Soon they would make camp for the night. It had to be now. She had no choice. She had heard the hunters talking and knew they would soon arrive at their destination. She looked into the woods on one side, then the other.

Hearing a cough behind her she quickly whipped her head forward. It was Elden. She knew what he wanted. He was telling her to do it, to use her cunning and strength and escape immediately. She was beginning to agree. The closer she came to their destination the more difficult it became to breathe. The air seemed to press the very breath from her lungs. The sensation was overwhelming. Another cough and she smiled. Looking up at the sky she knew it was now or never.

Slowly, using only her fingers, she gathered the reins, inch by inch, bunching them in her fists. Pausing, she took a deep breath and then raising her heels, brought them down viciously against the horse, yanking the reins fiercely to the side as she did so. The horse reared in fear, obeyed the angry pull of the bit, and plunged off the trail into the woods. Rowan slammed her heels into its sides again and the horse leapt through the air as it increased its speed. She hunched low over its back.

Elden sat on his horse watching her fly into the dark woods and disappear with an uncanny suddenness. The leader sat as if stunned by a stone, his mouth slightly open, his hands in mid-air as he watched the lass vanish in an instant. His horse danced sideways and the rider snapped to attention.

"Get her!" The words exploded from his mouth. Gathering the reins, he kicked his horse in the direction of her flight. His moment of surprise had been long enough for Elden to push his horse directly between him and the path of Rowan's flight.

"Out of my way," the man roared. Gabbing for his riding whip, he sliced it through the air, missing Elden's head by an inch. Enraged, he yanked the reins trying to back the horse around Elden and slammed into the two hunters who had rushed to follow the girl. Swearing, the man bellowed for the hunters to move, to get Elden out of the way and let him through. He swung his riding whip in the air not caring who he hit. They all deserved it. He bellowed his orders again but the two hunters continued to block his path as they fought their horses for control.

Flat on the back of the racing horse, branches whipping over-head, Rowan flew to freedom. Sensing its rider's fear, the horse increased its speed. Rowan pressed her legs to the animal's sides encouraging him to run even faster. Seemingly airborne, the lass and the horse shot through the woods heading north, away from her captors.

Colin remained quietly in his hiding place. The sounds came through the forest, louder, closer. Standing in the stirrups he strained to listen. Shouting. Perhaps bandits, a fight. Sitting quickly back into the saddle he began to kick his horse toward the noise when he heard something else, someone riding at break-neck speed through the woods, hard away from the shouts. Holding his mount steady, he waited. The rider was coming directly towards him. He loosened his sword in its hilt. Colin smiled. No doubt a bandit running away from the fray.

Rowan struggled to stay on the back of the soaring horse. The beast jumped a stream and plunged ahead. Gasping for breath she tried to control him and slow his headlong flight but he had the bit firmly in his teeth and her tied hands held no strength. A branch whipped her eyes then ripped over her back, almost unseating her. Tears streamed down her face as she tried to keep her balance.

Through the trees Colin saw the horse. A runaway! Shoving the sword back into its hilt he kicked his mount into action. As the runaway shot past him, he caught sight of streaming red hair. Narrowing his eyes, he gave chase. Gaining on the horse, he saw the flattened rider. A lass! Kicking even harder he urged his horse faster, gaining on the runaway. Inch by inch Colin pulled beside the pounding horse and neck and neck the two animals plunged through the dense woods, swerving around trees, jumping logs.

Rowan kept her head bent and gripped the horse with her knees. Sensing the presence of another horse beside her, she knew one of her captors was close. Moving her body back and forth she urged her horse even faster.

Colin saw the movement. He gave his horse one last kick bringing it slightly ahead. Reaching over he grabbed the runaway's reins and pulled back hard, yanking the bit from the horse's teeth. Rowan's horse swerved and stumbled, then regained its balance, slowing. Colin's horse, accustomed to battle, matched the runaway's slowing pace then swung to the side, planting its feet firmly, giving his rider a solid base from which to fight. Colin's arm throbbed as he fought to stay astride his horse and hold the reins of the other.

Rowan's horse, feeling the bite and tear of the bit reared slightly once, twice, then came to a trembling stand. Rowan clutched the horse like a burr, still flattened to his back. Her heart was pounding. They had caught her. She took a deep breath trying to plan. Colin kept hold of the reins and scowled down at the lass. His shoulder was on fire and he loosened his hold on the reins while he edged his horse closer to hers.

"Sit up." It was a command and a harsh one.

Rowan lifted herself up. For a moment she was astonished. She had no idea who this man was. But she knew he wasn't the leader. Gripping the horse with her legs for balance, she steadied herself then slammed her heels once again into the sides of her mount. Reins dangling, the horse set out at a dead run.

"Halt!" Colin's shout rang in her ears as she leaned over the neck of the running horse. Halt? She had no intention of halting. She moved her body again back and forth encouraging the horse to go even faster. Colin cursed under his breath. Kicking his horse to a slow run, watching carefully for low hanging branches and hidden logs, he kept the lass in sight. Whoever she was, she was going to break either her neck or that of her horse if she kept tearing through the woods at this pace. His mouth turned down in disgust. Just like a female to ride like a fury without regard for her mount, not caring if she killed it in her headlong flight. He increased the pressure of his legs and his horse picked up the pace. This was one lass who was not going to ruin a perfectly good animal.

Rowan heard Colin's horse approaching and she urged her mount even faster. Frantically she kicked her heels. Quickly she looked back to judge his distance. At the same moment her horse gathered himself and with a jolting push, leapt a deep running stream. Unbalanced, Rowan's bound hands grabbed at the air once, twice, and then she fell, landing hard in the water. Her mount streaked away into the woods.

Colin saw her hit and then sink. Racing to the edge of the stream, he reined his horse and jumped from its back. Red hair swirling with the current was all he could see. Plunging into the water he lunged for her hair then grabbed her tunic. Balancing against the current, he pulled her up and wrapped his arms around her waist. Slipping on the rocks he dragged her from the frigid water.

Quickly he laid her on the ground and knelt beside her. Bending over, he listened for a breath. There was no sound. He put his hand to her chest. There was no movement. She was stunned, her lungs full of water. Shifting his weight, he lifted one knee and placed his foot flat on the ground. Roughly he yanked Rowan up, turned her over and pressed her chest against his raised knee. He began slowly pushing on her back. Once, twice, three times.

Rowan panicked as she came to and tried to pull air into her lungs. Harshly her back was hit once, twice, three times and then as if startled into action, her lungs gave a gasp and drank in a huge gulp of air. Immediately she coughed then choked as water flew from her mouth. Abruptly she began to retch as water poured from her stomach. Her back arched with the effort and, as if from a distance, she felt a warm comforting hand on the small of her back, gently rubbing. Too dazed to make sense of the moment she gave a final cough - one last gag, then lay still, her breathing steadying, her eyes wandering aimlessly over the ground as she hung, draped over Colin's knee. Gratefully she continued dragging air into her lungs. Her brain began to clear. Her eyes fastened on a boot. A man's boot. The hand on her back. Swiftly she jerked up and smashed the back of her head into Colin's nose.

With a howl he dumped her on the ground and jumped to his feet, holding his hand to his face. Quickly Rowan scrambled up and faced him, her legs spread apart in fighting stance, her right hand straining against the wrist bindings automatically trying to go to her boot where the dirk should have been. Colin stopped in mid-shout and stared at her. It was the lass from the falls, the one he and Arden had seen take flight as if she were a bird, the one in the keek-stane.

Evening light glowed on her wet tangled hair. Colin narrowed his eyes and continued his inspection. Leather boots with long ties, the boots of a hunter. Intrigued, he let his eyes rise and he smiled as he saw once again the slender well-formed legs encased in tightly fitting wool. His eyes lingered on her leine. It was torn and wet. The shirt underneath was sheer with water. Her breasts were delicate yet firmly formed. Looking up he saw the murderous gleam in her eyes, the tilt of her chin, and the squareness of her jaw. Suddenly the light in those green eyes faded. Staggering, Rowan fell back against a tree, sliding down its length to the ground.

Colin started forward then paused, seeing the lass breathing easily. She would be fine. He would let her stay there for a moment while he assessed his own damage. Gingerly he tried to move his nose to one side, then the other. It stayed in place. He gave a sigh of relief. It wasn't broken but it certainly was bruised. Lowering his hands from his face he let his eyes travel over her once again and caught his breath at the angles of her cheekbones, the clean lines of her throat. His eyes moved to her chest checking her breathing, and again he noticed how the wet shirt strained against her. This was no soft creature from a castle, pliant and round as a newborn chick. The muscles in her legs and arms spoke of running, climbing, and hunting. His eyes traveled to the boot where she had reached for something, most likely a dirk, and his thoughts flashed back to the scene from Briac's keek-stane. The captive red-haired woman on horseback. This one was the image of her. She had to be the once abandoned bairn, somehow now fleeing through the woods like a mad woman. He thought of Gwynneth sending the hunters. His heart tightened, closed, and became hard. Aye, his wife had been raised ill and her parents had been killed but there was no excuse to hunt this beautiful wild creature now lying unconscious on the forest floor. Bending down he carefully untied her wrists.

Rowan felt tree roots pressing into her spine. Slowly she opened her eyes and met those of the man. She flexed her wrists and felt them unbound. Placing her hands on either side she pushed into a full sitting position. Dizziness returned and she closed her eyes briefly, willing it away. Colin watched knowing how she felt, knowing that she might jump up to run but that she would drop her in her tracks after only a few feet. He stood and waited. Rowan opened her eyes and again looked at the large man patiently standing a few feet away. Who was he? A vague memory nagged at her but fled when she tried to examine it. Pushing it aside, she noted his well-made clothes, for all they were the clothes of a hunter. Her eyes traveled over his face and she saw the wide blue eyes, the firm mouth. Quickly she looked down. A breeze swept through the woods and Rowan shivered in the evening air, the wet clothes cold against her skin. Colin, seeing her movement felt the sting of cold himself and walked toward her.

"Here. We should find a clearing and make a fire."

Rowan sat on the ground looking up at him, weighing her options. She knew she was in no condition to run away and she was enough of a hunter to know that she couldn't stay in her wet clothes overnight. She looked up at Colin and assessed the chances that he was another hunter sent for her or simply some-one who would do her harm. Colin returned her look with an arched eyebrow indicting that she really had no other choice. Trying to push up from the ground, the sickness came again and Colin moved to her side, kneeling. Quickly Rowan shrank against the tree. Colin gave her a smile and reaching out his arms spoke much as he would when gentling a colt, "I'm going to carry you."

Rowan tightened her lips and gave him a hard stare. Colin looked back at her calmly. "You dinna have much choice you know." It was not a question or a plea. It was a statement of fact and before she could respond, Colin swept her up and began walking toward his horse.

Rowan strained against his arms and he tightened them in response. She strained again and Colin stopped dead in his tracks. "If you fight me, I'll put you down and let you walk. You canna do it. And you know it."

Rowan pushed against him once more and, without a word, he opened his arms and spilled her onto the ground. Her breath flew out of her chest and her head spun. Leaning on her arms she tried to push herself up. Colin looked down marveling at her stubbornness, admiring her desire to stand under her own power. The dizziness increased and Rowan sagged, overcome with nausea. Seeing her wilt, Colin swiftly bent over and scooping her in his arms once again, walked to his horse. A soft nicker welcomed them but it was from his horse alone. Rowan's mount was apparently still at a dead run.

Riding away from the stream, Colin held Rowan in front of him and her nausea began to recede. She thankfully took deep breaths of air, letting it clear her head. The wind blew against her wet clothes and unconsciously she moved back against Colin's chest, her body instinctively seeking warmth. Colin, feeling the slight movement, smiled as he rode. She wasn't quite as tough as she thought she was. Tightening his arms around her, he felt no resistance and smiled again as he saw a clearing in the distance.

***

The waxing moon sent its feeble light slanting through the leaves. Cursing, the lead hunter pushed his horse deeper into the woods. Pulling his mount to a halt, he paused to listen. Silence. Cursing again he turned and headed back to where one of the other hunters kept Elden under tight guard.

"She's gone. I canna pick up the trail."

The third hunter rode into the clearing looking at the leader "It's getting too dark to see." He gave Elden a sideways look of apprehension "It's as if she has vanished into thin air."

Elden silently returned his stare. Did they really believe Rowan was a witch? The escape had been something any average man would have been able to do. As for her disappearing into

96

the woods without a trace, she had been doing so since she could walk. Elden gave an inward smile remembering the times she had run from him knowing his inability to follow her trail. Early in their life together he had realized when she disappeared into the forest, she would return only when she was ready and would not allow herself to be found until then.

"Where has she gone?" The question from the leader was harsh, demanding. Looking up Elden saw the worry in his face. So, this lady inspired as much fear as Lady Stannard had done those many years ago? The leader's face blended with that of another man, one drawn from memory belonging to the man who had captured Fiona.

"I have nae idea where she went." Elden spoke coldly. Perhaps it would be to Rowan's advantage for them to believe that she had special powers. He refused to speak further. The leader turned his horse in a circle gazing out into the deep woods as if he might by chance spot her. With grim determination he dismounted.

"We will make our camp here for the night." The men began removing their bedding. Elden leaned back against a tree and the lead hunter sat down beside him. "We have to find her you know. There is nae way I can return to the castle without her and even now I'll wager Lady Lochalsh grows impatient."

"She is like Lady Stannard then?" The quiet question caught the man off guard. Elden gave a faint smile and continued. "Och aye. I know of your former Lady." He turned his eyes to the woods as if seeing her again. "I know her and have felt her anger." The hunter stared at Elden in astonishment.

"When? I have hunted this area for the past ten years and I have never seen you."

"It was the time of the highland witch."

The man gave a start and narrowing his eyes, studied Elden. "The village is full of such stories. No one has ever known the complete truth of it. Not like you and your powers being widely known."

Elden kept his eyes to the woods. So, they did not come to get him and Rowan because of Fiona. As far as the hunters knew, they were simply two people living in the highlands who were supposed to have powers. He gave a nod to himself. And no one was going to know the connection if he could help it. He spoke, "Aye, I saw the witch. I was a young man and fascinated. You know how it is with young men. I spoke without thinking and said she should be let free. I felt the cut of Lady Stannard's whip along my back for my trouble."

The leader nodded his head. Relieved, Elden saw the man accept his explanation. Good. The man rose to his feet and gave a stretch then a yawn. "We will sleep early tonight and be up at dawn. We will find her then." He said the last words more to himself than to anyone else. Elden watched him walk away and silently sent a message to Rowan for her to run through the night.

***

"Here. This should do." Colin pulled a blanket from the back of his horse and walked over to Rowan, leaning down to give it to her. Shaking out the wool cloth she began to drape it over herself when Colin reached out his hand to stop her. "You know better than that. Even with this fire," he gestured at the snapping blaze, "you need to get out of your wet clothes before you take chill. There," he pointed to a large group of bushes, "go behind the juniper."

Rowan sat on the ground and stubbornly looked up at him. It made sense, drying her wet clothes, but the fact that he told her to do it made her want to balk. She hated that she'd had to be carried to the camp, and had sat while he gathered wood, had been weak. Colin stood above her looking down, his arms folded in front of him. "You can walk now. You proved that a few minutes ago when you tottered from the horse." He smothered a grin at the look on her face and continued. "If you dinna get up and walk over to those bushes and remove your wet clothes I will do it for you."

Rowan saw he was not jesting. Slowly she raised herself from the ground and turning away from him, tilted her chin and walked toward the bushes. Colin smiled as he watched her go. There was little chance she would make a run for it tonight. She was woodsman enough to know the value of dry clothes, a warm fire, something to eat. He kept an eye on the bushes as he stripped off his own wet clothes. Naked and shivering he turned to his horse and searched through the bundle on its back for something dry.

Rowan stood behind the juniper struggling to pull the wet wool from her legs. Hopping in a circle, one foot lifted in the air, her glance darted through a hole in the bushes. She froze. There, silhouetted against the fire, rummaging in the pack on his horse's back stood the man. She swayed for a second then became still. He hadn't a piece of clothing on anywhere. She lowered her foot to the ground, not taking her eyes from him. He pulled a tunic from the pack and moving into the firelight, shook it out. Rowan gave a smothered gasp. She had seen Elden many times when they had gone swimming in streams, as they had bathed one right after the other but she had never given it a thought. He was built much as the male animals she hunted. She knew why they were built differently and how they joined during mating season. Her eyes widened as she saw the man use the cloth to rub his body dry. She swallowed. Aye, she had seen Elden but he was nothing like this.

Safe in her hiding place she let her eyes travel over his body. He was large, a much larger man than Elden or even the hunters who had captured her. His back rippled with muscles as he moved. Turning, he moved his shoulders as if easing them and she saw the muscles in his chest tense and loosen. Her eyes dropped to his flat hard stomach and lower. She swallowed again. No. He was not like Elden in the least. A strange feeling crept over her and her breasts began to feel warm. Yanking her gaze from the man, she quickly raised her foot to pull at her leggings and stumbled, falling to the ground.

Colin heard the noise "You sound like a trapped rabbit. Do ye need any help?"

"No!"

Colin chuckled to himself as he pulled on his tunic then his trews. He fed some branches into the flames. "Finish what you are doing and come get warm."

Behind the bushes Rowan peeled off the remaining wet clothes and, draping the blanket carefully around her body, walked out to the fire. "Here." She held out her sodden garments. Reaching to take them from her, Colin's fingers grazed hers and she jumped as if stung. Colin stood still, watching her reaction. He spoke quietly "I did nae pull you from the water only to harm you."

Rowan stood just as still looking up at him. "Then why did you do it at all?" Her voice was hard, firm.

Colin continued to assess her. Aye, the question had the abruptness of a man but underneath its challenging tone there was the slight quaver of a scared female. He grinned thinking how furious she would be if she knew his thoughts. Rowan saw the smile and scowled at him. Refusing to answer, Colin turned his back and arranged the wet clothes on overhanging branches. Rowan turned and sat beside the fire, drawing the blanket closer. Why on earth had she taken off her clothes? Why had she given them to this giant of a man? Now she was completely defenseless, easily caught if she ran. And if she ran, where would she go? Home? The sight of the burning croft filled her mind. No. There was nothing for her there. Not even Elden. He was on his way to Lady Lochalsh. She lowered her head and rested it on her knees fighting the tears. She clenched her teeth and raised her head staring into the fire. What she had to do now was think. Think how to get away from this man. She trusted no male. He would most likely harm her despite what he said. Or perhaps he was indeed another hunter and would drag her to the castle to collect a reward. She closed her eyes concentrating.

Colin finished draping the wet clothes, rummaged again in his saddle pack then took his place beside her near the fire. Rowan shifted away. Smiling, he held out his hand and Rowan slowly accepted the piece of hardened meat. For a few moments they sat side by side staring into the fire, silently eating. Uncorking the lid from a flask, Colin took a deep swallow and handed it to her. Tilting back her head, Rowan took a huge gulp and sputtered as the mead burned down her throat. Coughing, she drew her arm across her mouth and looked up. He grinned at her. "Nae used to it are you?"

The liquid burned a path down into her stomach. Who was he? He dressed as a plain huntsman yet the cloth was of the finest quality she had ever seen, ate dried meat like a soldier but followed it with liquor she knew could only be bought with much coin. Her eyes narrowed and he watched her as she tried to pin a label on him, figure him out.

He spoke, "Who are you?" The question startled her and she looked up at him. He continued "Who are you and what were you doing flying through the woods on the back of that poor horse?" He wanted to hear her story, wanted her to confirm what he had seen in Briac's keek-stane, but Rowan kept silent. Colin looked at her narrowing his eyes. "Surely I deserve an answer."

"Why? I was in these woods minding my own business when you chased me. What was I supposed to do? Let some strange man in the forest capture me? As it is I'm the one who needs to know who you are." She stressed the last two words and sat back with her mouth firmly shut.

"You were nae in these woods minding your own business. You were riding as if your life depended on it with your hands bound in front. If it was my guess, I would say that someone other than me was chasing you." he looked out into the night, "and it seems as if I helped you get away." He turned and fastened a commanding look on her. "So now you will tell me who you are and what you are doing in these woods."

Rowan was not about to tell him that she was the one whom Lady Lochalsh wanted brought to court. Colin saw her fold her lips tightly and his anger stirred. How dare she ignore him? Swiftly he reached out and grabbed her blanket-covered arm. Startled, Rowan snatched her arm away then leapt to her feet, frightened, ready to run. Colin kept his hold of the blanket and suddenly in the dancing firelight, Rowan stood before him completely naked. Long red hair falling down her back, mouth parted slightly in surprise, she stood stunned, still as a fox gone to ground.

Colin sat frozen to the ground, holding the blanket in his hand, his eyes running up and down her body. He had been wrong about her being a lass. She was coming into womanhood. His gaze lingered on her breasts, pointing into the cold air. He felt himself stir. Taking a deep breath, Colin rose slowly. Rowan's eyes widened in fear. She couldn't move. She was barely breathing. Silently Colin stood in front of her. Lifting his arms, he draped the blanket around her, tucking the ends in about her neck. Standing only inches from her he looked down into the wide, fearful green eyes. Something touched him deeply for a moment. It was attraction, aye, of course, but it was something else, too. For all of her stubbornness, her muscles, her long legged ability to run, she was vulnerable. And she was scared. The fact touched his heart and he was moved to tenderness. A fierce feeling of protectiveness swept over him. If this was indeed the one Gwynneth hunted, he would never let her have the lass. It was as if he found a wounded fawn in the woods and was determined to nurse it back to health, determined to make sure no one harmed it.

Slowly he lifted his hands and Rowan's eyes widened even more. Softly he touched the top of her head letting his hand smooth her hair once, twice. Moving his hands to her shoulders, he carefully straightened the blanket. Stepping to her side, he placed his arm around her shoulders and gently guided her back to the fire.

Rowan moved with him. She should be afraid. She should be desperate to escape, having seen the lust in his eyes. The same look she had seen on the faces of men at the last clan gathering. She should be looking at how his horse was tied, thinking about how she would stay awake until he slept, planning how she would move about and not wake him. But none of this was going through her head. Instead, she was standing in front of him feeling safe. It was a rare feeling and a confusing one. True, she had felt safe with Elden but never with anyone else, instinctively knowing from the very moments of her birth that people could throw you from their lives in an instant. Safety was not something she was familiar with. And neither was the touch of Colin's hand on her hair. Unconsciously she had arched her neck like a young swan the second time he had stroked it. She walked back to the fire with him. His arm felt good, solid, comforting. Stopping near the flames she looked up at him, a question naked and fearful in her eyes.

Colin looked down and read her thoughts quite plainly. Again, moving slowly so she would not be startled, he lifted his hand and placed his fingers under her chin. Smiling down into her eyes, he spoke in low gentle tones.

"I am nae going to hurt you. I am going to take care of you, see that you are warm and dry, and see that you have a good sleep. No one will harm you while I am here."

Rowan looked up at him. Her eyes traveled rapidly over his face and into his blue eyes. Peering deeply, she saw the truth of what he said, heard it in the tone of his voice, felt it in the safety of his arm. Slowly she nodded her head and Colin's eyes crinkled softly at the corners. Gently he helped her sit beside the warm fire.

Chapter 14

Lochalsh Castle

GWYNNETH PACED AROUND her room pausing occasionally to look out to the woods. The moon rose in the evening sky and she frowned at the sight. So, he was not coming home again tonight.

Her fingers drummed an uneven tune on the stone window casing. Where were the hunters? Surely, they had caught that witch and were on their way here. Pushing herself away from the window she went to her door. Opening it, she called to a maid in the hall telling her to bring Silobah.

In the cavernous kitchens, Silobah looked at the cook and he gave her a smile of sympathy at the maid's summoning. There would be no easy conversation beside the kitchen fire tonight. With a sigh the old woman rose from her comfortable seat and walked slowly up the winding stone steps to Lady Lochalsh's chambers. Knocking softly, she let herself into the room and saw Gwynneth seated before the dressing table. Perhaps she only wanted her hair brushed. Silently Silobah walked to the table and, picking up the brush, she gently began the task.

The ritual was one that went back to the days of Gwynneth's childhood. Her hair was soft and fine, its long black strands running easily through the bristles of the brush. Her hair hadn't changed. If only Lady Lochalsh hadn't done so herself. If only she had stayed the same sweet little lass, then the laird would have found it easy to love her. There would have been no need for Gwynneth to send for a witch. The circle would have been broken.

"They aren't back yet." Gwynneth addressed the old woman in the mirror. Silobah nodded her head unwilling to get drawn into a conversation about the hunt. She had questioned

Gwynneth about it after her talk with Arden and had received a tongue lashing for her effort.

"I said that they aren't back yet. Do you think they have found her?" Gwynneth looked at the old woman in the mirror. "What is it?" Silobah shook her head and kept brushing the hair. Angrily Gwynneth reached up, grabbed the brush from her and threw it against the wall. It hit the stones with a sharp crack and bounced back to the middle of the room. Silobah moved to pick it up but Gwynneth turned on the stool and grabbed her arm.

"I know your face. I know when something is wrong. What is it?"

Silobah put her hand on Gwynneth's and loosened the young woman's fingers. Slowly, she raised her eyes and stared straight into those of her mistress. Silobah held the stare until the young woman dropped her eyelids. Silently Silobah moved to the fire. Gwynneth turned on her stool and watched the old woman. She started to speak but Silobah shook her head.

"You must call off the hunt," the old woman said. Seeing the stubbornness in the young woman's eyes, Silobah asked, "How much do you really know about the highland witch?"

"Enough," came the sharp reply.

"Indeed? Then if you know the story, why are you determined to follow in your mother's footsteps?"

Gwynneth pulled her eyes from the old woman and looked into the fire. "I'm not following anything or anyone. I'm simply having this witch brought here so she can cast a spell over the laird and I can have a bairn. I know she has powers. They say she has the markings and I will have her do my bidding."

"What if she can nae?"

"She must. She will have no choice."

The words sent a shaft of fear up Silobah's spine. They were the same words that Lady Stannard had spoken in this very room and on a night much like this. Closing her eyes, she tried to make the picture go away but she could not.

"You mean to have revenge at any cost, nothing can change your course?" Lines were etched deeply in the old woman's face and her eyes carried a haggard look.

"Stannard blood will rule this castle for generations. I will do whatever it takes to see that done."

Silently and in defeat, Silobah turned and walked from the room.

***

The moon drifted silently across the sky. Deep into his sleep, Elden shifted on the hard ground pulling the blanket up higher. Images flitted back and forth in his dream world. It was Fiona again but this time she was not troubling him; this time she was not warning him. This time she did not hold out her empty arms with her palms extended pleading for him to guard against evil. No. Tonight she was standing on a cliff, the wind sending her long red hair streaming out behind her. She was looking into the distance, her face turned up to the wind. A half secret smile played on her mouth. Elden, in his sleep smiled in return and fell deeper into his dreams.

***

Rowan sat silently beside Colin in the deepening night. They watched the flames, neither wanting to break the moment of quiet, of peace. Earlier Colin had scouted the area. It seemed as if the hunters had moved their pursuit in a different direction. All was still. A cry came through the darkness and Colin raised his head.

"A night hawk."

Rowan nodded her head.

"But then you knew."

Rowan nodded again with a faint smile.

"You are familiar with the sounds of the woods." Rowan looked up and Colin continued, "By your clothes. The leggings. The way you looked for your dirk in the top of your boot." He gave a quick bark of laughter, "but nae by the manner in which you rode your horse."

Rowan straightened her shoulders and glared at him. "And what manner was that?"

Colin fed another branch into the fire. "Aye, the manner that guaranteed you would break the poor beast's legs if you did nae kill him from exhaustion first. And then there was your graceful seating on the mount." Colin's appraisal of her lying flat on the horse's back while the beast clamped the bit between his teeth made Rowan smile. Colin watched the corners of her mouth turn up and he smiled too. They sat and continued to watch the fire. A few moments passed and Colin spoke again. This time he did not tease.

"I know what running from an enemy looks like and that is exactly what you were doing."

"And you know this because you have fled from enemies of your own?"

Colin stared at her "No. It is because I have watched my enemies flee from me."

Rowan arched her eyebrow, and Colin shook his head. This was getting them nowhere. He had tried to start the conversation on a civil note, hoping that his earlier promise of protection would smooth the way. What he needed now, was to know for sure by her own words and not just from keek-stane visions that Rowan was the daughter of the highland witch. Quickly he reached out and grasped her left hand. Startled, she tried to yank it back. Colin held it fast. Turning it over, he pried her fingers loose from the balled-up fist. Smoothing her fingers out on his knee, palm side down, he touched each finger in turn. It took him six times. Silently he kept his eyes on her hand, looking at the small sixth finger. Indeed.

Rowan quickly clenched her hand and he let her snatch it away. Colin placed a finger under her chin and lifted her face, watching it carefully. Rowan refused to meet his eyes.

"You have six fingers."

Silence.

"That is the sign of a witch."

Silence.

"Look at me when I speak."

Rowan lifted her eyes against her will. His was a voice to be obeyed. She stared into his eyes giving away nothing.

"It is Lady Lochalsh's men you are running from."

It was a statement, a fact. Rowan nodded her head unable to speak. She closed her eyes. He knew, had probably known all along. She pulled the blanket closer as if it could protect her from the man at her side. So, he would be the one to take her to the castle, not the hunters. Her eyes traveled to her wet clothes hanging from the branches. Even if she were to make a wild dash for them there was no way she could pull the wet wool over her legs before he would be on her. She closed her eyes in despair. This was not a man to sleep deeply if he had something to guard. Her lip trembled from her thoughts, from her tiredness, from the strain of the past days. Slowly she drew her knees to her chest and rested her head on them.

Colin sat watching her, reading the emotions that played plainly across her face. So Briac's seeing stone and his own suppositions were right. This was the witch. He saw the muscles in her hunched shoulders highlight the strength and sleekness that came from hunting in the highland forests. He watched as the fire played over her red hair, his thoughts on the green eyes that had flashed so brightly in anger then unexpectedly had gone dull. It was the same fading of light that he had seen when watching a deer die, a rabbit take its last breath. He looked down at the delicate arch of her neck gleaming through the red hair. She sat silent and still as if waiting for the whip to fall.

This was the one Gwynneth hunted. His eyes hardened as he thought of this wild creature captured and placed into the hands of his Lady. Images of the lass' mother lying bloodied on the cold stone floor of the castle rose in his mind's-eye. Looking down he again saw the defenseless neck, heard her give a soft sigh and he swore to his gods that Gwynneth would not have her witch.

Clearing his throat he spoke, choosing his words carefully. "It was wise that you escaped."

Rowan raised her head and looked at him, startled. Colin gave her a smile and nodded his head. "Aye, I heard talk about this hunt. You did the right thing to ride through the woods like a mad fox." Colin looked away. "You will receive nothing but harsh treatment from Lady Lochalsh."

"My brother Elden was captured with me but he did na escape," her voice trailed off.

"He is the seer," Colin said.

"Aye." Rowan looked into the fire as she spoke. "He told me that a circle was coming around again. That I am hunted because of him. That they kill witches in the castle," she continued, "Lady Lochalsh, have you met her? Is she as bad a woman as my brother says?"

Intrigued, Colin asked what her brother had told her.

"That she is covered in the colors of black and red and has a destiny that willna be denied."

"Lady Lochalsh," Colin paused and briefly closed his eyes. It hurt him to say these things out loud. It was as if by finally giving his thoughts a voice, he was acknowledging the sum of who Gwynneth truly was with her hate, her anger, and her unstoppable desire for revenge. And acknowledging his own part in letting her continue on that path. "Lady Lochalsh is no one to tangle with. You must continue in your escape."

"But my brother."

"Your brother will be fine. As you said, he knows who Lady Lochalsh is. He is a seer and can most likely find a way to please her, but you," his eyes traveled over her and she blushed at their intensity, "you will anger her." He saw more questions form on her lips and forestalled them by shaking his head. "That is enough talk for tonight. You need a good rest. Tomorrow, I'll wake you early and send you off." Rising, he went to his horse and pulled another blanket from its pack. Walking back, he handed it to her. "Stay wrapped in your blanket and cover yourself with this."

Rowan looked up at him and shivered as a breeze blew through their small camp. "And you?"

Colin smiled at her. "I will use my cloak."

"You know that won't be enough. The blanket is large enough to share."

Colin raised an eyebrow and was pleased to see her scowl return. Rowan spoke sharply, "You will be cold as the night wears on. The dew falls heavily towards dawn and you need a blanket if you are going to be of any use to me tomorrow." With that she began to lie down. Pausing, she spoke again "Well?"

Colin stood over her and saw that she expected him to obey. Smiling to himself, he slowly lowered his body. Lying between the dark woods and the lass he carefully stretched out, being sure to avoid touching her, and drew the blanket over them both. The fire cracked and danced in the night as Rowan fell into a deep sleep. Seeking warmth and safety, she unconsciously snuggled her body into the curve of Colin's and gave a soft sigh. Colin looked out into the darkness, ears tuned for any disturbance, sleep a far-away thing.

Chapter 15

THE HUNTER LOOKED through bleary eyes back into the woods. He had been up since first light trying to track the lass and again there had been no sign. Returning to the camp, his irritation had flared when he found the two other hunters had returned well before him and were sitting beside a warm fire, a hare cooking over the leaping flames.

"Get up!" The words rang through the air.

Slowly, Elden rose from his blankets. Flexing his shoulders against his stiffness he looked at the leader, "You are never going to find her, you know. Your best bet is to take me to the castle at once and give me to your Lady. At least you will be able to bring her something."

The leader turned and walked to the fire mulling over the advice. Elden raked his hand through his hair and willed the man to do it. If they gave up the hunt and went on to the castle then Rowan would be safe. But exactly how much did his lady's wrath weigh against the coin that would be paid? If she was like her mother, they had much to fear indeed. Elden saw the man glance out once again into the woods, then back at the two hunters busily eating the hare. He looked over at his captive and turned to the hunters. "Kill that fire. We have a day's ride until we reach the castle."

"We dinna hunt the lass?"

The leader turned to his horse averting his eyes, "We dinna hunt the lass."

Elden saw the two men look at each other in fear. He took in a deep breath and prepared to meet Lady Lochalsh.

***

The pale morning sun poured through the window. "My Lady, they are coming," Silobah spoke quietly. Jumping from her bed Gwynneth ran to the window, pushing the old woman aside. Squinting, she peered towards the woods. "I don't see them." Turning she grabbed Silobah's arm, "what do you mean they are coming?"

Silobah yanked her arm away from Lady Lochalsh's grasp. "I dinna said they were here, My Lady, but I know that today they will come."

Gwynneth looked closely at Silobah. The old woman gave a shake of her head. "No. Dinna set your sights on me as your next witch. I am nae seer. It is just a feeling I have." With a deep sigh, she turned back to the window and muttered to herself, "The circle is calling." Gwynneth stood silently and looked at the old woman. She glanced over at the journal that lay on the floor beside the bed. Silobah followed her look. Spying the book, the old one walked over and grabbed it up. "Where did you find this?"

"With my mother's things."

"Why did you nae tell me about it?"

"I had no need to."

Silobah looked down at the journal she had seen in Lady Stannard's hands for so many years and knew it contained the woman's most private thoughts, plots, and plans. Silobah clutched it to her breast as if she could make the book disappear. Gwynneth laughed out loud.

"I have read it many times. It is highly instructive." She laughed again. "You clutch it like a bairn." Turning to the window, she smiled knowing she would be successful where her mother had failed. She would keep control of Lochalsh and so would the generations of Stannards who would follow.

***

The roasting fox crackled and spit over the open fire as the chilled morning mist began to lift. Sitting beside the flames, Rowan reached out and tore a bit of meat from the cooking animal. Tending his horse, Colin looked over at her and gave a smile. "Kindly save some for me." Rowan smiled through her chewing. Colin walked over, and ripping a bit off for himself, sat beside her, their backs against the raw morning air.

"When did you catch it?"

The laird smiled and swallowed. "At first light."

"You should have woken me. I could have gone with you."

"No. You needed sleep."

Rowan gave a frown. Sleep? Did he think she was a child? She imagined him getting up with the first ray of the sun and looking down at her indulgently, as one would look at a bairn in its basket. Her spine stiffened.

"If you had taken me with you, we would be feasting on something other than this scrawny fox."

Colin paused, the meat halfway to his lips. Slowly, wiping the back of his hand across his mouth, he hid a smile. Prickly this morning, was she? Didn't like to be treated like a female, did she? He lowered his hand being careful to lose the smile. "Nae doubt. But you seemed tired from yesterday and anyway, doesn't the fox taste good?"

Rowan quickly searched his face for sarcasm but found none. She turned her attention back to the meat. It was good, more than good. The hunters had pushed hard and she and Elden had fared poorly. Thank the gods this one knew how to hunt. She paused in her chewing. He was a hunter but who was he? He certainly knew who she was. She swallowed then spoke. "Who are you?"

Colin gave her a bland look and her voice sharpened. "Who are you?"

Colin sat for a moment gathering his thoughts. He replied, "A hunter."

Rowan clenched her teeth. "I know that. But who are you, what is your name, where are you from?"

"I am known as Arden." Colin gave an inward grin at the thought of his friend hearing this, "and I live near the sea."

"Is that how you know about Lady Lochalsh?"

"Aye," Colin gave Rowan a look and continued, "and you?"

Rowan smiled. "You know who I am, why Lady Lochalsh wants to capture me. What else is it that you need to know?"

"Your name."

"Och. Aye. Well, I am known as Rowan."

"The same as the tree that guards against witches?"

Rowan laughed, "Aye. The very same. It seems that my brother gave me the name to ward off the power of my sixth finger."

Colin smiled. The rowan tree. The tall ash that grew in the mountains. It suited her well. Colin sat watching her, studying the angle of her chin. In the morning light she was even fairer than she had been yesterday afternoon or even last night. The picture of her standing naked with her hair streaming down her back flashed into his mind. Well, almost as fair as last night.

Suddenly Rowan wiped her hands on her wool trews and stood. "I need to be on my way."

Colin looked up at her and nodded, rising to his feet. Tossing the remains of the meat into the flames, he moved about the clearing, gathering leaves still wet from the dew. Throwing them onto the fire, he waited a few moments as the flames sputtered, then died. Turning, he helped Rowan roll the blankets and carried them to his horse, deftly tying them behind the pack. Checking the bridle, he walked around to the other side and mounted. Settling himself into the saddle, he leaned down and reached out for her.

"And we are going where?" Rowan stood with her arms folded over her chest.

Colin looked down at her in surprise. "We are going to look for your horse. Then you are free to go where you choose."

Rowan stood; her arms still folded over her chest as the large horse shifted from foot to foot. Colin controlled him with his knees and looked down at her in exasperation. "Come on. We have nae time to waste."

"You'll be true to your word?" she challenged.

Colin closed his eyes then opened them glaring at her. "Aye. I will keep my word. Here." Impatiently he held out his hand again and seeing her with her arms still crossed he deepened his voice. "Even if I did nae keep my word, what could you do about it?"

Rowan backed up a pace and Colin moved his horse a step forward and continued, "You are smaller. I am stronger, faster and know these woods like the back of my hand. You really have nae choice, do you?"

Rowan gritted her teeth. He was right. She thought about his promise to protect her. Indeed, he had not harmed her last night. Reason said she could trust him, but her heart wasn't so sure. Elden would certainly berate her for being prickly, unapprecia-tive. She straightened her shoulders. This wasn't last night. She wasn't exhausted and bereft of her clothes. If he tried to take her captive, she could certainly fight her way clear. Turning her face up to his, she smiled.

Colin sitting on his horse, ready for a fight, was taken aback. If he had thought her fair this morning, it was nothing compared to what she looked like when she truly smiled. Rowan lifted her hand in the air like a princess and tilted her chin. Laughing, Colin reached down and helped her up onto his horse. "Now. Let's find that beast of yours and get you on your way."

***

The late afternoon sun pierced the gloom of the great hall, highlighting the utter silence. Dust motes danced in the slanting light, swirling past the hanging tapestries to land near the vast wooden doors closed against prying eyes. Gwynneth stood in front of the large stone fireplace, her black gown falling from her shoulders, her white face still, motionless, beyond anger. Kneeling in front of her were the two hunters, their eyes on the stone floor. The leader stood to the side, his eyes straight ahead. Behind them stood Elden, his back straight, his head up, his thoughts racing.

So, this was Lady Lochalsh. Gwynneth. The name flared in his head, leaving a trail of smoke in its wake. Daughter of Lady Stannard, the killer of his mother. Ice-cold rage surged through him and the scene before him turned red, as red as the floor beneath his mother's lifeless body. The searing image cut through his mind and he closed his eyes willing it away. It was done. Go past it, he commanded himself, and concentrate on how best to deal with this Lady.

He opened his eyes and found her staring at him. He returned her look. Gwynneth narrowed her eyes. He noted she had the look of her mother, with her long black hair and dead white skin. His own skin crawled as he continued his assessment of her. Shifting his gaze from her long tapering fingers to the hollows under her cheekbones, he met her eyes and held her stare.

Gwynneth stood silently appraising the man, this seer, this brother of the witch. She had expected something other than this very ordinary man with his short powerful build and plain brown hair. The leader made a move as if to speak and she snapped her fingers for silence. The man gratefully hushed. He knew when things were in the balance. Lady Lochalsh seemed torn between her desire to whip him with her anger and her eagerness to question the seer. He breathed in and out lightly, slowly, trying to make no sound.

"Come here." The voice was cold, flat. Elden kept his eyes on Gwynneth as he walked toward her. He stopped a few feet away.

"So, this is the brother of the witch." Gwynneth looked down for the telltale sixth finger then raised her eyes at him in question. Her head jerked back slightly at the sight of his eyes, their not-so-ordinary tawny yellow gleaming back at her.

"You willna find a sixth finger on me." Elden's voice was abrupt and harsh. The leader moved slightly away. Gwynneth beckoned Elden closer. The hunters held their silence wishing they were back in the woods. Gwynneth's eyes were cold, her body still, her face devoid of expression. Nervously the leader looked from Gwynneth to Elden and inched even farther away.

Elden kept his eyes locked on Lady Lochalsh. For all that she looked like her mother; she was not Lady Stannard. Though he could see she was trying to be. He could feel her determination to have her own way but his determination was just as strong. He advanced closer, his steps firm and measured.

Gwynneth spoke. "You see things." Elden inclined his head. Gwynneth continued, "What things do you see?"

"I see the sky, the trees, and the sun just as any other man."

Gwynneth's eyes glittered in anger. The hunters threw glances of longing at the closed doors. Lady Lochalsh clenched her hand into a fist. Elden noticed the movement and smiled to himself.

"Do not mock me. What do you see?"

"I see only when I am asleep. Even then it is nae like every day seeing."

"Explain yourself."

"Vague stories come to me when I sleep. I remember the dreams then try to find out what they mean."

"Is it the future you see?"

"I see many things." Elden gave her a vague answer, hoping to prolong the conversation and keep the subject on him rather than Rowan.

"And just what are these things?"

"Normal things. Strange things." His voice became lyrical. "Things that tell their own tale, things that sing in the night, things that dance in the flames, things of a nature that is most private."

Gwynneth gave a grunt of disgust, "I have no time to waste. You will answer me when you are hungry enough." Giving a thin smile she turned to a guard and gave her orders, "Take him away. To the cellar. No food or water and see that no one approaches him." Elden gave a slight bow in mockery and her lips tightened. Watching as he was led from the hall, she turned back to the hunters. Her attention singled out the leader. A deathly silence again filled the large room.

"Where is she?" He started to answer but she raised her voice.

"Why do you not have her?"

The great hall echoed with her words and the leader cowered beneath her anger. Tales of Gwynneth's mother putting to death those who displeased her raced through his mind. He breathed in and out, trying to lessen the pounding of his heart, rapidly searching for an answer. No amount of money was worth this. He should have dumped the man at the castle gate and ridden away.

Gwynneth interrupted his thoughts. "I suppose she used her arts and disappeared?" Her sarcasm rang through the air while the leader silently thanked the gods for this escape.

Taking in a deep breath, he began, "My Lady, she did nae disappear in front of our eyes but she got away when she should nae have been able to. Her hands were tied, the horse was tied to a bush." As he lied, he saw Gwynneth's intense interest and he warmed to his tale. "She called out and the horse broke his tether.

Then it seemed as if the ropes just fell from her hands. We tried to stop her but it was as if our limbs would nae work. Somehow we were frozen to the ground." He saw Gwynneth lean forward. "When we were finally able to move," he paused for dramatic effect, "no trace of her could be found."

Gwynneth clasped her hands together, her eyes looking into the distance. Silobah, having been roused from an uneasy nap by the cook, rushed into the hall as the leader finished his speech. Stopping by the huge door she paused and closed her eyes. She knew the leader was lying to save his skin. Anyone would. And here was Gwynneth, ready to believe.

Spying Silobah, Gwynneth ordered the men paid, then swept from the room. Coins in hand, the hunters could not leave the castle fast enough. Silobah watched their hasty departure then went in search of the boy she had not seen for sixteen years.

***

The land around Fionn Ben was harsh and tiring. They had circled the huge stone mountain for hours looking for Rowan's horse, but instead had found two red deer and signs of wolf. As the sun began its slant toward the west, Rowan sat behind Colin, her body leaning forward, resting against his. During the morning hours she had held herself upright and away from him, but the large fighting saddle they shared was slanted inward, to hold a man close to his horse when wielding a heavy sword. As the day dragged on, Rowan had become increasingly tired, and finally gave in. Colin wondered how long she would be able to hold out and had been careful not to react when she at last leaned against him. It was difficult not to reach behind and give her a comforting pat, but he valued his hand.

"Over there. Listen." Rowan pointed to a stand of birch trees.

Colin pulled the horse to a stop and listened as instructed.

"There. Again."

Colin tilted his head and gave a nod. The sound of large teeth tearing grass came clearly to their ears. Flicking the reins, he urged his mount in the direction of the sound. They made their way around the trees. Rowan had been right. The runaway raised his head and gave a nicker.

Quickly Rowan slid down and walked over to the horse. Snorting, he nuzzled her hand and Colin watched as she stood quietly by the animal's side, stroking its mane. Rising up on her toes, she checked the contents of the saddle pack. Colin sat on his mount, watching her long slender fingers rummage through the leather bag. His eyes caught sight of the sixth finger. The feeling of determination that had risen in him so strongly last night, came over him again. He let his eyes travel up her slender arm, an arm that for all of its strength would undoubtedly fail against Gwynneth's cruelty.

Feeling Colin's gaze, Rowan turned her head to speak. But seeing the harsh look on his face, she quickly turned back to the horse. Gathering the reins in her hands, she pulled herself into the saddle. Fussing with the bridle, the saddle, her hair, Rowan kept her eyes away from the man, trying not to think of how comforting it had been to lean her body against his, trying to push away the memory of how he had looked in the firelight as he dried his body. Taking a deep breath, she dragged the image of the hunters into the forefront of her mind and her spine stiffened. Raising her eyes, she looked directly into those of the laird. Her words were formal, clear, and direct.

"Thank you."

Colin raised an eyebrow. Rowan took a breath and continued, "You did nae have to help me and you did. You could have taken me back to the hunters or to the castle and you did neither. Thank you."

Colin sat on his horse, admiring her. The huntress, it seemed, was back. The scared and tired lass had disappeared. Seated on her horse, her confidence renewed, he nodded to her, respecting her words even as he felt a loss at the return of her composure.

"I would never have taken you to the castle. That you must know."

Rowan gave him a smile and he returned it. The only sounds were the shifting of the horses, the creak of the saddles. Colin cleared his throat and spoke. "Do you have food enough in the saddle pack?"

"Aye."

Silence again. Rowan fidgeted with the reins and Colin leaned over to check a strap on the saddle. The horses nickered; a bird twittered. Rowan slid one hand through her hair and looked up at the sky. "It grows late. I need to be gone."

Colin looked at her. "Where will you go? You canna return to where you came from. That is the first place they will look."

Rowan shrugged her shoulders "I could nae return there even if I wanted to." Seeing his questioning look she continued. "They burned it, all of it. Elden said they did so to let us know that we would never have need of it again."

Colin gripped the reins so hard that his knuckles went white. His words were clipped, harsh. "So, you have nae home?"

"Nae home, clothes, possessions. Nothing." Rowan looked up at the sky and stopped speaking. Colin sat on his horse seeing the way she straightened her shoulders and a disturbing thought flashed through his mind.

"Nae. Dinna do it. Your brother can take care of himself."

Rowan took a deep breath and answered in a neutral voice.

"Aye. I know he can. I have nae intention of going to the castle. Why should I go to a place where I was trying to escape being taken?" She turned a smile on him. "I'll go deep into the highlands. All the way up to Smoo Cave where Elden's clan lives." She smiled. "We trade them visions for candles. They will help me." Shifting in her saddle she gathered up the reins then met the laird's eyes. "Thank you, again." She lifted her shoulders indicating that she had no more to say.

Colin nodded his head, knowing she needed to go. He could not go with her. He had to return to the castle and deal with Gwynneth. There was nothing he could offer Rowan except this chance to escape. "Bidh curamach."

"Aye, careful I will be." Backing her horse a few steps Rowan pulled on the reins and turned to go. As she kicked the horse into a trot, she turned her head once and looked at Colin. He raised his hand in farewell and watched as she rode into the distance.

For a few moments he sat gazing at the spot where she had disappeared. His horse, feeling the reins go slack, lowered his head to graze. Colin concentrated on reassuring himself. She would go to the highlands as she said. She would not go to the castle to rescue her brother. He recalled the warnings he had given about Gwynneth. He had said enough. He was sure she was headed to the highlands. There she would be protected, hidden, and live in safety. Pulling on the reins he turned his horse in the direction of the castle. Another night near Fionn Ben then a day's ride to Gwynneth. His eyes held a troubled look as he kicked his horse into a trot.

Chapter 16

Lochalsh Castle

EVENING WAS APPROACHING as Elden sat on the cot and looked at the bare walls, his eyes tracing patterns in the stones. With a sigh he rose, and walking to the window, looked through the bars. All was still. He could hear nothing; it was quiet as death. He leaned his head against the stones and closed his eyes. It was almost too much to bear being back here. Memories assaulted him at every step. The great hall where he had stood beside his mother facing Lady Stannard, the stale room in which he had first been locked, the small storeroom where Silobah let him live in hiding after his supposed escape.

"Let me see your face."

Elden jumped at the words and whirled around. Silobah stood at the doorway. At the sight of him her, eyes opened wide then closed tightly. It was he. The small one she had kept safe from Lady Stannard. The one she had rescued from the malice that stalked the castle halls. The one she had sent away before she left for Corrieshalloch Gorge with the bairn. Memories rose up and overwhelmed her. Putting her hand out for balance she stumbled and Elden moved swiftly to her side, catching her, and leading her over to the cot.

Barely noticing his help, Silobah was lost in the grip of her memories. She had always believed Thomas the Rhymer and his prophecy. Believed so strongly that she had pledged herself to the destruction of the circle, and thus, to a lonely life bereft of family and friends. But mistakes, by all the gods had been made, warning signs missed. In keeping watch over Lady Stannard, she had received not reward but blood on her hands and memories that tore through her. She opened her eyes and saw the face of one who was once more locked in castle Lochalsh.

"I prayed to every goddess I know that it would nae be you."

"Well, you see how much they helped." Elden's voice was harsh with memories. "Are you here to renew old acquaintances?"

Silobah looked at him for a few moments in silence. When she spoke again, her voice was soft. "It was I who hid you then kept you close to your mother. It was I who kept you safe from Lady Stannard."

"Aye and it was you who let my mother die."

Silobah closed her eyes as if she could shut out the stark memory. Elden saw his words hit their mark. He gave a contemptuous smile to himself. Did she really think that her kindness to him those years ago could erase the fact that she was still here, tending to Lady Stannard's daughter? Thank all gods that she never knew he had followed her to the sacred gorge.

Silobah watched the emotions playing over his face. This was one to keep an eye on. He always had been. She took a deep breath. "I thought perhaps you were dead although I prayed that you were nae."

"Death would have been too easy. As you can see, I made good the escape and have spent my life in the highlands. And now," he gave a short harsh laugh, "I suppose I shall await Lady Lochalsh's pleasure. It won't be the first time I have done so for a lady of this castle."

Silobah ignored the barb, concentrating on her question, "Who is this lass that Gwynneth wants so badly?"

"She is my sister, of sorts. When I escaped here, I returned to the Dalchork Wood. The clan from Smoo Cave took me in and the laird claimed me as his. It is his youngest daughter that Lady Lochalsh seeks," Elden kept his eyes level as he mislead the old woman.

"Won't the clan be close on your heels to bring her back?"

"No. She was cast out because she had the sixth finger and the clan leader's second wife claimed she was doing her harm. I lived on my own then, so kindness bade me take the lass in. Besides it was my duty to repay her father for taking me in."

Silobah watched him, trying to find the truth in his words. He gazed back at her blandly. She spoke, "Times are different now. Lochalsh has a laird who is strong." Elden looked a question at the old woman and she nodded her head. "You know the hold that Lady Stannard had on her lord. It is nae the same with her daughter."

Elden leaned against the stone walls, crossed his legs, and looked at her, "Tell me."

"He is Colin of Dunrobin, third in line to the Laird of Dornoch. He earned the right to Castle Lochalsh by fighting well at the battle of Bannock Burn. Colin was ordered to take the castle as a reward but the Lady Gwynneth came with it."

Elden gave no sign he already knew most of what she said. Silobah shifted, smoothing the cloth of her skirt over her knees. The silence continued and she raised her head, "I am here to help you. I know I canna undo what has been done or my part in it. But that does nae mean I want to see it happen again."

The words pierced Elden. Pushing himself away from the wall he quickly moved to her side. Leaning over he grabbed her by the shoulders and shook her as he spoke.

"It willna happen. I willna let it."

Silobah wrenched herself out of his hands. "Put your memories aside and listen! You may have no choice. It is revenge she wants and to get it she must have the desire of the laird." Elden looked puzzled. She continued, "Aye, it's Colin in her bed that she wants. That is why she searches for a witch. For someone who can make Colin come to her."

"The laird does nae do this on his own?"

"Och he is a man of normal appetites. It is just that he doesn't have an appetite for Lady Lochalsh."

"Why?"

"He has seen her anger and knows she harbors a taste for revenge. He avoids her. And the more he avoids her the more she is determined to get him in her bed. It's his child she wants. And through this child, she will keep Stannard blood ruling Lochalsh, and have her revenge. It has become a madness with her."

"Madness runs in the blood."

"Aye it does."

Her matter-of-fact words made Elden's heart turn cold. The words he thrust at her were just as frigid. "And what stake do you have in it this time?"

For an instant Silobah bent her head under the attack, then raising her eyes she answered, "The honor of an oath." Elden began to speak but Silobah interrupted, "The more the laird turns away from her, the more determined she becomes, and the more she becomes like Lady Stannard."

Elden walked to the window and looked out at deepening sky. Run, he whispered under his breath to Rowan. Run like the wind. Silobah began to speak again. Elden turned from the window and gave her his full attention.

"I will stay by Gwynneth's side and try to keep her from tracing her mother's steps. It is the least I can do, having failed before."

"And me?"

"You will leave here and never return. I'll tell the laird's friend, Arden, that you are being held here. He will help you get away. Then it is up to me to make sure that events dinna play the same as they have before."

Silobah stood and looked at Elden. "I have nae more words. My hand in the death of your mother was unwitting. I followed my heart and prayers and took the barn to Corrieshalloch Gorge. I had no choice."

"So that is what happened? Was it a lass or wee man?" Elden feigned ignorance.

"A lass. I gave her to the gods. That is my only comfort."

127

"It is no comfort to me." The words were harsh.

"Aye. But this time I know what I am up against. And I will fulfill my promise of long ago." Giving him a sad smile, she turned, opened the door, then closed it softly behind her.

Elden walked from the window and sat heavily on the cot, the talk with Silobah having taken his strength. Silently he sat and closed his eyes and leaned back against the familiar stone walls.

***

Colin reined in his horse beside the loch and sat wearily. Castle Lochalsh. He could see it in the distance and the closer he got the more it felt like a collar, tightening around his neck. How he wished he were at Briac's cave instead of here. He closed his eyes and the face of his old friend rose in his mind. Colin could almost hear the sound of the Falls of Shin, could almost smell the smoke from the cave's banked fire. The horse shifted uneasily beneath him and he returned to the present. There would be no such comfort now. Briac had told him all that he needed to know. The path of ignorance was now closed.

He looked up toward the castle and saw gannets swooping around the square tower before heading to the sea to capture dinner. The sky gave off a deep hue and he realized it was almost the end of the day. Had it been only a few days that he had been away from the castle? It felt more like weeks. He thought of Rowan's red hair and wondered what it would look like framed against the deep color of the sky. A smile drifted across his face, but vanished as he remembered Gwynneth and her hunt for the witch. Yanking on the reins he kicked his horse into a canter. He wanted to know if the hunters had returned. His mouth turned down as he thought of the reception his lady would give them. He kicked the horse even harder and galloped through the evening.

***

Arden heard the familiar hoof beats and put down the brush he was using on his horse. What was Colin doing back so soon? There was no way he could have made it to and from Briac's cave in this amount of time. He gave the horse an affectionate pat on the neck then hurried out of the stall. He needed to be the first to reach his friend.

"You're back early." He watched carefully as Colin swung himself from the saddle.

"Aye. It was time to come back. I was tired of sleeping on the ground." His reply was cautious, neutral. He didn't want to speak here in the courtyard. Arden nodded his head in understanding, "Here, give me that beast. You've most likely ridden him half to death."

The laird shot him a look then laughed. "And what makes you think you know what's best for my horse?" Bantering, barely hearing a word the other spoke they walked into the stable.

Leading the horse into the stall Arden lowered his voice. "We need to talk."

"We do indeed. I'll go the back way to your room."

"I'll follow right away."

The urgency of Arden's voice was enough. Walking to the back of the stable, Colin passed through the battered wooden door leading into a small waiting chamber in the castle wall. Moving across the empty room he reached a stone stair. Silently, he walked up the steps, then down the hall to Arden's rooms.

"What is your news?" Colin rested his back against the fireplace watching Arden pour them both a goblet of wine. He wasn't sure how to begin his own tale and needed time to gather his thoughts.

"The hunters have returned," Arden said, watching Colin's reaction. "They are back and without the witch. Gwynneth is nae pleased." Colin winced at the understatement. Arden continued, "She has the seer locked away. I was just going to see him when you arrived."

Colin started forward but Arden stopped him and recounted the events. Colin leaned against the wall and listened intently. When he heard that the leader had attributed Rowan's escape to her magical powers, he gave a snort of disgust. "That's ridiculous. The lass has nae special powers. She's merely clever, that's all." Arden raised an eyebrow and Colin snapped his mouth shut.

"And just how would you know?"

Colin didn't answer. Silence filled the room and Arden let it build, then pushed again. "In case you did nae hear me, I asked, what would you know about the lass being clever? And how do you know she is a lass, nae a woman?"

Colin clenched his jaw in frustration. Damn everything. He was off guard, still reliving the events in the forest. The laird met Arden's eyes squarely. "I know because I have met her."

Arden blinked in surprise. Looking at his friends' face closely, he said slowly, "Aye. You have, haven't you?"

Colin gave a weary sigh, as he moved to a chair beside the fireplace.

"It looks to be a long tale." Arden said. Walking over to the fireplace he worked at building the evening's fire, waiting for Colin to begin.

As he recounted the events of the last days, Colin tried to keep it simple for now, leaving out his meeting with Briac and the twining threads that connected Rowan to the witch who died at Lady Stannard's hands. As the tale ended, he sat back closing his eyes, exhausted. The fire glowed deep orange, the embers flickered dully against the dark of the chamber. A chill crept into the room and Arden pulled himself from the chair where he had sat entranced by Colin's story. Leaning over, he placed another log on the fire, settling it so it would catch the flame. A burst of yellow filled the air and he watched as the log blazed. So, Colin had met the witch. A frown crossed his face as he recalled the tone of voice Colin had used describing the lass. He glanced over at his friend who was now staring into the fire. Arden didn't like the look on the man's face. It was too soft, and Colin's eyes appeared as if they were half-asleep. He knew what that look meant. He had been friends with Colin too long for him not to recognize when the man was smitten with a woman. He closed his own eyes and suppressed a groan. He hoped the lass was miles away by this time. He shied away from the thought that she might be caught.

"Where is she headed?"

"To the north. To a clan that lives beside Smoo Cave."

"It's good she's been given a head start. As far as I know Gwynneth has nae sent out more hunters to get her but I have little doubt that she will. She is convinced it was the lass' powers that helped her get away and is more convinced than ever that the lass is a witch. And dinna forget, this witch has crossed Gwynneth by escaping."

Colin nodded his head slowly and leaned back in his chair, absently rubbing the tops of his thighs, pushing away Arden's words. "I met Briac."

Arden laughed, "Dinna tell me. The lass really is a witch and spirited you to the cave and back." Colin looked at his friend in disgust.

"No. Briac met me in the woods at Corrieshalloch."

It was a testament to how much the men believed in Briac's powers that Arden didn't question the old one's appearance. Colin continued, deciding that the more Arden knew, the better he would be prepared for what might follow. It was time for the whole story. "Remember that lass we saw at Cassely? The hunter with the red hair?"

"Aye."

"That was Gwynneth's witch. Her name is Rowan."

Silence hung in the air as Arden tried to close his mouth and failed. Colin laughed out loud at the sight, "You will catch flies." Arden popped his mouth shut and glared at his friend. Colin spoke. "Aye. It is the very one. And there is more. She is the daughter of the witch that Lady Stannard killed." He answered the unspoken question, "I saw it in Briac's seeing stone."

Arden digested this news then spoke "Silobah told me most of the tale but she did nae say that the bairn of the highland witch lived."

"I dinna think she knows. And it is better that she does nae." Colin took a deep pull of his wine and swallowed. "There is little reason to fan the flames with Gwynneth. If she knows that Rowan is the daughter of the highland witch, she will never stop pursuing her."

Arden gave a sigh. "What will you do? Surely Gwynneth knows by now that you have returned and have heard about the seer."

"It is simple. I will order the man released and she will be forbidden to hunt Rowan. She must give up this idea that a witch can help her, when all the magic in the world willna make me come to her bed if I choose not to."

Arden winced at the words conjuring up Lady Lochalsh's reaction. "Now?"

"Aye. Now." Colin looked up at his friend and gave him a ferocious smile. Reaching out he grabbed Arden by his shoulder and gave him a rough shake. "Take heart. I've been to war before." With clenched teeth, Colin strode from the room.

***

Shadows danced on the walls of the cave as Rowan hunched over the flames, keeping her body between the flickering light and the dark outside. Feeding another branch to the fire, she gratefully felt the increased warmth. The night was silent and Rowan shivered with loneliness. It was not just that she was out in the woods in the dark. She had spent many such nights, wilder and colder than this alone in the woods. No, it was something deeper. When she had been in the woods before, Elden had always been waiting back at home; the fire warm, her bed turned back, food ready. Even as she had crouched by a smoldering fire with leaves from the trees dripping cold water on her back, she knew that she had somewhere to go, someone who waited for her, someone who would try to find her should she be too long away.

She lifted her head and gazed at the muddy walls of the cave. That's exactly what Elden had done last year. He had found her with her foot caught beneath a fallen tree. Hungry and tired, she had watched in fury as he pulled the tree to the side with one hand. A smile crossed her face as she remembered the night; remembered how he had carried her back to the croft, dressed her leg, fed her then sung stories to her until she fell asleep, exhausted.

The wind outside the mouth of the cave picked up its mournful sound pulling Rowan from her memories. Shivering again, she reached out for another branch. Her hand hovered in the air, her thoughts holding her still for a moment. Elden had always come looking for her when she had not come home. Elden had rescued her and dressed her wounds. Sixteen years ago, he had followed the woman who took her to Corrieshalloch and saved her from death itself. And now that he was captured, what was she doing? She was running away. Angrily, she grabbed the branch and flung it into the fire. How could she think of running away when Elden was trapped at that castle? She frowned in disgust. Aye, he had told her to run, aye she had promised to do so but she had been wrong. He needed her. Only the gods knew what Lady Lochalsh was doing to him. Hadn't the man, the one who called himself Arden, warned her against the woman? She glared at the fire. Her choice was clear. She could no more abandon Elden than he had abandoned her. She would return and help him.

The wind rose again outside and Rowan tossed another branch onto the flames. Moving to lie on her side, being sure to keep the fire between her and the night, she tried to close her eyes and sleep. She would have need of the rest if she was going to travel the distance back to the castle, then rescue Elden, somehow. The chill of the air pushed into the cave, and she scooted closer to the fire. Her eyes searched the flames looking for answers, while her ears rang with Elden's words about the Lady Stannard and the witch she had killed.

***

"My Lady."

Gwynneth whirled around and found herself staring at Colin. Her eyes widened in surprise then deepened with satisfaction.

"You are back from the forest, I see."

Colin nodded his head and carefully looked around the room. Silobah was nowhere to be found. The serving maids were absent. He was alone with his lady. He winced inwardly at the thought but was glad the discussion would be held without servants hovering outside the door, their ears fastened to the wood. He took a deep breath and looked down at her.

"Aye. I am here. For one reason and one reason only." Gwynneth's eyes narrowed at the tone of his voice. Turning her back on him she walked to her chair. Swirling her skirts, she slowly sat and took her time raising her eyes to meet his. Colin watched her movements, deliberate, and designed to provoke. He let the silence drag for a moment. Gwynneth sat staring up at him and waited.

Colin's eyes hardened. "The man, I want him released."

Gwynneth raised her eyebrows. "Who do you mean?"

"How many men do you have locked up, Gwynneth? You know exactly who I mean. The man you sent the hunters to capture. The one you dragged from his home and hounded through the woods. I want him released."

"And just who told you this tale, Silobah?" Gwynneth gave a shrug of her shoulders and continued, "She is old and fanciful."

"Arden."

Cornered, Gwynneth changed tactics. "The man is here at my pleasure. I have need of him."

"Need?" The word was sarcastic.

Gwynneth got up, and clutching her skirts, she walked to the window. Looking out as if addressing the night, she continued, "Yes, need of him. He is here to help me." She kept her back to the room and didn't see Colin take quick strides towards her. Reaching out he grabbed her shoulder and yanked her around, holding her arm in a tight grip.

"I know what you want him for. And I will have him released." Flinging her away, he walked back to the other side of the room, facing the fire.

Gwynneth pushed herself from the stone wall that had checked her fall, and watched, as Colin stood with his arrogant back turned to her. The anger in her head expanded and her voice lowered, "I will keep him. You will not release him."

Colin spun on his heel and took two strides toward her, grabbing both shoulders in his fury. "You willna have him! You may be Lady Lochalsh but I am the Laird. I will be obeyed." He saw a flicker of desire in her eyes and pushed her away disgusted. Gwynneth stumbled back a step, then stopped. A small smile played on her lips. Colin noticed the smile and drew back watching her. What was going on in that mind of hers? Surely, she couldn't be pleased that he was angry.

Gwynneth saw him study her and the smile widened. It didn't matter what he said. It didn't matter what he did, she was going to keep the seer in the castle. Look what had happened with just the man's arrival. The laird had come into her bedroom uninvited. He had grabbed her. He cared enough to be angry at what she was doing. She had his attention now. He would be watching her every move. And she didn't even have the witch yet. The smile on her mouth widened.

Colin watched as Gwynneth stood momentarily lost in her thoughts. Her smile didn't bode well for either his peace of mind or the man whom she had locked away. He narrowed his eyes and broke into her musing. "I am ordering his release tonight," Gwynneth made no response and Colin continued, "and orders are being given that all searching for this supposed witch will cease. No men will be sent to find her."

Gwynneth looked up at him. Dipping her head she gave him a demure smile "As you wish, My Laird."

Nonplussed, Colin gave a puzzled look at her sudden capitulation. Nodding his head at her for emphasis, he turned and left the room. Gwynneth watched him go and smiled to herself. Stop looking for the witch indeed. Never! Let the seer go on his merry way? Hardly! She hurried to the bell and rang it furiously. Opening the door, she looked impatiently down the hall and went to ring the bell again.

Chapter 17

THE LIGHT FLICKERED on Gwynneth's face as Silobah stood by her side, silently watching. She had seen this look on the young woman's face before, just as she had seen it on the face of her mother. The old woman shivered and drew her shawl around her. It wasn't that the room was cold. Indeed, it was too warm, the maids having stacked wood on the fire in hopes they would not be called later in the night. By now they knew the laird had ordered the seer set free, and they were waiting for Lady Lochalsh's fury. Gwynneth stared intently at the fire, keeping her eyes on the dancing lights as she addressed her servant.

"Bring Ewan of the Little Head to me." Silobah shook her head and Gwynneth ignored the movement. "I said bring him here." The old woman opened her mouth to speak but Gwynneth forestalled her, whirling around with eyes that glittered more brightly than the fire. "Do not question me on this."

Silobah again began to shake her head no when Gwynneth reached across the distance between them. Grabbing the old woman by her shoulders, Gwynneth tightened her fingers in a cruel grip. "I know what you did with the highland witch. I know you watched her held captive, helped her die. Compared to that, bringing Ewan to me is nothing. Come by the back stairs. Let no one see you."

Silobah wrenched herself free. Her words came out thin and strained. "I did nothing. It was your mother. She was the one who let the woman die then ordered the death of that thin and wailing child. Aye, I stood by. Aye, I let it happen, but that is where it ends."

Gwynneth gave the old woman a cold smile. Silobah gathered her shawl around her shoulders as Lady Lochalsh's voice came through the air, bitter and clear. "Rumors swirl but only you and I know what happened to the witch, and I can always tell the laird that it was you who had her killed."

Silobah rocked back on her heels knowing full well that Gwynneth would do just that and take pleasure in it.

Gwynneth continued, "And if I know my laird, he would be repulsed by you, and, I believe, would feel it only right to banish you from the castle." Gwynneth noted the old woman's reaction and smiled. Of course, she would do as she was asked. She really had no choice. No one in the clan, in the village would take her in. For years they had heard tales of the things she had done for Lady Stannard. There was too much fear associated with Silobah for anyone to offer her shelter. Gwynneth held the old woman's eyes and smiled. "You go and do as I say and I will not tell such a tale to our laird."

Silobah closed her eyes and saw Thomas the Rhymer. The old one's face dissolved and, in its place, came that of Fiona, the highland witch, her long hair mingling with the blood from her body as it splayed across the stone floor. Red upon red. Death after death. The prophecy. The circle. The old woman prayed to her gods. If she were cast out of the castle, she would not be able to keep her eyes fixed on Gwynneth. But how could she give in yet again? How could she summon Ewan, knowing he would be sent to track Elden, helping with Gwynneth's plan. She would not, could not let the circle come around again. Gathering strength, she closed her eyes and looked inward. An imaginary keek-stand glowed in the dark. Gazing into its black depths she opened her mind. Suddenly, there it was. A pathway. She smiled. Looking up at Gwynneth she spoke.

"Nae. I willna fetch Ewan. And you willna tell such a lie. Stop and think. If you did, wouldn't I, having nothing to lose, speak to the laird of other certain truths and let him decide? To start, how do ye think you would fare with him knowing his food has been flavored with ground testicles of rabbit to make him soft and timid?"

Gwynneth stood rubbing her hands as if to keep them from circling Silobah's neck. The old one had found her resolve, and the threat rang true. She would have to speak with Ewan herself, hoping the dimwit would stay silent about the command. Casting a sharp look at the old woman, Gwynneth gestured for her to leave the room. Silobah was fast outliving her usefulness. Gwynneth turned back to the fire.

***

The following afternoon, Rowan moved her horse carefully through the twilight woods pausing now and then to take stock and to listen for the sounds of being followed, hunted. She sat on the horse waiting for the wind to bring her any unusual scent. The horse shifted impatiently and Rowan tightened her knees, stilling his movements. The air was free from the smell of smoke. Good. No fires had been lit. Perhaps they weren't going to resume the hunt. Perhaps Elden was enough for Lady Lochalsh. She bit her lip at the thought. Elden, locked up in the castle at the whim of that evil creature. She gave a sudden shiver. Aye, Lady Stannard had killed a witch but this was Lady Lochalsh, and Elden wasn't a witch, just a seer. Perhaps he will tell her what she wants to hear and she will let him go. The horse shifted again and Rowan pulled herself from her thoughts. She wouldn't trust the fates for that. She had to go to Elden herself.

Quietly clucking to her mount, she backed him out of the bushes and onto the trail. Squinting at the sky she knew she was headed in the right direction. Shifting her weight, easing her seat on the horse she put her heels to his side and increased his speed.

***

Colin strode down the stone corridor to the barred door. Grabbing the handle, he shoved the wooden plank from its latch.

Elden, looking out of the window, heard the sounds and was glad for the interruption. The night had been long and this day had dragged endlessly. Turning to face his visitor, he knew without being told that this was the laird. No one else would stride into the room in such a manner, no one else would have the bearing, the arrogant tilt of the head, the determined assured light in his eyes. Not around here, not with a lady such as Gwynneth. Elden studied the man standing in front of him. What manner of man was this who had married Gwynneth in return for Lochalsh? Aye, it was told that he had won battles and shown honor on the field, but what type of man was he truly?

Colin looked at the captured man and ran his hand through his hair in exasperation. He should have come down here last night and set the man free himself, but he hadn't. He had given orders; confident they would be carried out. He struggled to control his anger. Colin was sure this wasn't the first time that, unknown to him, Gwynneth had countermanded his orders and the guards had obeyed without a second thought. Thinking the man released and well on his way, Colin had spent most of the day with his men on the training grounds, working out his frustration, his anger. It was late in the afternoon when Arden strode into his chambers with the news that the seer still languished in captivity.

The laird tried to put his anger behind him as he looked at the man. He didn't look like Rowan's brother or even like what a seer might be. And there was no way to see this man in the young boy that Colin had envisioned in Briac's keek-stane. Colin took in Elden's humble manner of dress, the nondescript color of hair.

"It does nae take one with the vision to know who you are, My Laird."

Colin gave a wry smile and nodded his head. Elden nodded in return and continued to speak. "I was wondering when you were going to come to me. It is well known that you are a man of honor, one who nae would stand for someone to be unjustly locked away." Elden studied the laird carefully and waited.

"Nae, you see correctly. This," Colin waved his hand vaguely around the chamber, "should never have come to pass. You were to be released last night. I will see that you are given food and drink, some clothes, and a mount. You are free to go." He paused, recalling what Rowan had told him about their capture. "Although where you will go I dinna know. It pains me greatly that your home was burned."

Elden tilted his head to the side in surprise. The fire. How did the laird know of his burned home? Had he played a part? Elden gritted his teeth and willed the gods to let him into the laird's mind. He needed to know if this was a man of honor or if the laird plotted with that mad lady of his. Elden closed his eyes. Gathering his powers, hoping against hope that he would be successful, sent his mind searching into the laird's thoughts. An image of Rowan flashed before him, standing beside a fire wrapped in a blanket. A shadow moved beside her; the image of another person appeared, the person standing before him now.

Opening his eyes, Elden found the laird staring at him. A surge of dizziness overwhelmed him and he reached out for the wall, steadying himself. Nausea gripped his stomach and he closed his eyes once more, breathing deeply. The gods were taking their due, more so than with any nighttime vision. For a moment all was quiet except for Elden's ragged breathing. Gradually the dizziness passed and Elden slowly stood straight, his thoughts churning. So, they had met, and if there was any truth to the feelings and images he had seen in the laird's mind, it was a meeting filled with more than just the rescue of a maiden in distress. He peered deeply into the man's eyes and was pleased to see a flush appear on the laird's face.

Colin shifted from one foot to the other. Damn the man. Could he really read thoughts? Gingerly, Elden rubbed his forehead. Colin turned and walked to the other side of the room; his hands clenched behind his back. It was Elden who broke the silence.

"She is lovely is she nae?"

Stung, Colin whirled around and glared. His voice lowered an octave. "She is a hellion, a complete wild thing. She almost broke my nose."

Elden gave a short bark of laughter but quickly bit it off. He tried to apologize. "My Laird, she has ever been thus. She was raised by me, but I think she learned her manners from the creatures of the forest." Colin gave a grunt acknowledging the fact. Elden continued, "So you met her and helped her escape." It was not a question; it was a fact.

The laird nodded his head in acknowledgement then asked, "Can you see where she is now?"

Elden shook his head. "Nae. I canna see across great distances. I can only see what the visions bring me at night."

"And what is in people's minds."

"Only on rare occasions, My Laird. It's nae a power I can easily use. I am seldom able to do so."

Colin, seeing truth in the words, nodded and studied the seer carefully. He could find no resemblance between this one and the lass. The man was of middle height at best, with ordinary brown hair and eyes a strange yellow-brown. He wasn't anything like Rowan with her flowing red hair, long legs, snapping green eyes. The laird's face softened and Elden watched it closely. Yes, not only had he met her, but he was also smitten. Good. The gods were indeed protecting her. If the laird was even half the man he was supposed to be, then he would be protection indeed.

"My Laird, I can only guess where she has gone. I told her to run for the high country. It is where our mother is from."

Colin spoke, "You dinna look alike."

"We had different fathers."

Colin nodded his head absently as the information registered. Aye, of course. The rape he had seen in Briac's keek-stand. He pushed the ugly picture aside. Right now, all he wanted to do was get the man out of the castle and on his way. Surely with his powers he would find Rowan and keep her safe. He remembered her standing beside the fire, her eyes round with fear. He tried to banish the sight and glanced out of the window at the darkening evening.

"Will you stay the night?"

Elden shot the laird a look "This is an invitation?" The sarcastic words were not lost on Colin.

"It was nae by my order that you were hunted and captured." Elden kept silent and watched. Colin continued, "I am here now and you have my word. The door is unlocked and a night under a roof might ease your journey."

"I think not." Elden gave a slight bow to Colin ending the discussion. The laird raised his hands, palms out, then abruptly turned and walked from the room. Elden turned to watch the falling dusk. Rowan. The name sang in him and he drank a deep breath of the darkening night. Rowan. He sent his mind out, searching the woods, even though he knew he didn't have the power left at the moment to find her. "Rowan." The name fell from his lips as a blessing.

***

"He will be fine. I saw nae signs that he was worse for the capture." Colin stood beside the fire, his back leaning against the stones of the fireplace. Arden sat before him. Taking a swallow of his wine, he arched an eyebrow at the laird and answered. "Aye. You're quite right. There is nothing wrong with the man other than his home was burned, he was hunted through the woods like an animal, captured, and then dragged here to face the lovely Gwynneth. Actually, he was quite lucky when you consider it." The words came out with withering sarcasm and Colin frowned. Arden saw the frown and didn't care. He liked this man. If the word love could be used between two men, then he supposed he loved Colin like a brother, but there were times he would like to take his fist and knock some sense into his friend, laird or not.

Colin looked down at Arden and gave a heavy sigh. "There is nothing I can do about that. Gwynneth gave the order. I knew nae about it. At least I've finally made sure he is free. I told him he could stay the night."

"The man agreed to stay another night?" Arden asked incredulously.

"Nae. He is already gone, vanished in an instant."

Arden wearily rubbed his hands over his face. "And no wonder. You told him that you met the lass?"

"Nae."

Arden looked up and Colin nodded his head. "It is true about him seeing things. He knew that I met her without being told."

"And did you think that he was nae going to make sure that you never do so again? Colin, it doesn't take a vision to see that you're smitten with the lass. So now, not only does your lady want the lass for the spells she supposedly can perform, but also you want her for other things. The man would have to be mad to linger and give you the chance to follow him."

Colin turned his back on his friend and stared down at the fire. Of course the man had vanished immediately. He should have taken precautions to have him locked in his room until the trackers were ready but he simply could not make himself do it. He wanted the seer followed not to see Rowan once again, he assured himself, but to make certain Elden found her, and that they were safely on their way north.

Arden watched the reasoning flash over Colin's face and easily read his mind. Shaking his head, he took another sip of wine, then stared down into the goblet. That a man so battle sure and so powerful a leader could be so blind to his own feelings, his own reasons for acting the way he did, amazed him. A sudden movement broke his thoughts and he raised his head only to see Colin's back as he stalked from the room.

***

Ewan of the Little Head kept to the side of the castle, wrapping his cloak securely about himself. The wind tugged at the corners and he fastened it even tighter and waited in the evening dusk. His thoughts raced. If he was successful there was no telling what favors he might ask of Lady Lochalsh. He knew about the seer being captured, about the young woman escaping, about how angry Lady Lochalsh had been. He frowned at the thought of her going against Colin of Dunrobin. The laird was a good and fair man and had the loyalty of most in the castle and village but when Lady Lochalsh gave an order, you jumped to make sure that order was carried out. After all, the laird was reasonable and might be brought around to your way of thinking if you explained your actions properly. Lady Lochalsh was another matter. She was just like her mother. She didn't want to hear excuses. She didn't want to hear reasons. She just wanted her bidding done and punishment was swift and sure if it wasn't. He smiled again at the simplicity of it all. The people liked the laird but they feared the lady. Fear was stronger than liking in his book any day. He yanked himself back from his thoughts as he saw a movement near the hidden back entryway of the castle. It was just as my lady had said. The man was easy to spot. Medium height, a bit hunched, but with powerful shoulders and a swift and sure stride. Ewan nodded to himself. Moving out of the shadows, the chase was on.

Gwynneth stood at the castle window and a flurry of movement caught her eye. It was a man, no two. Stepping into the window alcove, she drew the hangings shut behind her.

Enclosing herself in the small dark space she peered into the fading light. Yes, two men. A smile crossed her lips. She stood quietly for a few moments, watching the figures pass into the woods, then pulled the hangings aside. Stepping back into the room she gasped. Colin was standing beside her writing table, his eyes scanning the surface.

"My Laird." Her words caused Colin to jump. Stepping quickly back he tried to compose himself. If he had seen her in the room, he would never have entered, even though he needed to see if there was a message sent, an order given to have them man followed. But he had found nothing and was left standing foolishly beside her writing table. Gwynneth kept a smile on her face. She knew this laird well. He had not come looking for her. He had come looking for other things. Her mind clicked and turned. Surely, he guessed she had sent a man to follow the seer. She kept her smile wide and guileless and approached him.

Colin moved aside as she stepped forward. The movement was not lost on her. Gritting her teeth, she went to the chairs before the fire and gestured for him to sit. "You wanted to see me my laird?"

Colin nodded his head but declined to sit. "Aye. I wanted to see you and make sure that you have nae given an order once again opposing mine." His words were cold and clipped.

Gwynneth made her voice soft. "I have given no orders contrary to yours."

Colin's voice was impatient. "Have you given orders that the man be followed?"

Gwynneth opened her eyes as wide as she could and tilted her head up sideways to his. Smiling softly, she replied, "No, My Laird. You were quite firm. I have learned my lesson well and will never go against you in any matter again."

Her words grated on Colin's ears, her manner making him feel as if he was covered with honey and his skin could not breathe. Giving her a nod, he began to walk from the bedroom.

Gwynneth made as if to speak, and Colin turned and waited. As she rose from her chair he backed towards the door. Gwynneth stopped in her tracks and gave him a bright smile.

"I was only going to ask you if you would not stay with me for a while, share a glass of wine?"

"Nae. There is much I have to do. I bid you goodnight." Turning on his heel he quickly left the room. Gwynneth kept the pleasant look on her face until the door closed on his back. Her smile faded abruptly and dark fire flashed from her eyes. The door opened again and Gwynneth fashioned the smile once more, only to lose it as Silobah entered the room.

"So, you spoke with that pea-headed servant of yours." It was a statement not a question. Silobah walked to the fire and held her hands out for its warmth. It looked as if she had aged overnight. Turning her head she stared at Gwynneth, and the younger woman felt, for the first time, a twinge of uneasiness. Silobah, seeing her discomfort, merely turned her gaze back to the fire. She felt like death, indeed should be dead, but perhaps it was just the part of her that had been afraid that was now dead. The part that wondered and dithered and fretted was now gone, buried, nonexistent. Tired, yes beyond belief. Finally determined? Indeed.

Earlier in the evening, as she sat in her room, shoring up her resolve to honor her vow, her mind had begun to wander. She remembered Elden answering questions about the lass. He had been so protective of her, refusing to divulge any but the slightest details. Strange to act so about someone he had taken under his wing as a simple favor. It appeared like he was safekeeping information about her as if she were his very own. A flame flashed in her head and air rushed out of her chest. The thought slammed into her with the force of a blow and she staggered, almost falling.

She had not seen it. She had absolutely not seen it. She had all of the facts at hand and still she had been blinded by her worry over Gwynneth, her concentration on the prophecy and all too eager to believe Elden's story of the lass being a clan leader's daughter. How could she have not known that the lass was the bairn she had left in the woods so many years ago? She had sent Elden from the castle after Fiona had died, but he must have hidden, then followed her. Of course he did, and then rescued his sister. The gods who protected the sacred gorge must have heard her pleas. They had answered her prayers and now they must be laughing. She drew in a deep breath and visualized Thomas the Rhymer. The circle was now. Her path was set. She was stunned but relieved that the waiting was finally over.

And now she stood in Gwynneth's bedchamber staring into the fire. Gwynneth watched her, feeling a shiver up her spine. There was tiredness and pain in the old woman's eyes, but something more. This old one looked like the men Gwynneth had seen returning from battle; bodies beaten, covered with exhaustion, but with an air of determination not quite extinguished. She hugged herself despite the warmth of the fire. She was eager to get the old woman out of the room.

"I won't need you tonight. You may leave." Gwynneth turned and found herself speaking to thin air. Frowning, she moved away from the fire and paced the room once, twice, then came to a stop beside the window. Stepping into the alcove, pulling the hangings around her, she was one with the night. A cloud crossed the moon. Ewan would have moved into the woods by now. There was no use looking for him, just as there was no use remembering the image of Colin leaving her room. Always leaving. Her fists clenched, knuckles turning white with the power of her anger. A sudden cold smile crossed her face. Out there in those woods, headed to the safety of the highlands, were the man and the witch. As soon as she had them, the laird, instead of moving away, would be moving forward. Into her bed. Giving her a child of her parent's blood. And then he would have no more need of life. Unclenching her fists, she ran her hands through her black hair and, turning from the window, pulled the curtains closed behind her. Smiling, she walked back to the fire.

Chapter 18

THE CASTLE SLEPT deeply, draped in darkness, guard's footsteps the only sound breaking the silence. Colin lay in his bed, his eyes open in the dark, searching. He heard a movement and his warrior's heart increased its strong beat. Slowly, and without noise, he slid his hand from under the covers and brought it to rest on the hilt of his sword resting at the side of his bed. His fingers curled around its shaft. He waited for the noise to come again and reveal its location. Suddenly someone stumbled against a chair. Colin saw a figure highlighted against the dying fire. In an instant he was out of the bed, his sword raised, his body ready to attack.

"Dinna swing at me, My Laird." The words caught him up short, the voice familiar. Slowly Colin lowered the weapon and concentrated on breathing steadily, stilling the thumping of his heart.

"May I add a log to the fire?" Silobah moved to the fireplace. Colin walked over to the bed and grabbed a blanket, wrapping it around his nakedness. The log fell on the fire, and flames shot up highlighting the old woman's face. Colin stopped in his tracks. Her face resembled a skull. He stood gazing down at her. Giving a sigh, she turned from his scrutiny and sat in a chair. Colin raised his eyebrows. No one did that in his presence without his permission. Perhaps Arden, but that was another matter entirely. Curious, he adjusted the blanket, walked to the fire, and lowered himself in the chair beside her, giving her an appraising look.

Silobah sat quietly, simply staring into the flames, and Colin, seeing the weariness on her face, the slump of her shoulders, let her sit. He watched the light flicker over her face. Gwynneth was the only reason Silobah could have for entering his room. It had to be vital for her to do so in the middle of the night. Perhaps it had to do with her pledge, so many years ago, to True Thomas. Colin sent a silent request for guidance to Briac.

"What is so important that you would risk death by creeping in here?" He made his voice rough, hoping to shake her out of her trance-like state. Slowly the old woman raised her head and stared into his eyes. Colin sat back at the look. Exhaustion was there, yes, but a bright fierce flame burned as well. He shifted uneasily in his chair and opened his mouth to speak, but Silobah raised her hand for silence. Colin's forehead wrinkled. No one had done that to him since he had become laird. It was his gesture to use, not hers, but somehow it seemed tonight she had the right. He clenched his jaw against what she would tell him and waited.

The words came slowly. It seemed as if it gave her great pain to say them, but they fell from her lips, nonetheless. Colin watched, fascinated at the play of emotions over her face. He held his peace throughout the telling, though he longed to rise to his feet and shout with anger.

Gwynneth had sent a tracker anyway.

Abruptly he stood. "And what are her plans after she finds out where the man and lass are?"

Silobah snapped her eyes up to his. "You know as well as I that Gwynneth will do as her mother did. Try to use the witch for her own ends." That was as much as she would tell him. She owed him no more information than that. Her debt was to Thomas the Rhymer. She would never tell Colin the hunted lass was the daughter of the highland witch. She held her secrets closely, unaware that the laird knew them already. She pulled herself from her thoughts and spoke plainly. "Her craving for revenge has twisted her. She sees nothing but her own wants, her own desires. She is blinded by her rage."

Colin took several steps away from the fire, then back. He was restless, angry, wanting an end to the situation. "I will take care of this." The old woman looked up at him, not wanting her betrayal of Gwynneth to be known quite yet. He shook his head. "You dinna have to worry. No one will know what you have told me. But listen to me well. When that creature of Gwynneth's comes back, I want you to come to me. If you canna find me then I want you to tell Arden. The lass must nae be trapped."

Silobah's ears caught the change in his voice. What was this? A soft almost wistful sound coming at the end of all that anger? She looked up at the laird and Colin flushed a dull red. A thought entered her mind but she tossed it away. How could he have feelings for someone he had never met? It was most likely his knowledge of what might happen to the lass that caused the curious quiver in his voice.

Silobah nodded her head silently. Giving a great sigh, she rose to her feet and silently walked from the room. Colin watched her as she left, wondering what it was, truly, that caused her to finally betray Gwynneth. The fire popped and cracked. Absently he walked over to it and tossed on another log. He watched as the flames flicked the wood, weary of dealing with Gwynneth. The color of the fire reminded him of Rowan's hair and he frowned, worried anew.

Even now Gwynneth's tracker hurried noiselessly through the woods, dogging Elden's heels. Somewhere in the night, Rowan sat beside a fire, lonely and headed to the highlands.

The thought reminded him of that last look Rowan had flashed at him as she sat astride her horse. The unthinkable whipped through his mind. No, no, he told himself. She would never do that. He had convinced her that Elden would be set free, hadn't he? Certainly she had seen that his warnings were based on reason, based on fact. He had told her more than once what Gwynneth was like and how she was best avoided. But he also remembered Rowan fighting him even as he tried to rescue her. He softly pounded his fist against the stone wall. This was no milk and whey maid. This was a lass who hunted and killed and was fiercely loyal. This was also a lass who had been hunted herself, captured, and who trusted no one no matter what words were said. How could he have ridden away, thinking she would do anything but return to the castle to set her brother free? Who had he been to give her such advice? Just another hunter in the woods for all she knew. Turning swiftly, he grabbed his clothes and roughly pulled them on, already planning what he would say to Arden.

***

Rowan pulled the blanket tightly over her cold body. Shivering, she huddled under the covering of dry bushes she had fashioned into a shelter. She had no fire. She was headed toward the castle and didn't want to chance being seen. Suddenly she stilled, holding her breath so she could hear more clearly. Aye. There it was. The faint sounds of someone making his way through the woods on foot. Silently she willed the horse to hush. All became quiet save for the rustle of the brush being pushed aside in the distance. Slowly turning her head, she looked up at the sky. It must be hours before dawn. It was too early to hunt, and she had seen no guards patrolling this far from the castle. The fact that someone was near, boded ill for her. Breathing softly, she listened again, but the person had gone past her and was headed away into the deep woods. In the distance, a bird gave a cry into the night. Rowan nodded to herself, whoever it was had indeed moved away. Breathing a sigh of relief, she settled down to wait for the light. Only then would she make a fire to get warm.

***

Elden pushed deeper into the woods, a frown on his face. He could have sworn that for a few moments he had felt Rowan near, but it had been too close to the castle for that feeling to be right. It was most likely just his relief at being away from Gwynneth. The name made him shiver even though with each step he put distance between himself and Lady Lochalsh. A bird rose from a branch and gave a sharp caw. Elden jumped, his heart pounding. Catching his breath he gave himself a mental shake. "Get a hold of yourself! Jumping at every sound won't help anything." He needed all of his concentration, all of his powers now to find Rowan. For a moment he stood quietly, letting his mind search the dark. Nothing. Not a scent, not a feeling. He was not surprised. He had nothing left from having used his powers with the laird, and even then, it had been a gift from the gods rather than any power on his part. Shaking his head, he again pushed quickly through the forest, rapidly heading north.

***

"Wake up."

Arden pulled away from the grasping hand, mumbling.

"I said wake up!" Colin raised his voice. The tone pierced through the fog of sleep and Arden sat up abruptly, his hand snaring that of the laird's.

"For God's sake dinna break it." Angrily Colin yanked his hand back and Arden shook his head, still half asleep. Focusing his eyes, he saw Colin at the side of his bed and his thoughts cleared completely.

"What's wrong?"

"We have to go."

"Where?"

"Into the woods."

"Now? Tonight?"

"Aye. Now. Here get dressed." Colin tossed Arden's trews at him.

The man jumped from the bed and began pulling them on. "Why?" he asked reaching for his boots.

154

"Gwynneth."

Arden stopped, the boot held in his hand, and looked at the laird, "She's gone into the woods? Well, what's your hurry? Good riddance, I say."

Colin gave a growl, "Nae. It isn't Gwynneth who is in the woods. It's the man she captured, Elden."

"As well he should be. It's a wonder he didn't sprout wings and take flight."

Colin folded his arms over his chest and Arden, recognizing the kingly stance, gave a sigh. "So, he's gone. Why are we jumping about in the middle of the night?"

"Because Gwynneth has sent someone to track him."

Arden nodded his head. Aye. It would seem the logical thing for Lady Lochalsh to do, knowing her. He looked up at the laird and Colin continued.

"You know the man is going to find the lass!" Colin's voice roughened, "It's plain and simple. Elden will lead the tracker to the lass. That's who Gwynneth really wants."

"So let her bring the lass back."

"Have you nae brain? Remember Briac's words?"

"Aye."

"Then what are you balking for?"

Arden pulled on the other boot and reaching for his cloak, paused, searching his friend's face. "Who told you Gwynneth sent someone?"

"Silobah."

"Well, that old one knows more than she lets on." He paused then continued, "You realize that whether or not the tracker brings the lass and the seer back, this is the point where things canna go on as they have. Only one of you will win."

"I will win."

"Aye, but then Gwynneth will have to lose." Ending the conversation he fastened the clasp on his cloak, and pointing at the door, followed the laird out.

155

***

An exhausted Elden paused, leaning beside a tree. He was pushing himself hard. He needed to catch Rowan although how he could do so, since she was on a horse, made him realize the futility of his continuing without rest. Steadying his breathing, he desperately wished he could connect with her through his powers, but it was only in dreams that he was shown what he needed to know. The thought hit him between the eyes and he wondered at his stupidity. Here he was blundering through the woods, searching first this way then that when what he should have been doing was building a fire, gazing into it, and letting it put him to sleep. Then and only then would he be shown where she was. Cursing at the wasted time, he quickly began to search for wood to build his fire, eager for the dreams.

A bit later, sitting beside the dancing flames, gazing into the fire's depths, he thought about Rowan. Where was she? What was she doing? Was she scared? That caused him to smile. She might be angry, hurt, fiercely determined, but scared? He'd only seen her scared once when their croft had been burned. And even then, it had been a fleeting thing. He couldn't remember a time when she had been so. He moved uneasily. Something was wrong. A deep frown crossed his face and he shifted. He thought he had felt her nearby earlier but now he felt himself moving away from any suggestion of her presence. He opened his eyes and looked into the flames again and concentrated, to no avail.

***

"Come on. You're taking as long as a lass." Colin sat on his horse grumbling. The animal danced sideways, pulling at the bit and the laird gave a savage yank on the reins. The horse, feeling both the pain and the command, settled down momentarily.

"I'm ready. You're just faster, you always have been. Besides, you were awake." Arden said the last words with a laugh, tightening his saddle. The laird forced a smile in return. Lifting his eyes to the sky he noted that dawn was still some time away.

"Hurry. We can make it past the loch and well into the woods by full light if we leave this instant."

"He must realize that he is hunted." Arden swung into the saddle and adjusted his seat.

"I'm sure he does. I just hope he finds Rowan before she makes her way to the castle." The comment took Arden by surprise. Pulling his horse in line with the laird's, he arched an eyebrow by way of a question. Heading out of the gate, Colin answered, "I would bet my last coin she is headed to the castle to help her brother." Arden shook his head no and Colin continued, "You have nae met her. You dinna know who she is." Colin continued. "I know this lass, I tell you. And she is nae one to seek her own safety while her brother remains in the hands of Gwynneth. She is nae one to run away."

"So, you're convinced she is headed back to the castle to rescue him?"

"Aye, but even if she isn't, the man Gwynneth sent to find Elden is sure to find them both. It's the girl Rowan that Gwynneth wants."

***

Silobah woke with a start, her heart pounding. She had been dreaming she was back in the tower room of the castle, the one she tried never to think about. Lady Stannard had been there, and so had the highland witch. The old woman closed her eyes and rolled over on her bed, pressing her face against the pallet, but the sight would not go away. The witch had been on the floor, lying on a blanket-covered pile of straw. Sweat poured down her face as she strained with the pains of childbirth. Silobah pressed her face into the covers but could still hear the shrill cry of the woman as the bairn had ripped out of her, could still remember the blood gushing out onto the floor. Memories of what had happened next made the old woman lift her hands to the sides of her head, as if she could squeeze the memory from it: Lady Stannard's face twisting in fury seeing the witch dying, her rage at seeing the babe a lass, dashing the bairn out of its mother's arms onto the stone floor.

The last image pulled Silobah upright and she staggered to the window. Gasping for fresh air she leaned on the casement. Out of the corner of her eye she saw a movement at the castle gate. She squinted. Aye. Two. There were two of them and they were on horses. From the size of the men, the mounts, she knew it was the laird and Arden. The pain in her head eased a bit. Taking a deep breath, she watched as the figures rode into the waning night. Her determination had hardened but her body was weak, and she knew it would be easier if Colin could find the lass before Ewan did and take her somewhere, anywhere not within Gwynneth's grasp. The laird's words from earlier flashed into her mind, and again she heard the sound of his voice as he had mentioned the lass being caught.

That had not been the sound of a dispassionate man. It had been the sound of someone who not only knew the person he was talking about but felt deeply for. His path somehow had crossed that of the lass. There was no other explanation. She could hear the gods laughing anew and she cursed them soundly. The laird would not take the lass home to the highlands, would not help her and her brother build a new home far away. Nae, this man would bring the lass back here. Silobah would find no easy way out of breaking the circle. Her thoughts went to Gwynneth and fear crawled up her neck. What would happen then? Visions of Lady Stannard raced through her head and she prayed to the same gods she had just cursed.

Chapter 19

AS THE NEXT day dawned, purposefully but carefully, Ewan of the Little Head made his way through the woods, quickly determined to reach his goal. Afraid of Gwynneth but also thinking of the reward she promised him, he focused completely on the skill of the hunt. His lady seemed much like her mother. At the thought of Lady Stannard, the man gave an unaccustomed shudder and quickened his pace. Now that one, she had been a nightmare. When she had chosen you for a task, you were blessed by the gods if you succeeded. Failure meant punishment both swift and forceful. Lady Lochalsh seemed to be living up to the blood she carried in her veins. A noise distracted him from his thoughts and he stopped.

Crouching close to the ground he tilted his head to the side, listening. The sound came again. Ewan smiled to himself. It was the noise made when someone was carefully breaking sticks. He knew what that meant. Looking up at the sky he noted shafts of light streaking the sky. Someone had spent a cold and lonely night and was eager for dawn and a fire. There was only one reason they would wait until the light of day to do so. They didn't want to be seen. This was as easy to figure out as Elden's track had been to follow.

The seer's path had run almost directly across that of a path made by a horse and rider. But the paths had not joined. It seemed the two had not met. The seer's path had veered off into the deep woods, and the path of the horse and rider looked as if it was heading toward the castle. Ewan sat for a moment, thinking. The lass had escaped her hunters on a horse. Was it possible she was heading to help her brother? If so and he found her instead of the man, his reward would be huge indeed. He had decided to follow this new path and now a smile crossed his face. Rising from his crouch, he crept silently toward the sounds of the breaking sticks. Hunkering down once more, he peered through the bushes. A lass. It was her all right. Carefully he sat back on his heels, waiting for the right moment. The more sticks she broke without anyone leaping out of the woods, the more confident and unguarded she would become. He could hear her moving freely about now, convinced she was alone, unobserved. He waited, giving her plenty of time to feel safe, to let down her guard. It was only then that he would make his move.

***

The same dawn-streaked sky arched over Elden as he slept fitfully beside the fire. The flames had died down to mere embers and provided little warmth but even at its brightest, it had given just that, warmth, and no visions. For part of the night, he had gazed into the flames. Nothing had come to him but a feeling of unease; a feeling of blackness closing in and he didn't know if it was a true feeling or one born of circumstances. Hoping sleep would bring a vision and finally, worn out by the events of the day, he had dropped off into a restless sleep.

***

As the sun rose, Rowan sat beside the fire, drawing closer to it for comfort. The warmth was good, but her stomach grumbled with hunger. She had been too concerned with approaching the castle and not being caught to have thought about simple creature comforts, but she did now. Trying to distract her stomach, she focused on the warmth of the flames, but they failed to penetrate. And that was surely because the castle was near. The closer she came to it, the colder she got. It was a coldness of the boncs and the heart. She shivered and tried to move closer to the fire. The heat burned her face and her cheeks reddened with it. Pulling her knees to her chest, she wearily rested her head. A small sigh escaped her. She missed Elden. She was tired. She was hungry. She didn't want to go to the castle and rescue him, but she had to. There was no choice. Elden had saved her, raised her, and could have easily given her to any of the local clans and been done with it. And then there was the matter of their blood bond.

The thought hardened her resolve to rescue her brother. Deciding to raise an infant was not a choice most men would make, even if the infant were their sister. Her thoughts went back to their last conversation. They were brother and sister, only by half, having different fathers but the same mother. The thought of her mother gave her pause and she stared into the flames wishing Elden had told her more. Who was this mother? How had she died? And who was the man who was her father? The questions burned in her heart, hurting her deeply. Closing her eyes, she dropped her head onto her knees. The warmth of the fire flickered over her skin and she pushed the questions to the back of her mind. Elden would tell her. He would tell her when they were safe and far away. Her mind drifted with her thoughts and she dozed.

Ewan sat patiently, waiting. Seeing Rowan put her head to her knees, he eased into a standing position and stretched his muscles. She would be an easy catch with the warmth of the fire, the lack of sleep, the weakness that accompanied hunger. Slowly he placed one foot in front of the other, careful to not startle her drowsing horse. He could have rushed noisily through the brush and taken her by surprise, but he had seen the muscles working in her slender arms as she snapped the tree branches for the fire; he was wise enough to respect them.

Rowan sat dreaming, half-asleep, thinking of the home she had shared with Elden. The unmistakable sound of a twig cracking under a boot shot through the air. Leaping up she whirled around, her hand reaching down for her dirk, grabbing emptiness. A large rough hand closed on her right wrist. Twisting with her back to the side of the man, she broke his hold. One step forward toward escape but instantly he grabbed the back of her neck. Yanking forward she broke the hold, whirled around, and kicked out. Ewan grabbed her boot. Frantically she yanked her foot, arms swinging in the air. For a moment she felt him release her ankle but it was only to painfully grasp her calf.

Lifting her leg into the air he tumbled her to the ground. As she hit, she rolled trying to tear her leg from his grip. Cursing and muttering Ewan held on but was forced to his knees. He jerked back as she brought her body up to hit him. Swiftly he grabbed the other calf and jumping up, flipped her onto her stomach. The next instant he launched himself over her, pinning her face down to the ground, shoving the air from her lungs.

She lay still, unmoving. Holding her firmly he whipped his head around, tensing, making sure there was no one waiting to join in the fight. The only sound was Rowan's panting. Ewan gave a satisfied grunt. Slowly he rose up on his elbows, keeping her trapped with the rest of his weight, and looked down at her.

Feeling the movement, Rowan gritted her teeth and swiftly raised her head, slamming the back of it into the man's mouth. With a howl Ewan rolled from her and Rowan sprang to her feet. Taking a running step, she was once again checked as his hand closed on her ankle. Kicking, she tried to smash his face with her other foot. Quickly he reached out and grabbed it. Seizing both feet, he yanked her to the ground, knocking the wind from her once again.

Rowan lay in the dirt, trying to make her lungs work, her face mottled and red. Ewan carefully sat up and gingerly worked his front teeth. Nothing was loose, but there was plenty of blood and it hurt like the very devil himself. Flinching with pain, he crawled over to her and placed his heavy legs crossways on top of hers. There. He checked his teeth once again.

Chapter 20

SILOBAH ENTERED THE room silently. Closing the door softly behind her she looked over at the window, realizing that she needn't have been so quiet.

"Come in." The words were cold and addressed to the view outside.

She noticed the bed had not been slept in. "You have nae been to bed all night?" Silobah tried to make her words sound like they always had before she had conquered her fear and betrayed Gwynneth to the laird.

Lady Lochalsh whirled around, "I am waiting for the witch."

"You dinna truly know the lass is a witch."

"She escaped from the hunters, it is said she has a sixth finger, her brother has the sight. She's a witch all right." Gwynneth turned back to the window, her eyes scanning the edge of the woods and continued, "She is a witch and I intend to use her."

Those had been the very same words used by Lady Stannard and Silobah struggled to keep her voice even and without emotion. She changed the subject. "You have been at that window all night and your gown is soaking with dew." She roughened her voice, hoping the scolding note would overshadow the transformation she felt in herself, the renewed purpose, the call to thwart the prophecy. Gwynneth gave a small smile and turned from the window.

"You never could let me get by without a scolding now, could you?"

Silobah gave a silent sigh of relief. Gwynneth hadn't noticed the change in her. Perhaps it didn't show in her voice, but it was certainly there in her heart. If she could lull Gwynneth and watch her every move, maybe she could keep all of them, the lass, Colin, and the rest from following the circle's path. Pulling away from her thoughts, the old woman clucked and scolded, bustling about, peeling the damp gown from Lady Lochalsh's body. Drawing Gwynneth away from the window, Silobah stood her beside the fire to get warm.

"It's nae use staying up all night watching. What will be, will be, and no amount of you staring at the forest will change that."

Gwynneth stood in the warmth, the familiar words of her nurse flowing over her like a balm. She felt safe and warm. Nothing could stand in her way. Gwynneth turned her head toward the window and smiled. Soon the witch would be here. Giving a tired sigh, she let Silobah drop a fresh gown over her head and lead her to bed for an early morning nap.

***

Elden sat up quickly beside the dead fire. Tilting his head to the side, listening, he bit his lips and concentrated. No. Nothing. A sudden cold shaft of fear shot up from his stomach to his chest and he froze to the spot, his heart pounding, and his pulse racing. Closing his eyes, he tried to see what it meant. It was the same reaction he always had when he dreamed a forward dream of death and destruction. Struck to the heart he looked in the direction of the castle, then back to the deep woods. He shivered. He hoped the feeling was wrong.

***

Drawing breath back into her lungs, Rowan opened her mouth but Ewan quickly covered it with his rough palm. "Dinna scream." Feeling the movement of her lips he quickly arched his palm so her teeth barely grazed his skin. He gave a grin as he saw the hardening of her eyes. Disappointed, was she? Well, just wait until she got to the castle. There she would find someone to fight. He kept his hand over her mouth and kept his legs over her body. He spoke gruffly, "Now this is the way it is to be. I am going to take you to the castle." His eyes searched hers for a response. Finding none he continued, "Lady Lochalsh has commanded me to bring you to her and I am going to do just that." The mention of Gwynneth brought a movement however slight from the lass and he was satisfied with the response.

"When I was told to find you, nae one mentioned how I could pass the time with you until we returned to the castle."

Rowan went completely still and the man gave a dark smile. Scared, was she? She had a right to be. She was alone in the middle of the woods, unprotected and lying there with that long red hair, those long legs, that beautiful face. He felt himself stir and harden. Shifting uncomfortably, he roughened his voice, more to distract himself than to scare Rowan. After all he was no fool. Och he would give many a coin to lay with one like this, but he knew what would happen if he brought back the lass ravaged and hurt. No matter how strong his desire for the maid, his fear of Lady Lochalsh was greater. He shifted again to ease himself and continued to speak.

"Lady Lochalsh willna care one whit if I drag you into the great hall by that long hair of yours, without your clothes and begging for mercy. Indeed, she might like you presented to her that way." He looked at Rowan and saw that he had her attention. Good. "I am a reasonable man sent to do a reasonable job. I have caught you and I am taking you back. Make nae mistake about that. Now we can do this so you can be rested and ready for whatever it is Lady Lochalsh has in store for you, or we can do it with you fighting the entire way. It makes no difference to me one way or the other, because I will win. You willna escape."

He looked at her to see if his words were registering and continued, "If I were you, my lass, I would want to arrive rested and fresh. If you dinna know about Lady Lochalsh, you soon will, and it would be best for you to have your wits sharp."

Rowan reluctantly nodded her head. His words rang true. There was little chance she would be able to get away from him.

He was too strong, too fast, and didn't seem one to drop his guard however slightly. She would play his game, pretend defeat, and reserve her strength. She had been on her way to the castle anyway. It was just that now she would have to rescue not only Elden, but herself. She gave an inward sly smile and drooped her shoulders in a pantomime of resignation.

Ewan saw the slump of her shoulders and nodded to himself. Good. She was going to use some sense then. Clearing his throat he commanded her attention once again, and held her eyes with his, "That is the way it is to be then?"

Rowan lowered her eyes and nodded her head up and down. Carefully pulling his hand back, the tracker watched for her reaction. He would not have been surprised to see her leap to her feet and make a mad dash for the forest. Rowan lay still, wanting to make her move, but she tamped it down. She knew she stood only a slim chance of getting away from this man, and even if she did, his tracking skills were as good as hers. It was better to use her capture to rest and make plans.

A sudden thought made her quail. What was it the man had said? Something about not knowing what Lady Lochalsh had in store for her. Her mind raced to the warnings that Elden had repeated over and over since they began this journey, the same warnings that the man, Arden, had given: Lady Lochalsh was like her mother before her and that mother had killed witches. Rowan shook her head. Surely this Lady would not do the same. Surely, she had learned from her mother's mistakes. And besides, the castle was in Scottish hands now, not English. Surely the laird knew what was going on under his nose. She had heard of him, as had everyone else, when word of the Bannockburn victory spread through the highlands. He was supposed to be a fair and just laird, nothing like the English usurper who built the castle.

Ewan eased the pressure of his legs over hers, cautiously, watching to see if she would try to escape, but her thoughts were far from flight.

The man Arden, who rescued her from the stream said he lived near the castle. Her mind raced trying to recall exactly what he had said. From the manner in which he spoke, carried himself and treated her, perhaps he was a member of the court. If so, maybe he would help. Surely her capture and presentation to Lady Lochalsh would not go un-remarked. He would hear and come to her aid. She recalled the protective way he had treated her and more importantly, that he seemed to hold no liking for Lady Lochalsh. Aye, she would look for him at the castle. He would help, of that she was confident.

Her thoughts lingered for a moment on the man who had found her, cared for her, then let her go. She closed her eyes, letting the memory of his face fill her mind. She recalled the blue eyes, the color of his hair and his muscular body. A small blush stained her cheeks as she remembered seeing him without his clothes. With a shake of her head, she pulled her thoughts back to the reality of her situation.

Rowan looked into the eyes of the man who now held her captive. For all of his height and strength, he had quite a small head. It gave him an ominous, feral aura. She rubbed her hand along the side of her thigh, nestling the small sixth finger out of sight. Nodding her head at him she spoke, "You can release me. I know why Lady Lochalsh wants me and I am willing to go and face her. I willna try to escape, but neither will I face the woman tired, unkempt and with an empty belly."

The imperious words brought a slight smile of admiration to Ewan's face. Perhaps she would do well with Lady Lochalsh after all. The thought of Gwynneth drove the smile away. He rose to his feet. "Good. Then we are of a mind, you and I."

Rowan allowed him to pull her to her feet. "Give me a blade and I'll hunt with you."

A loud guffaw rang through the forest, "And would it be me that you'd be hunting?" "Nae. I dinna think you'd taste very good."

Ewan laughed as he wound a rope around her wrists, tying her hands in front of her. Looping another rope through her wrists, he lashed her to a tree and hitched her horse to a large bush. That should keep her secure while he went for a quick morning's hunt.

***

Elden stood looking toward the direction of the castle. What he knew Rowan would do, and what he hoped she would do, were two very different things. She was as hardheaded and determined as the boar she hunted. He understood now she had ignored all caution and had doubled back. The feeling that almost felled him in his tracks moments ago had told him so. She was moving toward danger and death. Despite all of his warnings, she was going to try to help him escape. His stomach knotted and he pressed his fist against it, trying to calm himself, hoping against all hope that she had not done anything so fool hardy. His stomach continued to knot and bile rose in his throat as he moved through the forest.

His thoughts turned to Gwynneth. Damn her. He knew what she wanted. She wanted Rowan just like her mother, Lady Stannard, had wanted Fiona and wouldn't rest until she had her. Rowan certainly fit every description there had ever been of witches. She lived most of her life in the woods, healing animals when she wasn't eating them. He gave a small laugh at the thought. She had red hair and green eyes; a male seer in the family and aye, there was that sixth finger. There had never been anyone born with the sixth finger that did not have some sight, some power.

As he made his way, he thought of the laird. A good man. A solid man, although one who had chosen to let himself be maneuvered into marrying Lady Lochalsh. How did such a man bear living with a woman like Gwynneth? The memory of how he had spoken about Rowan began to make sense. The thought of Rowan in the castle with Lady Lochalsh hating her and the laird having tender feelings made Elden pick up his pace.

Leaping a fallen tree with his thoughts on Fiona, he failed to see a hidden branch. Sharp prongs snagged his leggings, trapping one leg behind. Arms flailing in the air, Elden plunged forward landing heavily on one leg. His foot twisted sideways. His ankle gave a vicious twist. Shouting with pain, he fell onto the forest floor and rolled in agony.

Moaning, catching his breath, he tried to sit up. The sky swung in a sickening arc over his head. He closed his eyes and lay back, letting the dizziness pass. A few moments elapsed and carefully he pulled himself into a sitting position. Pausing for the brief flare of nausea to recede, he reached toward his foot. The swelling had already begun. Quickly and ignoring the pain, he tugged off his soft leather boot. A few moments longer and he would have had to cut it away. Sitting on the forest floor, he watched his ankle darken and expand. The flesh bulged in an area where there had been no such knob before. Carefully he tried to move his foot but couldn't. He had either broken a bone or had pushed one far out of place. He let his fingers trail over the deepening blue flesh, then curled his fist in anger. Why now? What was it that these gods wanted? Another witch dead at the castle? What was it that cursed Lochalsh? What good were the deaths? He gave a shudder then forced himself to turn to matters at hand. It was going to be a long day and an even longer night. Looking around, he saw enough fallen wood within reaching distance to make a fire. He thought of Rowan and swore angrily and at great length that he could not reach her and let her know she need not brave that black castle.

***

Colin pulled his horse to a stop. Holding up his hand he motioned for Arden to do the same. Arden complied and looked at his friend with a question in his eyes. What had he heard? Tightening the reins, Arden tried to keep his horse still. Colin spoke. "Did you hear that?"

Arden motioned no, then tilted his head, concentrating. Colin did the same. It came once again. A familiar noise. A fox going to ground.

"It was nothing. A fox." Arden said.

"So, I'm hearing things?"

"Most likely you want to hear things."

Colin pulled at the reins of his horse. "If you're so smart then you lead for a while." Arden gave a grin and prodded his mount ahead of his friend's. It was just as well. The man didn't have his mind on what he was doing, and every crack of a twig or call of a bird made him jump like a maid. Arden shook his head while scanning the forest for signs that someone had recently passed by. Several times they had thought they saw signs of Elden's trail but found themselves at a dead end. It was no good looking for the lass like this. From everything he had been told, she was too experienced a woodsman to leave a trace of her trail. He kept his eyes moving from the low branches to the forest floor hoping to find something, anything that would end this search. He eased the tension out of his shoulders as he rode. By all the gods, he wanted to find the lass and get her on her way. She didn't need to be at the mercy of Gwynneth or the beck and call of Colin.

"What is it?" Colin saw the emotion on Arden's face.

"Nothing." The answer was gruff and Colin knew from long experience that it meant there would be no further discussion.

Nodding to himself, Colin turned his thoughts inward and let his mind once again picture Rowan standing beside the fire, the light from the flames dancing over her long red hair, her slender waist, her long white legs. His thoughts kept him occupied as he and his friend rode through the forest.

Chapter 21

Lochalsh Castle

MY LADY, THEY are here." Silobah concentrated on keeping her voice soft, not showing the ice that covered her heart at having to say the words. Flinging her quill to the floor, Gwynneth jumped from her writing table and ran to join her at the window. Eagerly she leaned from the stone casement. Yes. Two people on foot, leading a horse, coming from the woods.

Silobah squinted into the sun, holding her breath as she watched the one with long red hair. Turning her gaze to Lady Lochalsh, Silobah saw Gwynneth quivering with excitement and the old woman hardened her resolve. This time there would be no death. Turning again to look out of the window, her heart closed into a fist.

Rowan looked at the castle looming in the sky and a slice of fear shot through her body. Giving herself a shake, she tried to reason it out. The fear was because of the warnings Elden had given her. There was nothing to fear. After all, it was not Lady Lochalsh who was supposed to be the witch, it was herself. Rowan gave a small smile knowing that she wasn't one either. If she were, then she would never have to hunt. She could just call the animals to the cooking pot. She smiled and felt better. Straightening her shoulders, she gave the castle an assessing stare. I've hunted scarier things than you, she thought to herself. She envisioned Lady Lochalsh and silently spoke to her; you are nae match for the likes of me.

Ewan tightened his grip on the restless mount's lead line and saw Rowan square her shoulders. He sighed. If she knew Lady Lochalsh as well as he did then she would realize her resolve was warranted indeed. He felt, rather than saw her gathering strength and his admiration grew. In the short time he had been with her he had grown to like her and hated the fact that he must turn her over, no matter how many coins he was paid. He looked up and saw the castle loom nearer. Gwynneth waited. There was no choice. Yanking on the lead, he led the lass towards her fate.

***

"It's getting toward dark." The statement went by without comment from Colin. Arden ignored the non-response and pushed his horse through the brush. In the distance he heard a stream running. Fine. That was as good a reason as any to stop for the night. Pulling his mount to a halt he swung from the saddle. Turning around he saw Colin still on his horse, riding away.

"Your Lairdship!" The words were sarcastic, loud.

Colin gave a start and pulled his horse up sharply. "We stop here for the night?"

Arden shook his head at the obvious question. Sweeping his arm out into an arc and giving a mock bow, he replied, "If it pleases Your Lairdship, aye."

Colin shot him a disgusted look and swung off of his horse. "Fine. Here is just fine." Turning his back, he began to take the saddle from his mount. Stopping for a moment, he ran his hand over the animal's side. The slanting sun glancing sideways on the black hair revealed wisps of red and he remembered the color of Rowan's hair. Inhaling he tried to remember the smell of her, the fire, the crisp air of the night they had spent together. All he got was a good sniff of horse.

"Why did you decide to stop here?" The words were sharp, edgy.

Arden looked at him. He knew exactly what was going through Colin's mind. Well, perhaps not exactly, but he was able to tell that the laird was thinking of the lass. It wasn't a difficult thing to figure out; first Colin's face would get soft, then almost immediately it would become hard. His next words would be harsh. Patiently Arden explained himself, "There is water nearby and the horses are tired having been at it half the night and most of this day, and all the gods know that we haven't found a trace of the lass or the seer. Perhaps we should rethink our direction."

Arden unsaddled his horse being careful to keep his expression neutral. Colin grunted and began leading his horse to the stream. Sighing, Arden set his saddle on the ground then arched his back, hands on his hips, casually looking around for firewood. Not seeing any, he checked his horse's tether and struck out in the opposite direction of the stream.

***

Rowan looked around as they approached the castle wall. The sun had almost disappeared and the shadows loomed blue and deep. She turned her head from one side to the other, a puzzled frown on her face. Why were they heading for the stone wall instead of walking to the gates of the courtyard? She turned and looked back. The woods were far away and even though they were blacker than the shadows that lingered close by, she longed to be there. Biting her lip, she turned again just as Ewan jerked her to a stop. Glancing at the stone wall she threw a questioning look at her captor. Silently he motioned for her to dismount. Quickly tying the horse, he began to push her forward.

A sudden movement in the dense mass of juniper bushes growing beside the walls made them both jump. The sound of a door pushing open came to their ears. The bushes heaved again and after a moment, Gwynneth walked into view. An old woman followed behind. Rowan stood as silent as death. She struggled to pull air into her lungs. Her eyes fastened on Gwynneth and didn't leave. Ewan shifted uneasily from one foot to the other. A twinge of conscience flashed through him. If all of the rumors were true, he hated to think of the lass being here in secret with no one to protect her. He watched Gwynneth walk forward and he stepped back several paces, trying to distance himself from the scene.

Silobah stood silently, simply looking, drinking in the sight. Her eyes settled on the lush red hair flowing down the lass' back. She knew how it would feel to run a comb through it. It would feel just like Fiona's when she had combed her hair those many years ago. Unconsciously she took a few steps closer. Shifting her eyes to Rowan's face, she gave a low moan. The nose, the set of her head, the green snapping eyes, the chin, sharp and firm; there could be no doubt. She had hoped beyond all reason that her conclusions had been wrong; that the bairn was truly dead. The winter had been so cold and she and been so sure the snow would be the bairn's shroud. Silobah continued to stare at Rowan. Aye, this was the one she had left to die. Fiona's child. Feeling eyes on her, Silobah turned to find Gwynneth studying her.

"What is it that you see?" Silobah shook her head and did not answer. Gwynneth's voice sharpened, "Answer me. I said what is it that you see?" Silobah had no intention of giving her a truthful answer. "She is younger than I thought she would be."

Moving slowly forward, Gwynneth kept her eyes fastened on the girl, her face hardening as she took in Rowan's long slender form, the shapely legs clad in tight wool trews, the chest straining against the short leine.

Fascinated and repulsed, Rowan watched her approach. It was exactly the way she felt when seeing a beautiful but deadly adder slither through the woods. The comparison became more apt as the woman drew closer. Unconsciously, Rowan held her hand so the sixth finger did not show. She began to operate on instinct, every sense alert, screaming danger.

Gwynneth spoke to Ewan. "Are you sure this is the witch?" The servant's throat closed. His conscience fluttered once, twice, then caved in under the fierceness of Lady Lochalsh's stare and the knowledge of what she would do if he played her false. He cleared his throat and answered. "Aye, My Lady. It is her in truth. Look at her hand. You will see."

Rowan stiffened at his words. Her hand clenched into a fist.

Gwynneth saw the movement and quickly stepped to her side. "Show me your hand."

Rowan didn't move. She tightened her fist. Gwynneth's eyes snapped with anger and her voice roughened. "Show me your hand." Rowan stood unmoving. Gwynneth took a step forward as if to grab her tied wrists only to find her way blocked by Silobah, who pushed between them. The old woman's voice was a soft contrast to Lady Lochalsh's as she reasoned with Rowan. "It is no use to disobey. Give her your hand, lass."

Rowan looked at the wrinkled face. The dark eyes held hers and Silobah nodded her head up and down. The soft words came again. "Aye. Give it here." Reaching out she grasped Rowan's wrists. Gwynneth stepped closer. Ewan stepped backwards. Slowly Rowan unclenched her fist. Gwynneth drew in her breath. Silobah slowly closed then opened her eyes as if in pain. Rowan simply looked down at the sixth finger.

"Indeed." Gwynneth greedily reached out for the hand but Rowan quickly snatched her hands back, balling them into fists. Gwynneth's eyes turned to slits at the movement but decided to let this small show of rebellion pass. Turning to Ewan, she spoke.

"You are back sooner than I thought. And with the witch instead of her brother. I will increase your reward when you attend me tomorrow morning," Ewan waited. Gwynneth continued, "The horse is yours for finding her so quickly. Later tonight I will send something to help you celebrate your success. Mind you," Gwynneth roughened her voice, "celebrate it with your mouth closed and attend me tomorrow. You will not speak of this." It was not a question but a statement. Gwynneth drilled the man with her eyes.

Ewan nodded his small head thanking all the gods that she was pleased with what he had done. He would be more than happy to keep his mouth shut and collect his due. Gwynneth watched him for a moment, then drew Silobah aside with a quiet voice. "Put her in the tower room." Silobah stood perfectly still and stared at Lady Lochalsh. Gwynneth ignored the look and continued, "The one my mother used. Make sure you are not seen." Silobah started to speak but was interrupted. "I said to do it and do not speak to a soul. I want to deal with her on my own terms and without interference." Silobah nodded her head and Gwynneth continued. "And that means the laird. Do you hear me? When he arrives back at the castle, he is not to know that she is here." Her eyes bored into those of the old woman. "You will obey me in this. You think you have seen punishment handed out when you attended my mother. Well, I am capable of much more. Mark my words well."

Turning, Gwynneth gathered her skirts, pushed her way through the bushes and moved quickly back through the hidden door. Walking up the stone steps inside the castle wall her thoughts churned. She had noted the way Silobah had spoken to the girl. She would have to watch her. No one could know the girl was here. She thought of Ewan and hurried to her next task.

Outside of the castle wall Silobah, stood beside Rowan. Her words were quick and quiet. "Take every care that you dinna anger this lady. Others have done so and have regretted it." Silobah kept her eyes locked onto Rowan's and made her voice hard, convincing. "I will do all that I can to help. Whatever you say, dinna admit who you are."

The old one's words made no sense to Rowan and she brushed them aside. All she could think of was Elden. The name came out of her mouth and Silobah stopped stone still. The young woman spoke quietly but with an edge.

"Dinna look at me so old woman. The man brought in by the hunters. He is my brother. He is here is he not?" Silobah gave a start at the sound of Rowan's voice, so husky and low. Fiona had spoken with a voice such as this. She closed her eyes and shook her head.

"He is gone. The laird let him go."

"He is gone?" The husky voice held a slight quiver.

"Aye. The laird made Lady Lochalsh release him."

"Where is the laird now? I wish to see him." The imperious tone of her voice made Silobah snap up her head. So this one had strengths that weren't at first evident. She would have need of such strength to face Lady Lochalsh.

"He is away and may not be back for some time."

"Where did he go?"

"I dinna know where he went or how long he'll be away."

"The moment he arrives tell him I am here."

Silobah sighed. The highland witch had demanded the same thing and Lord Stannard had indeed been told, but it had not helped. The old woman sent a quick prayer up to her gods. It was different now. Colin was strong, not a weak Englishman in the grip of his wife. She looked at the lass and again was struck by the likeness to her mother, dead these past seventeen years. If Elden had not found Rowan, she would not be here and this situation would not exist. Silobah gave a bitter smile at the self-delusion. This would be happening no matter what. It was the circle struggling to complete itself once again. Silobah, aware that Ewan was listening, shook the thought away. "I willna disobey Lady Lochalsh." Grabbing Rowan's arm and gesturing for the man to take the horse and depart, Silobah led Rowan through the wooden door.

Quickly crossing a small musty chamber, they pushed through a heavy door and climbed a dark stone stairway. At the top they entered a dim hallway, lit only by the fading light coming through high slotted windows. Rowan noticed the dirt gathered on the floor and cobwebs heavy with dust hanging from the ceiling. Silobah pointed up more stairs.

Slowly, holding her hands in front of her, making sure not to stumble on the rope hanging from her wrists, she began climbing the narrow stone treads, the old woman trailing behind. Her thoughts were no comfort. Elden was gone. He was safe and she was not. She began to take careful note of where the old woman was leading her. It certainly appeared to be towards the tower of the castle. Apprehension crawled up her spine as she saw the long spiral of steps wind high above their heads. No one had seen them arrive. Only Lady Lochalsh, the old woman and her captor knew she was here. Her thoughts fastened on the man. Perhaps his tongue would loosen with drink and he would brag about his reward.

Rowan stopped abruptly. Pale light illuminated a wooden door held by large, metal hinges. Pushing ahead of Rowan, the old woman took a key from her pocket and placed it in the lock. The door swung open before she turned the key. A frown crossed Silobah's face. Cautiously she pushed into the room and saw that Lady Lochalsh had preceded them.

"My Lady?" Silobah took a step toward Gwynneth as Rowan looked at the room. It was indeed the tower room, and a cold one at that. Wind blew through the huge window that stretched from floor to ceiling. The thick walls were bare of hangings. A straw pallet with a meager covering lay on the stone floor. To the side was a table and chair. It was on this table that Gwynneth had set a small leather chest. The open box held several vials, a pedestal, a crushing dish, and some herbs.

Gwynneth turned to Silobah with a smile. "I am making a reward for Ewan."

Silobah watched Gwynneth add another drop from a vial into a small pot of mead.

"My lady. You are preparing the mead as a reward?" Gwynneth nodded her head and concentrated on her task. Silobah continued, "But the vial you are using contains foxglove."

Rowan bit back a gasp. Everyone knew it was a plant that could kill as well as heal. Lady Lochalsh kept mixing. Rowan eyed the open door but Silobah quickly pushed it shut behind her and moved to the woman's side. Grabbing Gwynneth's hand, she pulled the vial away from the rim of the container. Lady Lochalsh looked up at her and smiled.

"Yes. Of course. You are right. If I used more, it would taste sour. He would never drink it then."

Silobah released Lady Lochalsh's arm and stared. Gwynneth answered the look. "Don't you see? He cannot let others know that she is here. He must be silenced."

"My Lady, you must nae do this. The man acted in good faith. He will keep his word. Hasn't he done your bidding before? Hasn't he kept secrets to himself? You canna do this."

Gwynneth wiped the edges of the pot and gave Silobah a hard glare. "I know what needs to be done. Attend to your duties. Get the girl settled."

Rowan stood stock-still watching, hoping the old woman would keep quiet. Rowan needed her. After all, she had given a warning about Lady Lochalsh; perhaps she would help her escape. If Lady Lochalsh were bent on killing the tracker, then the old woman would be the only other person who knew that Rowan was here.

Gwynneth gave the mead a final stir and smiled. "There." Turning to Silobah, she arched one eyebrow. "Now you will give this to Ewan for me."

Silobah clasped her hands and held them tightly behind her back. It was a conscious thing, not simply instinct. Rowan saw her movement and slowly let out her breath, waiting. Gwynneth held the pot out to the old woman and kept the smile on her face. Rowan looked from one to the other, her eyes darting back and forth. Perhaps they would fight. She could run out of the door. She tried to remember where Silobah had put the key.

"I said to take this. Have your ears failed you?" Lady Loch-alsh's voice held an edge that was hard and cold. Slowly, Silobah unlocked her hands and let them hang by her sides. Gwynneth repeated her command.

As if snapping out of a trance, Silobah answered, "Certainly My Lady." Reaching out she took the pot from Lady Lochalsh's hands and turned to go from the room.

Rowan watched in horrified silence. So, this Lady had that much power over those she commanded.

"Here. Let us go together." Gwynneth walked to the door and held it open. Silobah, keeping a tight grip on the pot, slowly walked from the room. Following the old woman Gwynneth paused for a second, looked back at Rowan, and smiled. The door shut and Rowan stood still, hearing the key turn in the lock. Leaning her back against the wall, she closed her eyes in despair. There was madness here. The air around Lady Lochalsh was filled with malice, but a smile wreathed the woman's face at every turn. And the old one with the white hair. Going to do her mistress' bidding so easily? Rowan wished she had listened to Elden and stayed away. Why had she gone against her common sense? Opening her eyes, she lifted her wrists in front of her face. Unclenching her fists, she looked at the sixth finger. Bringing her hands to her mouth she began to pull on the rope with her teeth.

She whipped herself with her thoughts as she gnawed. There was not one person she had met who had not warned her against Lady Lochalsh. Her mind flashed back to the night she had spent with the man, Arden, in the woods. He had said Lady Lochalsh was an evil person. No, she corrected herself. No, that was wrong. He never really used the word evil, but he had hinted at it and had told her the castle was no place for her to go. She ran her tongue over her teeth and paused her efforts for a moment remembering that night. But it was not the words she was re-calling; it was the play of the fire over the hard planes of the man's face and how he had looked silhouetted against the flames. She made her mind focus on her present situation. She had no one but herself to blame.

Letting her wrists fall, she turned and walked to the large window. The rising moon clearly showed a leap to freedom would end in death. She would never choose it. Closing her eyes, she breathed in the night air and tried to imagine herself back in the woods; safe, wild, free. Sniffing hard she tried to recall the damp, dark smell of the forest at night, but smelled only the damp of the cold stones. Turning from the window she crossed the room and sank down on the chair, staring at nothing.

***

Elden heard the night owl cry and raising his eyes to the deep blue sky, saw the bird silently pumping his way through the trees. Reaching down, he touched his ankle and gave a grunt of pain. Still that hard knob jutting out. At least the skin wasn't pierced, but the ankle was hot to the touch and the pain flashed through him as he tried to reposition it on the ground. It worried him, this heat. What if he had damaged the inside and the flesh was turning bad? What if he awoke in the morning and still could not walk? What would he do then? He didn't know much about the deep woods, but he did know that weeks could go by without anyone passing through; that predators roamed both day and night looking for the sick, the disabled, and the dead. A shiver of cold went up his spine and he tried again to move his leg. This time the pain didn't stop at his knee; it flashed up through the center of his body and shot into his head. Nauseated, he leaned back against the tree and tried to clear his mind. All he could think of was what might be out there in the night, waiting. Keeping his eyes closed, he pulled his clothes even tighter against the night air and willed himself not to think. A rustling of juniper bushes made the hair rise on his arms, but the noise soon ceased and exhausted from pain and worry, he drifted into an uneasy sleep.

***

"You willna get through the night if you try and wait it out." Arden spoke from under his blanket. Colin sat beside the fire and did not answer. His thoughts were of another fire. Reaching out, he grabbed a stick and angrily poked at the flames. Sparks danced into the air and drifted to the ground.

"Blast it man." Arden jumped up brushing the sparks from his blanket and glared at Colin. "Get her off of your mind." A sudden silence filled the night. The only sound, a sleepy bird calling out and the crackling of the fire. There, thought Arden. There it was. Out in the open where it belonged. Placing his hands on his hips he looked down at Colin who stubbornly glared into the fire.

"I said get her off of your mind and turn your thoughts to dealing with Gwynneth."

Silence. Arden gave a sigh and began to gather up his blanket, ready to remake his bed. His friend was stubborn beyond belief. He paused. The words were so low he first thought it was the wind sighing through the trees.

"I canna."

Arden held the blanket unfolded in his hands not daring to move, afraid he would break the spell. The laird continued. "I canna forget her." Colin shifted his position and again jabbed at the fire.

Arden spoke, "So we track her brother, and when we find the brother, we find the lass."

Colin closed his eyes. "And then what?"

Easing himself to the ground, Arden carefully kept his eyes on the fire. "Then you must do the thing that is best. You will help them on their way." Colin nodded his head and a pause left an opening in the air. Arden stepped in to fill it. "You will send them on their way because there is nae other choice." Colin made as if to speak, but Arden held up his hand for silence.

"Dinna look at me that way. It is written all over your face what it is you truly want." Colin turned his face away from his friend and scowled into the fire. Ignoring the look, Arden continued.

"You want to find the lass and bring her back to the castle. Somehow you want Gwynneth, who by all appearances seems to be getting as mad as that mother of hers, to magically disappear and leave you free to be with this Rowan. Am I right? Shall we go to Briac for a spell, do you think?"

Colin sat by the fire not speaking. It was humiliating to have Arden read his thoughts this way, but then it had ever been so. And more, his friend was right. His thoughts had been focused on Rowan ever since he had sent her back to the highlands. Aye, he was out in the woods because he thought to stop her before she returned for her brother, and aye, he was here to thwart the tracker Gwynneth sent after Elden. But if he was completely honest with himself, he would admit that he was also here to see Rowan one more time, at least be in her presence if only for a moment. He shifted his position beside the fire and looked up at his friend. "I feel the fool, like a mooning calf."

Arden laughed. At least now the man was being honest with himself. Arden decided to push a bit further. "You know, even if we found her and Gwynneth somehow disappeared, and you brought this lass to the castle, she probably would not stay. Not if she is anything like what we saw at the waterfall. Don't you remember what she looked like then? A wild thing. She fairly flew away when we came upon her."

Colin spoke, "When I met her, it was as if she was a part of the woods and aye, you are right. She's nae one to capture and hold. The only way she could be held is if you had no chains on her." He looked over at his friend for the first time. "And anyway, there is Gwynneth."

"Then we canna do more. We continue to track the brother and hopefully find the lass."

Colin nodded his head "And I will put away the mooning." Arden laughed again.

"We start once more in the morning. You will need a good night's sleep." Both men settled in, rolling themselves in their blankets and closing their eyes against the night.

***

Gwynneth stood by the window in her bed chamber looking at the moon. Turning as Silobah entered the room, she spoke, "You did as I said with the mead?" The old woman nodded her head, "Aye." Closing the door behind her she asked, "You are nae in bed? There is a chill in the air."

"You have not brushed my hair."

Motioning Gwynneth to a stool, Silobah picked up the brush and began to pull it through the black hair. Gwynneth gave a groan of pleasure and closed her eyes. Silobah gave a smile, thankful that Lady Lochalsh's sharp eyes would not be studying her face. It was the second time that she had defied her mistress. But she was pleased with what she had done. The decision had been finally no decision at all, but the only path open to her. A vow was sacred, and now that she knew the exact path the prophecy would take, she intended to prevent it from coming to fruition.

She had taken the pot of mead to Ewan, and getting him alone, had quickly and quietly spoken. "There willna be any attendance upon Lady Lochalsh tomorrow for you. Mark my words well. The mead contains poison." Ewan started to speak, but she interrupted, "Tis true. She wants you dead because you know about the lass. Gather your things and leave tonight. It is the only way you will keep your life." The man gave her a sharp look. Silobah answered, "I am old and tired. She does nae frighten me anymore. Now go."

"You are brushing too hard," Lady Lochalsh complained. Silobah hastened to assure her. "I am sorry my lady. I will do better." The old woman saw a smile cross Gwynneth's face and she thought to herself, 'Aye, my lady, smile as you reprimand me. Smile at the thought of poor faithful Ewan drinking the mead mixed by your hands. But you willna succeed.' The brush moved through the long black hair.

Chapter 22

THE COLD LIGHT of dawn reached through the trees and played on Elden's face. Moving his head to avoid the light, his back shifted from where it had been resting against the tree and he slipped to the ground. A shaft of fire shot up his left leg. Groaning, he tried to curl up into a ball to ease the pain. The movement only increased the throbbing and blackness descended upon him.

***

Colin sat beside the sputtering fire, staring into the black ashes. The dawn's light played through the trees and he gave a sigh, watching it dance over the darkened logs, his thoughts as black as the burned wood. If Rowan was indeed headed back to the castle, shouldn't they have found some sign of her? And what about any sign of her brother? It was as if they were witches indeed and had vanished into the air. He shook aside his fanciful notions. This was a massive forest. He and Arden could have passed within one mile of either of them and not seen any trace. And it wasn't as if they would call attention to themselves. No. They had most certainly moved along animal trails, avoiding the traveled routes. Perhaps they had found each other and were miles away, galloping on Rowan's horse. If that was the case, then he should let them both return to the highlands, and he should go back to the castle and be the laird and husband that his role demanded.

"Did you sleep at all?" Colin jumped at the voice and frowned. Arden threw his blanket aside and rose to his feet, stretching his arms above his head. He had woken silently and had spent the first few minutes watching his friend's face. It was apparent that the man had not slept. Arden kept his back to the laird as he folded his blanket. It was time to get Colin back to the castle. They had not found the lass and the seer. Undoubtedly, the two had crossed paths and disappeared into the deep forest. Good. It was best that way. He said as much as he finished folding his blanket. "We can be back by tonight if we ride fast." Colin silently listened as his friend finished. There was no more to be said.

***

The door opened and Rowan jumped up from her pallet, her legs braced, her hands clenched in fists. The noise had torn her from a troubled and anguished sleep. She had been in the woods fighting a wolf, trying to keep it from gnawing on a prone and unconscious Elden.

Silobah stood stock-still looking at the lass, noting her stance, the way her eyes flickered around the room, the rope that had bound her fists on the floor. This was a wild one. The old woman gave a deep sigh. "I have brought you some food."

Rowan unclenched her fists and watched warily as the old woman placed the food on the rough table. Slowly she relaxed her legs. Silobah backed away from the table, and Rowan approached the bowl. Still keeping her eyes on the old woman, she began to eat quickly, neatly. Still standing. Silobah watched as she did so. The lass reminded her of an animal; alert, cautious, unwilling to let her guard down for a moment.

The old woman turned, making sure the door was tightly shut, then approached the lass, her voice low, "You must take note of what I'm going to say. I have been with Lady Lochalsh for all of her life and I know her well."

Rowan raised her eyebrow as she chewed her food and nodded for the woman to continue.

"She is becoming more and more like her mother as the days go by."

Rowan nodded again, and Silobah took a deep breath.

"You know about the highland witch."

Rowan swallowed her food and cautiously took only a small sip of the mead. Wiping her mouth with the back of her hand she spoke, "Was she the one who was killed here?"

Silobah looked deeply into her eyes. So, she really didn't know. It was time. Aye. It was time. Slowly she walked over to the chair and sat down. Rowan watched her. The old woman nodded to the pallet, "You will need to sit."

Rowan stared and the old woman nodded her head. "Aye. You must sit for this and you must listen without speaking. Once I am finished you may ask questions but there is little time and I must tell you these things."

"Why should I trust you? You took poison to the tracker. Is he dead now? Have you done her bidding?"

Silobah looked at the lass and her eyes hardened. "How easy it is for you to throw words at me, not knowing what is involved. Aye she gave me the poison and aye I have raised her from a bairn, but there comes a time when the circle must be broken. What I did last night will help break it."

Rowan looked closely at the old woman and Silobah continued. "I gave the mead to Ewan but told him it was poison and that if he valued his life he would leave, and quickly. Hopefully he has."

"And what will happen if Lady Lochalsh finds out what you did?"

"That I dinna know. She might go as far as to have me killed."

"But you said you have been with her since she was born!"

"Aye," she looked up at the lass, "but now I dinna think it will matter. She seems to be following in the exact footsteps of her mother, and the gods know her mother was bad enough."

"Her mother was the one who killed the witch?"

189

"Aye. In a manner of speaking, she did. And Gwynneth trying to poison Ewan means it is now beyond my attempts to reason with her. I worry not about myself but others who must be saved."

Rowan took a deep breath and cautiously sank down onto the pallet. "So, there is something you need to tell me? What more could there be? I know Lady Lochalsh will use me for her own ends and may try to kill me if I dinna do her bidding. What is there left to say?" Silobah looked at the lass and closed her eyes for a second. It would be a hard telling, especially the part that she herself played. But she was determined, firm in her decision, and she had had enough of death to last her a lifetime and more.

"I will tell you. It will be painful for you to hear. But you must know." Silobah took her eyes from Rowan's and looked out of the window, not wanting to see the effect of her words. Taking a deep breath, she began in the only way she knew how. Directly and straight from the heart.

"Aye, you could say that Lady Stannard killed the highland witch. She killed her by capturing her. And then when the witch refused to work her magic she locked her here, in this room."

Rowan looked at her bleak surroundings. "Go on."

"The witch tried to escape one night but ran right into Lord Stannard. Drunkard that he was, he was still capable of rape and she became pregnant. Lady Stannard was delighted with this turn of events. She hoped the witch would birth a son whom she could eventually pass off as her own, but that was not to be." Silobah paused for a moment, collecting her thoughts. "The witch suffered greatly with the birth. There was no one to attend her but my lady and me. To this day I believe she would have survived if she had been properly cared for, and if Lady Stannard hadn't flown into her rage."

"What happened?"

"She saw the bairn was a lass. And with the witch continuing to vow never to use her powers, Lady Stannard's hopes were destroyed in one instant." Silobah paused again, as if too tired to continue, but need pressed her on. "She kicked at the witch, so great was her rage. The blow landed on the side of her head. There was nae chance for her after that."

The tower room was silent except for the wind sailing by the tall window. Rowan sat still as a stone, her eyes wide and watching. Silobah wrapped her arms around herself for warmth. Slowly, she let her eyes meet those of the girl. "She did nae kill the bairn. I got to the child before she could. Once she recovered from her rage, she ordered the child taken away and killed. I took the babe days away to the great Falls of Measach and placed her beside the sacred Corrieshalloch Gorge. And gave her to the gods."

Rowan's eyes locked onto Silobah's. A deathly quiet filled the room, the only noise their ragged breathing. Rowan looked deeply into Silobah's eyes, and slowly the old woman nodded her head. Rowan jumped up and began rapidly pacing the room, her thoughts in a furor. She could barely credit it. If this old woman spoke the truth, then she was the daughter of the highland witch. The thought stopped her cold. She looked down at her left hand. Indeed. Her thoughts raced on. If this were true then she was the daughter of the hated Lord Stannard. Ice filled her stomach. This also made her the half-sister of Gwynneth. Rowan whirled around and bending down, peered into the face of the old woman.

"Gwynneth is my half-sister?"

Silobah nodded her head.

"Does she know this?"

"No, My Lady. She does nae."

Rowan gave a start at the change of address immediately. She had never been called 'My Lady' in her life. She bit her lip then asked, "How can you be sure it was me you placed beside the stream?"

Silobah looked at her and smiled. "The bairn had a sixth finger just as you do."

"Others are cursed with the sixth finger. Again, why do you say that I am the one? Perhaps others abandoned sick and helpless babes to the gods there also."

Silobah's eyes softened for a moment. "You are the image of your mother. She was beautiful. The hair, the nose, the eyes all are the same. Besides, I know your brother."

"Of course you know him, he was just here."

"He was also here those years ago. Elden came to the castle with Fiona. He was captured along with her. Lady Stannard ordered him locked away, but I feigned his escape then hid him so he could be near your mother. He lived in an empty cellar room and ate scraps from the kitchen tables. I protected him."

Rowan remembered the talk she and Elden had had right before her escape. She gave a bitter smile and nodded for Silobah to continue.

"When I returned from the gorge, I hurried to him to give him food and some coin to get safely back to the high mountains, but he was gone. And now we know where he went. He followed me. That's how he came to find you and raise you."

It was too much for Rowan to take in at once, and she stood silently, trying to process it. After a moment she spoke softly. "He said his dreams showed him where I was and it was the gods intervention that he have me. I guess he wanted to spare me the truth. But right before I escaped the hunters, he told me we shared the same mother. We were separated before he could finish the tale."

Silobah nodded her head at the words. "I would imagine he wanted you to think that you were the child of an ordinary woman." The old woman's words trailed off. It was a lot to know in so short a time.

Again, Rowan spoke, "So. I am the daughter of the old lord and the highland witch." This time it was a statement and not a question.

"That is correct, My Lady."

Rowan looked at the old woman and raised her eyebrow. The old one gave a small smile back. Rowan walked to the window and looked out at the rising sun. "What do we do now? I have to escape. I need to find Elden."

"The room is watched by those who will do Gwynneth's bidding for coin."

Rowan asked in frustration. "What is it she wants? What can I do to give it to her and be released?"

Silobah stood and walked closer to the girl. "Gwynneth says she wants the laird to give her a child. But that is only part. Yes, she wants a male bairn with her parent's blood to rule Lochalsh. But she also wants revenge on Colin. The laird stays away from her bed and would be rid of her had he not made a promise to Robert the Bruce to marry her, protect Lochalsh, and rule the land."

"I dinna care about the laird. You see how poorly he rules his wife. What does she want me to do?"

"She believes that you are a witch and would have you place a spell on the laird to make him come to her bed and make her womb rich with child."

Rowan gave a snort of disgust. "Surely she canna be so gullible as to believe that can be done?"

Silobah nodded her head. "Aye. She believes it. And you must trust me when I say that she is dead set on having her way. She will stop at nothing. She truly believes that you have power and she will try to bend you to her will."

Rowan looked at the old woman and realized she was dead serious. A question rose in her. "You raised her yet you go against her wishes and help me?"

"Aye. I have made a vow. I owe it to you and I owe it to your mother."

Rowan bit off her next question. Mother. The word was so completely unfamiliar. To her it was a word that held no meaning. It never had. Elden had been all of the mother that she had ever needed. Almost without thinking, the next words came out of her mouth. "What was she like?"

Silobah gave a small, sad smile and spoke in a low voice, "She was almost as beautiful as you. The same hair, build and jaw. She was tall and breathtaking."

"You said before I have her look. What was she like?"

"She held herself high. She was nae arrogant or haughty but there was an air about her that said she knew her own worth," the old woman paused as if searching for the right words, "She had a way with laughter and that stood her in good stead during the months she was here. And she was strong. Not physically but in her mind. She was absolutely unbreakable when it came to what she would and would nae do. Lady Stannard was just as stubborn, and she had power on her side."

"Power?"

"Aye. This castle was in the hands of the English. Lord Stannard had turned into a drunken fool. My Lady ruled with a hard hand and will of stone. No one disobeyed her. As the years went by, she became obsessed with the dark arts, wanting a male heir was only part of it."

Silobah paused, seeing that Rowan paid no heed to her words. The lass was lost in thought.

"Fiona." Rowan said the name to herself. She could not use the name of mother. "Fiona had power too, didn't she?"

"Aye, but it was nothing compared to having English troops at your beck and call."

Rowan turned her back on the woman and looked again out of the window. "And there was nothing you could do?"

Silobah answered the accusation quietly, "No. There was nothing I could do and not court death."

Rowan whirled around and glared at Silobah "But you would do something now?" Her tone was harsh, commanding, "Why?"

"I told you. I owe a debt to both you and your mother," her tone lowered and Rowan had to strain to hear the words, "and besides, My Lady, I made a vow many years ago that I was unable to fulfill. It has to be fulfilled now. Even if it indeed means my death."

Rowan looked carefully at the old woman and knew that her words were true. "Well then, what do we do first?" The door swung open and Rowan and Silobah both jumped.

Gwynneth stood in the doorway, looking back and forth between the two of them. Both struggled to keep their faces blank. Gwynneth narrowed her eyes and addressed Silobah, "Leave."

Silobah stood up from the chair and held her composure. "My Lady, I would stay to help you."

The voice came again hard, cold, "Leave. Await me in my bed chamber."

Silobah kept her eyes from Rowan and hurried from the room.

The door closed and both young women stood, watching each other. Rowan knew she should be frightened, intimidated, but the overriding emotion was equal parts fascination and repulsion. She searched Gwynneth's face for traces of familiarity. Aye, their mothers had been as different as two women could be but after all, she and Gwynneth shared the same sire. She could only think of Lord Stannard in those terms. The word father had even less meaning than that of mother. Rowan let her eyes travel over Lady Lochalsh's face and saw it tighten under her scrutiny.

Gwynneth, in turn, looked back at the witch. Yes, she was pretty if you liked that pale red-haired type, but that interested her not. It was the hand with the six fingers that fascinated and drew her close. She needed to see it again. Swift as a striking snake, she reached out and grabbed. Quickly Rowan tried to snatch her hand away but Gwynneth was too fast. Tightening her hold, she pulled Rowan toward her. Rowan held back for a moment but Gwynneth was insistent, digging in her nails. Using her other hand, she examined Rowan's. Gwynneth ran her index finger over Rowan's small sixth finger.

"So, you are a witch."

"Nae."

"Your hand says differently."

Rowan snatched her hand away and met Gwynneth's eyes. "I am nae witch."

"I say you are."

There was no reply. Standing in front of Gwynneth, she noticed a familiar look in the woman's eyes, the look of a predator having captured its prey. A cold tendril of dread wrapped around her heart. She tried to ignore it. Gwynneth noticed the change in her demeanor and gave a thin smile. Of course she is a witch. She has the look of one. She has a brother who is a seer. She has the sixth finger. And it is time to find out exactly what her powers are. "I see that you are finished eating. I have things to prepare and will return later. Then we will settle this question of your powers." Turning, she walked from the room. Rowan watched helplessly as the door swung shut.

Chapter 23

ARDEN RODE THROUGH the afternoon behind the laird, keeping his eyes on his friend's back. It was straight as a rod. The man smiled to himself. Colin knew he was being watched and there was nothing he hated more. Arden's smile broadened into a grin. He also knew the laird hated to admit defeat and he was doing just that by returning to the castle. Colin may think it defeat, but it was the best decision, the only decision the laird could reasonably come to. Surely by now Elden and Rowan had crossed paths and were on their way back to the highlands. And anyway, to find the lass would have been folly.

"Did you hear that?" Colin pulled his horse to a stop and held his hand up in warning. Arden reined his horse in and tilted his head in his usual listening stance. There it was. A slight noise. Colin gathered the reins and swung down from his horse.

"What is it?" Arden asked, but the laird again held up his hand for quiet. Arden gave a snort.

Ignoring his friend, Colin dropped the reins and walked into the bush. He knew that sound. It was one that an animal makes when it is caught in a trap and dying.

Arden watched the laird creep into the woods. Aye, he had heard the noise too, but it was nothing unusual for a forest. He could only guess that Colin was trying to put off his arrival at the castle. If this took any time at all, they would end up having to spend another night in the woods. Arden gave a slight smile. That would suit the laird just fine. Arden flexed his shoulders, easing the knots that had come from sleeping on the forest floor. The laird might be anxious to stay another night on the damp ground, but he was in no mood to do so. Anxiously he straightened his legs, lifting up in the stirrups to get a good view.

"Colin?" No answer. With a sigh, Arden sat back down on his horse. It was just a ploy to stay away from Gwynneth. No doubt about it.

"Arden!" The voice was harsh, demanding. With one swift movement Arden was off of the horse and running to the laird, his hand on his dirk. Tearing through the bushes he almost stumbled over his friend crouching on his knees. For one terrified moment he thought Colin was wounded, but then his eyes focused on the ground. A man was lying there. Quickly straightening up, Arden searched for attackers. He saw nothing. Ignoring his laird, Arden rapidly walked around the area looking for signs of a struggle, signs that anyone lingered. Nothing. Satisfied there was no threat, Arden walked back to Colin, squatted on the ground, and gave the man a look. He was not from the castle and by his dress; he wasn't from the village either. He addressed Colin. "The seer?"

"Aye"

Arden ran his eyes slowly over the man, seeing the ankle, swollen and black. A nasty thing and, if first looks were correct, the bone inside was broken. He reached out and touched the inflamed flesh. Another groan came from the man, but Arden continued his examination. No, not a break, but a bone was badly out of place. At least there was no flesh wound to putrefy. He raised his eyes to the laird. "It is a good thing that he is unconscious. We will have to push the bone back into place so he willna become a cripple."

"We?"

Arden ignored the question. "You will have to hold him while I push." He rose to his feet and started for his horse, considering what he could use to bind the ankle.

Colin looked at the unconscious man. Lifting his head he called out, "Where do you think the lass is?" Arden gave a grunt and ignored the question as he draped leather laces over his shoulder and broke a branch in two. Walking back to the laird, he kept his eyes on the man, hoping he would be able to reposition the bone without causing it to rip from the skin. Colin saw his friend's face and kept quiet.

"Here. Get up beside his head. Hold his arms. Men have been known to take a swing when this is done." Colin moved to comply as Arden placed his hands on Elden's ankle. Without so much as a pause he grabbed the leg in one hand, the foot in the other, and gave a mighty tug apart. From his stupor, Elden shouted with pain. Colin winced at the sound. The man began to thrash. Arden yelled for the laird to hold him down. Colin struggled, pinning Elden to the ground. "Blast!" The other foot had raked through the air and hit Arden's face.

"Damn you. I said to hold him still."

Colin gritted his teeth and increased his hold.

"Give me a hand."

"A hand? I dinna have a hand."

"Aye you do. Here, hold these." Arden gestured to the two pieces of broken branch.

Colin cast his body over that of the unconscious but thrashing Elden, effectively knocking the wind from him. Reaching down, Colin held the sticks in place while Arden bound the ankle with the leather laces.

"There," panting, "There. You can let go now."

Colin pulled himself from the man and sat back. Arden rested on his heels and looked at Elden's face. It was pale, sweating, but at least the man had not been conscious during the process. He moved up beside Elden's head and gently turned it one way, then back again. "I see no knots. It looks like he's unconscious from the pain, not from hurting his head. When he comes around, he should be fine. But he is in nae shape to travel. I suggest we make camp here tonight and keep watch over him."

Colin nodded his head in agreement, willing the man to wake up and answer his question. Did he realize that Rowan might have gone back to the castle in search of him? He watched his friend trying to make the man comfortable. With a sigh he began to gather wood for the evening fire.

***

"You are sure?"

The young male servant answered quickly, "Aye, My Lady." The boy took a deep breath. "He is nae where to be found."

"You are certain?"

"Well, My Lady, his cot is empty. He has nae been seen today. He just seems to have disappeared along with that horse he found in the woods." He steadied his voice and continued, "Do you want me to find another to attend you?"

"No. You may go."

The boy bowed to Lady Lochalsh and thankfully left the room.

Tapping her finger against her mouth, Gwynneth turned and walked to the window, looking out at the early evening sky. He had been warned. She knew it. It was as plain as could be. He should be dead in his bed but instead he was gone. When she hadn't heard news of his death, she had sent word to the kitchen for him to attend her. And this was the answer she received. A black rage began to slowly burn inside of her head. There was only one person who could have done this. The one who had so recently begun to second-guess every decision she made. Silobah.

Turning from the window she sat down at her dressing table and began to brush her hair, deliberately and with long pulling strokes. Yes, the old woman had betrayed her. Ewan should be dead. Dead! She threw the brush across the room and jumped to her feet, pacing. A sudden thought made her jerk to a stop. What if she tried to help the witch escape? The black rage burned even brighter as Gwynneth pressed the palms of her hands together trying to still her mind. Silobah had to be stopped. Whirling around she ran to the bedroom door.

***

"There. The fire is built. Is there anything else I can do, My Laird?" Colin's words were sarcastic and an acknowledgement of how Arden had been ordering him around since finding Elden.

"It's fine, thank you." Sitting back on his heels, Arden grinned. "You know if you ever decide to give up this laird business, I can help you find a place as a serving man. Colin scowled at his friend and sat beside the fire. Looking at Elden he noticed the man's eyelids fluttering. "Is he coming around?"

Arden bent over him, lifting one eyelid, then the other. "Not yet. I think he'll do it during the night." He put his fingers against Elden's throat and felt for the heartbeat. It was strong. Good. He looked down at the ankle to make sure the cloth and not been tied too tight around the swollen flesh. "Aye. I think he will rouse tonight but he willna be happy about it."

"Pain?"

"Och aye."

"But he will be sensible?"

Arden gave him a sideways look. "Aye. Sensible enough to answer your questions about the lass."

Colin spoke in anger. "You know as well as I that we have to know."

Arden calmly watched as Colin rose to his feet pacing back and forth, questioning out loud, "What if she has been hurt too? Or what if their paths never crossed and she is on her way to the castle? Maybe she's almost there?"

The look on Arden's face changed at the last few words. Colin saw it and nodded his head. "Aye. What then?"

Arden turned back to the man on the ground and, placing his hand on Elden's head, he gently moved it back and forth, seeing if there was a response. Elden groaned then lapsed into silence. Arden looked up at the laird. "Go get some cool water and let's see if we can bring him around."

***

"If you dinna do as she says you will come to harm." Silobah spoke in low tones, the words urgent. Rowan listened to everything she said. But why was the old one now acting like she would not be here to help?

"A guard is on the steps?"

"Aye. He knows nothing and willna even ask."

Nodding that she had heard, Rowan looked around the room, then shut her eyes briefly. The stone walls were impenetrable. The window, a large gap between floor and ceiling and way too far from the ground. Her eyes took in the door and again noted its strong thick beams. She glanced down at the food. "These are the leavings are they nae?"

Silobah nodded her head. "Lady Lochalsh took them from the kitchen saying they were for the laird's bitch. She does nae want anyone to know where you are."

"Ewan does."

Silobah smiled. Rowan continued, "It was brave of you to tell him."

The door slammed open. Silobah and Rowan jumped and turned. Gwynneth stood there glaring at the old woman. Rowan glared back. Gwynneth paused, the muscles in her throat working, her hands clenched, poised as if to leap. She looked to Rowan exactly like a wolf getting ready to rend its prey. Silobah stood completely still, her eyes locked on her mistress. Silence. Rowan's muscles tensed as she saw the rage on Gwynneth's face.

"Ewan is not dead. Is he Silobah?"

The words were even, quiet, deadly. The old woman flinched at them.

Gwynneth closed then bolted the door behind her. Slowly she walked into the room and stood in front of Silobah. A hand flashed through the air and the old woman was on her knees bending towards the floor, her hands over her face, moaning. Gwynneth stood rubbing her hand.

Instantly Rowan leapt across the room and grabbed Gwynneth's arms.

"No!" Silobah's shout rang through the air but Rowan didn't hear it. All she could see through her red rage was the old woman on the floor, crying. Quick as a whip, Gwynneth twisted to the side, turned her head, and bit. Jumping back Rowan grabbed her bleeding hand and sucked as if an adder had struck her. Panting, she kept her mouth to her hand and held her place, watching, waiting for Gwynneth to drop her guard.

"Get up." The words were cold and hard. Silobah stayed on her knees. "I said get up."

Silobah kept her head bent but slowly rose to her feet. Taking a deep breath, she squared her shoulders. Raising her head, she looked directly into the eyes of Lady Lochalsh. "Aye, I gave him the mead but I told him it was poisoned. I told him that you intended for him to die because he knew the lass was in the castle."

"Where did he go?"

"I have nae idea. I told him if he valued his life he would leave and never return. He could be anywhere, but I'll vow you will never see him again."

Gwynneth raised her hand and struck Silobah across the face. The old woman rocked back on her feet. Rowan launched herself through the air. Sensing the movement, Gwynneth turned and grabbed Rowan's arms. Using the force of the leap, she swung her around and propelled her into the wall. Rowan's head cracked against the stone. Silence. Light breathing. Gwynneth released her and Rowan quietly slid to the floor. Gwynneth turned back to Silobah.

"How dare you betray me like this!" Her voice rang with rage.

Lowering her hands from her face, Silobah looked at Lady Lochalsh. The old woman's eyes gleamed with deep contempt and a solid resignation. She spoke. "Evil in those walls will dwell. Beside the waters Alsh knows well. The red-haired one is hunted then. Beware the circle comes again."

Gwynneth jerked back, silenced by the words. Silobah continued. "Thomas the Rhymer said these words as he drifted into the shadow world."

Gwynneth stilled completely, caught by the name of the great seer. The old woman took a step closer to Gwynneth and lowered her voice. "Never again will I stand by and watch while others die. Listen to me well. Your parents built Lochalsh on ground sacred to the old religion. They were warned but did nae care. The grove was destroyed, the stones from the old site used to pave this castle's courtyard. And so, it began. The old gods were angered and cursed this place. Your father raped and killed. Your mother had a twisted desire to master the dark arts. She murdered. I couldn't stop them. But you, I will."

With a strangled cry Gwynneth swung her fist and struck the side of Silobah's head. The old woman dropped to the floor. As if from a great distance, Rowan heard the cry. Struggling with the darkness, she tried to focus her eyes, keep her breathing light, and remain motionless. She needed to gather her strength, concentrate on what was before her. Through lowered lids she watched Gwynneth like she would a mad wolf. The woman stood over Silobah, her breathing ragged, her fist clenching and unclenching. Feeling Rowan's eyes upon her she turned and spoke. "This is what happens to those who disobey me."

Gwynneth leaned down to the girl, her face only inches away. Rowan turned her chin to the side and pain raked up the back of her head. Reaching out with a powerful hand, Gwynneth grabbed Rowan's chin and yanked her head back to the front. Black lights jumped in front of her eyes and she strained to keep conscious. Gwynneth's voice sank to a hiss.

"You will not disobey me, will you? You will do exactly as I command. I will return as the moon rises. There is work for us to do while it is full."

Pushing Rowan's chin away, she turned and walked past Silobah, giving the old woman a push with her foot. There was no response. She looked back at Rowan and gave her a smile as cold as death.

"You will do as I say or you will join your friend." Without another word she walked from the room and bolted the door.

***

The evening sky settled over them like a soft blanket. Looking up, Arden squinted his eyes at the moon. It was full. A frown crossed his face. He hated a full moon. Hearing a groan, he looked to the side where Elden lay sleeping, fitfully. Leaning over, he touched his hand to the man's forehead. Aye, there was sweat, but no fever. The sweat came from the pain. Arden withdrew his hand and looked over at his friend.

Colin sat on the other side of the fire, moodily staring into the flames. Arden knew what was on his mind. He was thinking about Rowan. Feeling eyes on him, Colin raised his head. "He is better?"

"No. Much the same but we can be thankful for that. At least there is nae fever from rotting. He will live but I dinna know how well he will walk."

Colin felt badly about the man, after all it was Gwynneth who had had him hunted and captured. Colin rubbed his hand against his forehead. Aye, he felt guilty about the man, but what he really wanted was for him to wake up and answer questions about the lass. A nighthawk rose from a nearby tree and called out into the darkness. Colin started at the sound then spoke, "Where do you think she is?"

"I dinna know. Do you think she's gone back?"

"I think it a likely thing."

Arden nodded his head. Colin had met her and so should know. But it was something he felt too. "She is at home in the woods, you said so yourself. If they were together, she would have built a shelter and would have kept them supplied with food until his ankle healed enough to travel."

Colin nodded in silent agreement. Arden spoke "She has had plenty of time to either be well away, or back at Lochalsh."

Colin felt uneasy, as if an animal had run across his grave. "I want to start back to the castle tomorrow morning nae matter what shape Elden is in. If he canna move then you will stay with him but, I'm going."

Arden recognized the tone in Colin's voice. "What is it?"

"I'm nae sure. It's more a feeling than anything else. I just know that I need to be back there, now."

Arden continued to watch his friend, but Colin didn't speak, he just continued to stare uneasily into the fire.

***

Rowan sat on the floor, her head resting against the wall. She knew she should get up and do something about Silobah but she couldn't move. Her head throbbed, but it wasn't the pain alone keeping her as if nailed to the floor. Groggily, she turned her head toward the tray of food. She should have never eaten, it no matter how hungry she was. She should have known that Gwynneth would put something in it to make her weak, unable to fight. Rowan turned her eyes again to Silobah. Or had it been this old one who had drugged her, hoping to make her complacent and less able to struggle against Gwynneth's will so together they could plan escape? Rowan's mind was filled with fog. She saw the gentle movement of the woman's back, up and down. Good. At least she was alive. But there was no telling how long she would be insensible or if she would even live through the night, so fierce had been the blow to her head.

Rowan bit her lip and recalled the scene between the two women. For Gwynneth to have hit Silobah with that much malice, that much strength, she must be unhinged. This was the woman who had raised her from a bairn. She kept her eyes on the still form. But this was also the woman who had let the highland witch die, then left her bairn in the cold forest. Mixed emotions played through her groggy mind.

"So, you are feeling better after your meal?" Gwynneth gave a low laugh and Rowan drew back against the wall. She hadn't heard the door open. She must be drugged indeed. She tried to collect her thoughts.

"Good. Then get up." Rowan remained still.

"I said get up!" Gwynneth walked over to Rowan, and, grabbing a handful of her hair, pulled her to her feet. Rowan stumbled and shook herself free. The floor moved when she tried to walk, and she put her hand out to the wall to steady herself. Gwynneth gave another laugh at that.

"Do not play the idiot with me. You can stand; I gave you just enough goldenseal to keep you calm."

Rowan looked at Gwynneth. Her mind was beginning to clear a bit. She hadn't eaten as much as Gwynneth supposed and she was fighting to gain her wits. Adrenaline pumped steadily through her veins as she took a deep breath, trying to clear the poison from her mind. But it wasn't enough. Roughly, Gwynneth grabbed her shoulders and dragged Rowan toward an iron ring hammered into the wall. Quickly she bound one wrist, then the other, then raised them high and bound them to the iron ring. Stepping back she gave the girl a smile.

"Good. That is the way it is supposed to be. Now let us talk."

The sudden movements made Rowan dizzy, but her heart began to pound with rage. She wiggled her wrists but the ropes were tied tightly and well. She opened her eyes and looked into Gwynneth's eyes, remembering the warnings. Yes, she was the one who was always the hunter. But of forest predators. This human predator was a different matter. There was no predicting the actions of one such as this. A shudder went deep through her. Quickly she prayed to the gods for strength then tried to focus her mind away from the overwhelming rage.

"So now it is time for you to work your magic, gain me the affections of the laird and the babe to follow." Rowan looked blankly back at Lady Lochalsh. The woman's voice roughened. "You are not leaving here until the laird comes back to my bed."

Still Rowan kept silent. Her eyes wandered to the window, the strong wood door. Gwynneth gave a laugh. "No one knows that you are here. The guard below has been dismissed. He was told nothing. Ewan is surely deep in the woods by now, running like a scared hare and Silobah cannot help you."

Rowan looked at Gwynneth. The woman's eyes had gone strange. She took a deep breath, hoping her words would be heard and understood. "I am nae witch. Aye, I have the sixth finger but I dinna cast spells. I dinna turn people into frogs. I know nothing of these things."

"Your finger says you do. Your brother is a seer with great powers."

"It is nae real power, simply the ability to read faces. Only the simple people believe him."

Gwynneth walked closer to her. Shoving her face directly into Rowan's she spoke softly, with an undertone of menace. "Take care. I can use you as I will."

Rowan lowered her eyes. A long finger jabbed under Rowan's chin and forced her head up. Rowan's eyes met those of Lady Lochalsh and she winced at the light that danced in them. Gwynneth laughed, "So tell me. What is it that we have to do to get the laird into my bed?" Gwynneth reached out her other hand and grabbed Rowan's arm, digging her fingers into the white flesh. "Speak to me now or you will regret it."

Rowan pushed her head back against the wall as far as she could, trying to get away from the woman's face. Taking a deep breath, she repeated her last words. "I told you. I have nae power. Aye, I have the sixth finger but I have never used it in the way you think."

Gwynneth snatched her hands away, her eyes narrowing into slits and hissed, "You will obey me in this."

A flame of anger flared in Rowan's head and rage took over. She had been hunted for days. She had been trapped like an animal and dragged into the castle. She had been locked up, hit, drugged, and seen Silobah beaten. Enough. Thrusting her head out toward Gwynneth the words flew out of her mouth before she could stop them.

"Nothing. There is nae power in the world to make a man come to the bed of a woman such as you."

Gwynneth's hand whipped out and struck Rowan's face. The girl's head snapped to the side and she felt blood fill the corner of her mouth. Gwynneth lifted her hand again and waited, her eyes gleaming. Rowan slowly brought her head up straight. Licking the corner of her mouth with her tongue she tasted iron. The flame of anger that had burned in her turned to solid ice. She stared back at Gwynneth. Slowly she let her eyes travel from Lady Lochalsh's face to the upraised hand then back again, the look scathing.

Gwynneth's eyes widened in disbelief, then in anger. Her hand flashed forward again. Rowan clenched her teeth against the impact. The blow landed on her ear and for a moment she could hear nothing but a high ringing, then a dull pounding. Bending to one side she tried to ease the pain by rubbing her ear against her shoulder. The ropes around her wrists stopped the movement. Slowly she raised her head and tried to focus on the woman standing in front of her. The image was blurred. Closing her eyes she took a deep breath, and then opened her eyes again. Gwynneth was still there, a malevolent smile dancing on her lips.

Rowan answered the look. "It does nae matter what you order me to do. You could beat me to death and it would nae matter. I will do nothing for you. Do you hear? I will do nothing for someone as mad as you, someone who comes from mad stock."

Gwynneth's eyes hardened. "It is not I who is mad. It is you by denying me what I will. And you will suffer until you do for me what the highland witch should have done for my mother."

Rowan spat the words out, "The witch did nothing for your mother and was killed for it."

"You lie, witch. But you won't lie much longer. Try to take your rest. I will be back later in the night. Once the castle is asleep, we will have things to do." Backing away, and without a look at the inert form of Silobah still lying on the floor, Gwynneth walked from the room.

***

Colin sat with his back to the tree. He could not sleep. Something was very wrong. It went further than the trouble with Elden, broken and sleeping beside the fire. It went further than being married to Gwynneth. It was something else. He shook his head as if to banish the feeling, but it was no use. The night was too silent and there was nothing to distract him. Rowan. The name came to him as easily as did his own. The lass disturbed him. Aye she was beautiful and he would pay almost any price to be with her, but it was more than that. The brief time he had spent with her had filled an unfamillar void. Most of his adult life had been spent fighting the English. There had been no time for introspection and, after all, a warrior was not supposed to indulge in that sort of thing. What he was supposed to do was win at battle, conquer women, and sire sons. But meeting Rowan had stirred something else he didn't know was there.

Och, it was not that he was unaccustomed to women or that Rowan had simply turned his head. No, it wasn't simply the fact that she was a woman and had pleasures to offer that nagged at him. When he had been with her, he had wanted to protect her. Not protect and own her but protect without having to place his mark on her. She was weaker than he, yes, but it was not a weakness that filled him with contempt, it was the weakness that had its own particular type of strength. She knew her own mind and treated him as an equal whether he had liked it or not. He rubbed his hands over his face. It was confusing, this sleeping beside her without plunging into her, yet feeling satisfied on a level that he hadn't known was there. The thought made him restless and he rose to his feet, brushing away leaves and dirt.

"For god's sake get some sleep. You want to make the castle tomorrow and it will do no one any good to have you tumbling off of your horse and killing yourself." Arden had been watching Colin as he sat with his thoughts. Colin's restlessness had not been lost on his friend, and he knew well what was on the laird's mind. It was the lass. Ever since he had met her something had been eating at him, and it wasn't just his obvious attraction to her or his fear that Gwynneth would use her. He had never seen Colin taken with a female like this. Arden smiled to himself. This was a first.

From what Colin had told him, this lass was no compliant maid, one to bow and scrape and let her man lead the way. He could just imagine the sparks that would fly if Colin, used to having his own way, ever got a hold of this Rowan of the forest whom, it seemed, lived by her own rules. The grin abruptly left his face. What if the lass was indeed at the castle? Colin would make sure she was safe but would he be able to send her away? He shuddered as he thought of Gwynneth's reaction. Raising his head, he saw the dying flames of the fire flickering over the hard planes of the laird's face. If he was reading his friend right, Colin would want that lass to stay.

"How much longer until light?"

"Colin, it is just a few hours into the night. Dawn will not be here for hours more. Look. Lie down beside the fire and try to get some sleep. You have nae rested well in days."

"Dinna tell me what it is that I need."

Arden laid his head back against the ground. Fine. Let him fall off his horse tomorrow. Just what they needed, Elden senseless and unable to walk and Colin half-dead. He heard the jangle of reins and a bit. Pushing up on his elbows, he found himself staring at the laird's back. Colin was saddling his horse. Arden watched silently.

"I'm going. There is light enough with this full moon now. I know she went back to the castle to find her brother and you know how badly Gwynneth wants her. I have nae intention of letting that happen." Colin pulled himself into the saddle and plunged into the dark woods.

Arden sat up, stretched, and then crawled over to Elden. The man's head was still warm to the touch, but not too much. Getting to his feet, Arden threw more wood onto the fire. Sitting down, drawing his blankets around him, he prayed to his gods as his friend rode through the night.

Chapter 24

ROWAN STOOD WITH her head leaning back against the wall. The room was dark except for the moonlight streaming through the floor to ceiling window. Her face throbbed. Her arms and shoulders ached unbearably from their forced position. She tried to sleep but each time she drifted off, her knees would bend and her weight would pull against her arms. Slowly she tried to flex each muscle of her body. Doing so helped to pass the time and it also helped to keep her muscles limber. If Gwynneth untied her, she wanted to be able to move quickly.

She looked over at Silobah. The woman stirred. Rowan called out her name. Slowly Silobah pushed herself up from the stone floor. Pausing for breath she leaned on one hand and lifted the other one to her head.

"Silobah. Wake up." Rowan willed her to find the strength to stand. Moments passed and then, as if in answer to the silent command, Silobah rose to her knees, straightened her body then slowly shuffled forward speaking as if to herself. "She will kill you as surely as her mother killed yours if I dinna get you out of here."

"Hurry!" Rowan whispered but the old woman paused as if listening to the night. Rowan strained against the ropes. Silobah began to speak, her voice flat. "It is the circle, you know."

Rowan saw her sway as if in a trance. Making her voice rough and clear she tried to cut through the old woman's sudden weakness and defeat.

"Untie me. We will escape. I will take care of you. You will be safe." The words seemed to rouse the old woman. Rowan spoke desperately. "Now is your chance. You said that you did nae want any more killing. This time you can stop it. Untie me and Lady Lochalsh willna be able to kill. You can stop her."

"Aye. You are right. But then you were always right. Remember the talks we used to have late at night when Lady Stannard did not know I came to see you?"

Fiona. Rowan realized that Silobah was reliving the past. Rowan played her part. "Aye, I remember. They were fine talks. But now it is time to set me free. You can do it without Lady Stannard knowing. Here, it is the middle of the night and nae one is around. Now untie me."

Rowan gave a slight sigh of relief as the old woman approached her and began to untie her left arm. Both of them froze at the sound of the key in the door. Silently it swung open.

"So, you have wakened. I thought you might. And now you will let the witch go free?" Gwynneth's voice was low and soft, and Silobah came back to the present. Silently the old woman backed away from Rowan. Gwynneth walked slowly toward her. "You dare continue to go against me?"

Silobah looked at the woman's raised hand and then to her face, and her mind cleared completely. There was nothing she could see that resembled the lass she had raised, nothing of the young woman in whom she had tried to instill some shred of compassion or caring. The only thing she could see now was her own vow. And suddenly she knew how she could finally break the circle. It was the only way. She sent a silent prayer to her gods to guide her. She murmured under her breath to True Thomas. She was coming to him. Her vow would finally be fulfilled. Silobah continued to back away. Gwynneth continued to approach her. Rowan stood against the wall, helpless as she watched the deadly dance. The old woman moved slowly, deliberately, one foot placed squarely behind the other, her gaze fastened on Gwynneth, drawing her along.

"You are so like your mother."

Gwynneth took a menacing step forward and Silobah moved back from her.

"You will fail like your mother."

Gwynneth raised both hands. "Old woman, Ewan should have died peacefully. Not so you."

"You will fail." The words were mocking and Silobah moved back once again. She was only one step away from the window's edge. Rowan stopped breathing. Silobah waited for a moment, then spoke, "No witch alive could make the laird come to a bed such as yours."

Enraged, Gwynneth leaped forward. Quickly Silobah snaked out a hand and, grabbing the material of Gwynneth's tunic, twisted it in her fist, then took a final step backwards.

Silobah fell into the night. Frantically Gwynneth jerked back. Dropping to her knees she threw herself to the side of the window and braced herself against the jutting stone. Silobah's will was stronger than her grasp. Weakened by pain, age and exhaustion, the old woman's fingers scrabbled to hold the material as it slid through her fingers. Finally, she clutched only air.

Silence. Then a small sound. Like a grain sack falling from a cart. Staggering to her feet, Gwynneth stood, leaning over, her hands on her thighs for support, her breathing ragged. Rowan tried to make herself invisible against the wall. At once the room filled with a harsh wail. Gwynneth straightened, arched her back, then fell forward to her knees, weeping. Rowan tried to close her ears to the noise, her heart thumping with the force of what she had just witnessed. As quickly as the crying had begun, it stopped. Gwynneth pulled herself to her feet. Turning around she locked her eyes on Rowan.

"You did this."

Rowan stared at her in disbelief.

"You did this. I heard her talking to you. She thought you were the highland witch. You used your powers to fool her. She would have never so completely betrayed me. She loved me. She would never have left me. You made her believe you were the highland witch and now she is dead."

Rowan stared at Gwynneth and saw that all reason had fled into the night with Silobah. Silently Rowan flexed and released her muscles, easing them. She needed to be ready. She stayed quiet, knowing that nothing she could say would touch the mind of this woman.

Gwynneth approached Rowan and spat in her face as she spoke, "So now you have her death on you. How does it feel, witch? How does it feel to have sent an old woman to her end?'

Rowan tried to press back against the wall, away from the words. Gwynneth saw the movement and laughed. Backing away she looked Rowan up and down.

"You are not half so charming now, with that swollen face." A shout interrupted her. A second shout joined the first. Silobah had been found. Gwynneth hurried to the window. Carefully holding on to the sides of the wall, she peered out.

"I must deal with this." Turning back, she spoke to Rowan, "Ewan is gone and so is Silobah. Now only I know you are here. In time, you will do my bidding."

Moving quickly to the door, she slammed it behind her. Rowan listened intently but didn't hear the sound of the turning lock. Perhaps in her hurry Lady Lochalsh had forgotten to lock it, or more likely, she saw no need. Now if she could only get her arms untied. Taking a deep breath, she began to flex her arms and move her wrists back and forth.

Chapter 25

WHAT IS THIS I hear about Silobah?" Colin strode into Gwynneth's apartments at dawn. Startled, she sat up in bed, pulling the covers to her chin. Realizing it was the laird, she let the covers fall to her waist and Colin's mouth turned down into a frown.

"Good morning, my laird." Gwynneth said quietly as she placed a despairing look on her face. Colin turned away from the sight of her.

"What happened?" He walked to the window and stood looking out.

"I do not know. I was in my rooms when the servants came to get me. They said she fell from the tower room."

"What was she doing in there? The tower hasn't been used since," his words trailed off and there was an uneasy silence.

"Since the battle when my parents were killed." Gwynneth finished the sentence for him. Pulling on a robe, she walked to the window and, coming up behind Colin, she leaned against his back and slid her hands around his waist. "I am so very sad. She often went up there to pray to her gods. Perhaps she stumbled and fell."

Colin tore her hands from his waist and whipped around to look for the truth of her words. Gwynneth gazed back with a serene face. Frustrated, seeing he would get no meaningful response from her, he turned to the reason for his swift ride back to Lochalsh. "Did you send someone to follow the seer, Elden?"

Gwynneth kept her eyes steady, concentrating on stilling the bright red flame that pulsed at the back of her head. How dare he question her? She was Lady Stannard's daughter. She was the one who had English blood. She concentrated on keeping her voice soft and answered, "No, My Lord. I did not."

"I am nae lord. I am The Laird." The words were hard. Colin's eyes bored down into hers looking for the truth. Her eyes were flat and unreadable. Unease filled him. He walked some distance to the center of the room and turned. It was time; it was past time for this. He steeled himself.

"The lass who was with the seer. Where is she?"

Gwynneth opened her eyes in innocence and lifted her hands, palms up. "I know not what you mean."

In two strides Colin was across the room, his hands gripping her arms. Roughly he shook her and then repeated his question. Gwynneth kept her silence. Colin increased the strength of his grip, his words shaking with the effort of not striking her. "You had him hunted and his sister, too. Dinna give me that wide-eyed look. I know that you hunted both of them, and I know why."

Gwynneth inched her body closer to his, and in disgust, Colin shoved her away. Stumbling back, she reached out and steadied herself against a chair. The red flame sparked and consumed her. Words hissed from her mouth.

"If you know why, then why are you surprised."

Colin jerked back at the venom.

Gwynneth continued, her voice rising, "We both know that magic is needed to make you man enough to come to my bed."

The words spit into the air and hung there. Gwynneth put her hand out as if she would drag them back into her mouth. Colin stood looking down at her, his face a mixture of contempt and pity.

"That, madam, is something that will never happen again." His tone sharpened. "Is the lass here?"

"No."

Colin gave her an iron look. "Madam, you had best pray to your gods that your answer is truthful." He turned on his heel and stalked out of the room.

Gwynneth frowned as she watched him close the door. The bright flame had burned away most of his words and her thoughts turned and clicked in the old pattern. He had been away for days. He should feel the need of a woman. Clutching her robe, she rushed to the window and looked out into the woods. No. He was not on his horse heading for the forest to hunt. Good. She needed him here. Raising her eyes to the ceiling, she thought of the tower room and the witch who would soon have no choice but to cast her spell.

***

The morning chill settled on Arden and waking, he placed more wood on the fire. Feeling eyes on him, he turned around. Elden was watching every move he made. Arden, recognizing the look, spread his hands out by his sides in the age-old gesture of 'no harm' and spoke. "I am nae here from Lady Lochalsh. I am here from the laird. I want to get you well and on your way."

"You know who I am?"

"Aye. You are the brother of the lass, Rowan, whom Lady Lochalsh hunts."

"And who are you?"

"I am the laird's friend."

Elden gave Arden a questioning look. Taking his cue, Arden sat beside the injured man and explained how he and Colin had come to find him. As he paused in his tale, Elden spoke. "So, the laird has returned to the castle to see if he can find Rowan?"

"Aye. She was nae with you. And Colin feels sure that she returned to the castle for you." Arden saw the dark look on Elden's face and nodded his head sympathetically. "Aye, we are both worried, Colin and I," he paused for a moment then continued, "Dinna look so surprised. There is nae love lost between the Laird and Lady Lochalsh. If he had his way, he would never see her again. But he gave his word, and now he is bound."

"And what interest does he have in Rowan?" Elden wanted to see if this one indeed spoke truthful words.

Arden was silent for a minute trying to decide what to say. He didn't want to tell what he believed to be the entire truth, but yet he knew the man a seer and not easily deceived by a simple lie. He began cautiously, "Colin knows the history of your mother, Fiona, and does nae want it repeated."

"Nor do I."

"Does Lady Lochalsh know that she hunts her half-sister? Arden asked.

"Nae. Surely she would have said so when she had me."

Arden nodded his head, thinking that the gods must be laughing with glee. Colin had done what Robert the Bruce had wanted him to do all along. He had fallen in love with the English lord's daughter, only it was the wrong one. Arden turned practical. "Do you think you can ride?"

"Aye." The word came out quickly.

"Good. Then let's be off." Smothering the fire with leaves wet from dew, Arden prepared to break camp. Watching him, Elden gathered what little strength he had for the ride back.

***

"Drink it. Drink it I say." Gwynneth held the flask to Rowan's lips. The girl clenched her lips together. Frustrated and angry, Gwynneth took her hand from Rowan's chin and slapped her. Rowan's head snapped to the side then quickly she straightened up. Tears poured from her eyes and she tried to shake them from her face. Her whole body throbbed, and she ached from the lack of sleep, the lack of food. There had been no morning meal, just Gwynneth arriving with her foul brew. She grabbed Rowan's chin again, and this time, forced some of the liquid into her mouth.

"There. Swallow. Swallow." Gwynneth saw Rowan holding the liquid in her mouth, and, taking her fist, she punched her stomach. Rowan swallowed. The liquid burned a fiery path down her throat into her belly.

Clenching her teeth, Rowan tried to concentrate on the patterns of the stones in the walls, the pain in her body, anything just so she would not feel the effects of the liquid. Satisfied that Rowan had swallowed enough, Gwynneth backed away to sit at the table and wait.

"You know it would be wise of you to go ahead and start the spell."

Rowan raised her head and glared. Gwynneth gave a small laugh, "Oh, you will comply with what I want once the potion has taken effect."

Rowan turned her head away from the sound of Gwynneth's voice and tried to concentrate on other things. It was a habit she had acquired when she had to wait in the forest for long periods of time hunting. She let her mind wander, and all at once she was standing beside the fire, and it was night. She was looking through the bushes and there was the man who called himself Arden, the one who had saved her from her fall into the water. She was unaware that the liquid was starting to take effect, and as her body began to feel warm, a smile crossed her lips.

Gwynneth stood. "What is it that you have to smile about, witch? Are you planning something for me that will do me harm? Well, I promise you that no spell of yours can be half as bad as what I have in store for you if you fail to do as I want." Reaching up, she grabbed Rowan by the hair and peered into her eyes. Rowan looked blankly back at her. Lady Lochalsh nodded, satisfied. Now the witch would say what was in her mind. The mixture of lady's slipper and lowbush blueberry could unlock secrets from anyone. Untying Rowan's arms, she watched for resistance. There was none. Good. Gwynneth led her to a chair at the table. Rowan groaned as she lowered her arms to her sides. Gwynneth had indeed given her just the right dose. Enough to take away some of her will, but not enough to stop any pain that might be necessary.

"I know you can hear me and I know that you will answer me truthfully. My mother trained me well in the art of potions. There is a spell you can cast, to make the laird come willingly to my bed and get me with child. So now, weave your spell."

"He does nae love you." The words came out of Rowan's mouth of their own will, and she sat there, stunned. How had that happened? In a daze, she watched Gwynneth's face become hard and cold. Rowan's mouth opened and again she could not stop the flow of her words. "He does nae love you. He does nae even like you. He wants to be far away from you."

Gwynneth jumped up, the back of her chair slamming to the stone floor. She stood beside the table, enraged. Rowan paid no attention to her and the words continued to fall from her lips of their own accord.

"You know well that he promised Robert the Bruce to marry you. That is the only reason why he stays with you," Rowan tried to stop the words, but failed, "and you dinna love him. You only want him in your bed. A child. You want a child," Rowan's voice became clear and sharp. "And then you will kill him. Just the way your parents were murdered."

Gwynneth gasped but Rowan continued, "Aye, murdered. The arrow came from inside the castle. One of the clansmen who had been pressed into fighting for the English let it fly and find its mark. And your mother did nae trip on her gown. Hands came out of the dark in the stairwell. They reached for her back. They pushed."

Gwynneth's hands clenched into fists.

"So, you are a witch after all. I knew it, despite your denials. It is told that if this brew is used on a person, they will die, but if used on a witch, it will loosen her tongue and truth would be spoken. So, the laird hates me, does he? Well, it is up to you to change his mind."

"There is nae way to change his mind. He will always hate you. But it does nae matter, really."

Gwynneth bent down and peered into Rowan's eyes. They were dilated and looking into the distance. "Why do you say this? What do you mean?"

"It does nae matter. You willna bear a child of the laird. You willna live long enough to do so."

Gasping, Gwynneth pressed her hand to her mouth. The slow burning flame burst into her head. This could not be true. The only one in this room who will be dying is this witch. Taking a step closer to the table, she looked deeper into Rowan's eyes. There. A flicker of something. Aye. The witch was clever, she had just been pretending to be under the influence of the liquid, but Gwynneth could see the glimmer of control in her eyes. She knew it. She gave a smile to herself. She would cure this witch of her lies. Her hand clenched and swung up, catching Rowan on the chin, snapping her head violently back. Rowan felt the shot of pain. The room went black and she fell to the side. Feebly throwing her hands out she tried to catch herself but failed. Her head slammed into the stone floor.

Gwynneth walked over to the fallen girl and stood, looking down at her. A thin trickle of blood ran from her mouth. Bending over, she listened to Rowan's heart. Good. It was strong, steady. These witches were a hearty breed. Stooping down, She tied Rowan's wrists together behind her back. That would keep her for a while. Gwynneth looked around the sparse room and paused. If someone came to the tower to see the room from which Silobah fell and found the door locked, they would raise a cry and perhaps wake the lass. For certain they would tell the laird.

Gwynneth looked again around the tower room and smiled at the sight of the privy. A small dark slit in the stone wall led to a tiny, even darker room, with a stone seat and an opening for waste to empty down the outside walls. A perfect place for a witch. Dragging the pallet and then Rowan into the small space, she stepped out into the room and looked around. There. No trace. Glancing at the table she made a mental note of the things she would need to bring when she came up tonight. It was fate that had made her slap the witch, further adding to the drug's effect and rending her unconscious. She recalled her mother's writings and remembered the words noted that there was only one way to proceed with such a stubborn witch. She did not need her alert and well. She just needed her alive for the ritual. After that, nature would take its course. It seemed that this was going to be the only way of it. Gwynneth realized that her hand was hurting. Looking down she saw her knuckles red and bruised. Rubbing them to ease the pain, she reasoned that she had need to hold on to her temper if she was going to succeed. Turning again to survey the room, she gave a nod to herself and left the tower.

***

Colin sat in his chair, listening to what the man had to say. As the words flowed around him, he could feel their undercurrent. It wasn't what the man was saying, but how the man was saying it. He could tell there was much more to be recounted. Colin shifted impatiently in his seat and interrupted.

"What is it you are not telling me?" The words came out short, clipped. The man stood temporarily silent, his eyes pleading. Colin ignored the look. "Tell me what you are keeping back. I know men. I know when they have bad news to bring. Say it to me now and you willna be punished."

The man quailed under the order, his mind working rapidly. He knew that if he told, the laird would act on it immediately. But then there was Lady Lochalsh. If she ever found out who told these things, his life would not be worth the stone he was standing on. The man cleared his throat and looked up. His gaze met Colin's. In the laird's eyes he saw wisdom, kindness, and strength. He also saw a burning impatience. The man gathered his courage and spoke.

"If I could ask but one thing before I begin, My Laird."

Colin nodded his head and tried to soften his features.

"It would be a kindness to me if you would nae tell Lady Lochalsh, it was me who spoke to you of these matters."

Colin raised his eyebrows. The man quailed; perhaps he had misjudged the laird. He felt a moment of uneasiness. He truly did not want to be the one to bring news of the things his lady had done in his absence. Colin watched the man, easily read what was on his face and spoke. "You have my word."

The man looked up at Colin and prayed that he spoke the truth. Taking a deep breath he glanced around the room, satisfying himself that no one was listening, and began to speak. "The old woman."

"Silobah."

"Aye. Lady Lochalsh's woman. They say that she fell but some say they saw her standing at the window and she seemed to take a step backwards."

"You mean she was pushed?"

The man shifted uneasily from foot to foot. "No, they say that it seemed as if she took the step backwards like she wanted to," the man swallowed hard and continued, "and some are saying that after her fall, Lady Lochalsh stuck her head out of the window and looked down."

Colin sat not speaking, containing himself, nodding his head for the man to continue. He did.

"But when they ran to get Lady Lochalsh, she acted like she dinna know a thing."

Colin's face changed and became even more still, his jaw clenching and unclenching. "Is there more?"

The man looked at Colin and cringed at the thought of telling him about Ewan. The servant had confided in him before he left to track the seer, wanting someone knowing the truth in case his body turned up in the woods. No. Let the laird learn about the lass being captured from the woods on his own. He would not anger this man any more than he had to.

"That's all, Laird Lochalsh." He shifted uneasily from foot to foot but held firm. He knew he would always be remembered not for the help he gave, but for the bad news he brought. That was nothing against the laird. That was simply human nature.

Colin, realizing he could force no more information from the man, conceded. "Go. I willna speak of this to Lady Lochalsh."

The man backed out of the room and Colin sat with his chin resting on his fist. So, Gwynneth was with Silobah when the old woman stepped to her death. Why did she nae immediately fly downstairs and see if the old woman needed help? Why did she nae call out to others? Only the guilty ran away. But he shook his head mentally, Gwynneth wouldn't have killed Silobah. The old woman had raised her. He knew Gwynneth was whirling out of control, but murder? And murder of her old nurse at that? Colin straightened up. There was only one way to find out, but first he needed to make sure Rowan was nowhere in the castle.

Colin spent the afternoon prowling the deepest rooms of the castle. His first search had been of the tower room where Silobah had fallen to her death. But a quick glance past the door revealed only a table, chair. He stood quietly for a moment, listening, but no sound came to his ears. Turning, he walked slowly down the stairs and on to the lower levels of the castle, where, holding a torch high, he found rooms filled with grain, rooms bursting with wine casks, but no Rowan.

Chapter 26

THE LATE AFTERNOON sun streaked through the trees. Arden gave a worried glance over his shoulder at Elden. The man looked grey. There were beads of sweat on his upper lip but the air was cool. Arden leaned over and looked down at the injured ankle.

"It does nae good to look at it. I know." Arden straightened in his saddle and urged his horse faster. They needed to get to the castle as quickly as possible. The man looked bad and his voice had become weaker with the passing hours. Arden didn't have to question why. He had seen this happen when men fought great pain for hours on end. He felt Elden shift, then listened carefully as the man began to speak.

"I may not be sensible when we reach the castle."

"I'm listening."

"There are things you must know. Some of them you may already know about, but you must know the whole story so you see why you have to get Rowan away from this mad lady."

Arden nodded his head and Elden began to speak of the highland witch.

***

"You were in the tower room with Silobah." It was not a question, it was a statement, and the voice that spoke it, was cold and hard. Gwynneth stood up from her dressing table and walked to the window. Someone had seen her look out after Silobah had fallen. "You acted surprised when they came to tell you. Why, Gwynneth? What is it that you dinna want the people to know?"

Gwynneth kept her back to him and her mind raced. What could she tell him? What would make sense? Thoughts flew in and out of her head and she tried to grab them, but none stayed with her. She kept silent and pretended to look out of the window.

"Dinna keep your back turned to me while I speak. You might be Lady Lochalsh, and cherished highborn English blood might flow through your body, but I am the laird here and you will turn your face to me."

Gwynneth determinedly kept her back to Colin. She had no other choice. Thoughts were careening around inside her head and she was having trouble capturing them, examining them, and figuring out what to say.

Angry that she would not do what he demanded, Colin took several quick steps forward and grabbing her shoulder, twisted her around. Glaring at her face, he tried to look into her eyes, but she kept them lowered.

"Look at me. Now." His voice was rough, commanding.

Gwynneth did no such thing. Angered, Colin put his hand under her chin and forced her head up. Quickly Gwynneth raised her hand to cover her face. Unexpectedly, Colin loosened his grip on her chin and quickly captured her hand. Lifting it toward him he looked at the knuckles, bruised and red. There was only one way a hand could get such marks. Holding the hand in a death grip, he looked at Gwynneth's face. She stood silently staring up at him. His words came out low, almost soft.

"You beat her before you pushed her out of the window."

Gwynneth pulled her hand from his grasp. "No. No. It wasn't that way at all. We were arguing and she stepped back and fell through the window."

"Arguing about what?"

"It was just that she was not doing what I wanted her to do. She was defying me. She is a servant. I had to make her obey."

"Obey what? What was so important that it caused you to strike her with so much force it tore your knuckles?"

Gwynneth looked down at her hand and closed her eyes. The thoughts were slower now. She grabbed at one.

"I did not hit her. But when she began to fall, I reached out and grabbed her clothes, like this," Gwynneth held out her hand in a fist then continued, "and she pulled me to the window with her and my hand slammed against the stone," Gwynneth lowered her eyes and softly said, "and then she fell. There was nothing I could do. I couldn't bear it so I ran to my room. I knew she was dead." She lifted what she hoped was a believable face to the laird. "When the men came to tell me, I didn't know what to say, so I acted surprised."

Colin stood looking down at the woman he despised. It could have happened that way, but there was a part of him that knew better. There was a lie in the story, at least one lie and probably more.

Her gaze became calm. She had found the story she needed. She was on sure footing. All she needed was for night to fall completely. Then she would go to the witch, and the laird would not stand in front of her demanding, arguing, hurting her. He would come to her bed, gladly.

A small smile danced on her lips at the thought. Colin saw the smile and turned away in disgust. How could she smile when she had witnessed Silobah's death? A surge of anger flowed through him. He wanted to take the palms of his hands and put them on either side of her head and press until the truth was pushed out of her. Startled at the ferocious thought, he roughly wiped his wet palms dry and knew he had to get out of that room. He was aware of the violence in his blood. He was a warrior. He had killed more than his share of men, but to think of bloodshed in terms of any woman left him shaken. He strode quickly to the door.

Gwynneth barely saw him go. Already she was turning to the bed, rooting under the mattress. Her hand closed on leather and smiling, she pulled out the book and ran her hand over the raised letters on the front. Her mother's journal. Lady Stannard had written down every bit of information she had gleaned from every possible source. Gwynneth opened the volume and looked for the section that dealt with witches who could not be commanded. That was certainly the case with this one. Just look how she had tried to pretend she was overcome with the potion and then lied. My early death indeed. Her eyes scanned the page. There were no notes indicating that her mother had tried doing what she had written, but if she had included the information, then surely her mother had deemed it of worth. The directions were clear. If a witch refused to cast a spell, their blood would work just as well. This gathering of blood had to be the last measure because once done, the witch could not help you anymore. She would be dead.

Gwynneth made a mental list in her head as she read. The supplications to the gods were written with care, as was the ritual song. She would need a knife, a very sharp knife, and a bowl for the blood. Pausing, she lifted her head and wondered how blood would taste. Unknowingly, she rested the tip of her tongue on her lips before she bent her head and resumed making her list. Colin strode down the hall where the sun was making bright patches on the dark stones. He couldn't think of anywhere he had not searched, no one he had not asked. What was Gwynneth up to? What had she really done to Silobah? And was the lass truly not here? Colin walked into the kitchen.

The cook stopped in his tracks at the sight. "My Laird," the cook began.

Colin waved him to silence. "Do you know of a lass being brought to the castle?"

The cook shook his head no.

"There have been nae rumors? No one has spoken of this to you?"

Again denial.

Turning on his heel Colin stalked from the kitchen.

As the afternoon faded to evening, he slowly climbed the steps back to the main hall. Pausing, he looked out of a window at the rising moon. It was a full moon, fat and glowing. He furrowed his brow, a thought nagging at the back of his mind. What was it? Something that Briac had said about the full moon being the most powerful one for witches? It came in a flash. Blood sacrifices were made during the full moon because of its supposed strength during that phase.

A small fission of fear raced up his spine. He recalled the smile Gwynneth had given him. Turning on his heel he traced his steps back to her room.

***

"I wish it was nae the full moon." The words came from Elden and Arden grunted in acknowledgement. He knew about the moon. Knew what it meant. If Gwynneth had Rowan in her grasp, this was the night she would do what was planned. She was too much like her mother not to know this night was special.

"Hurry. We must get to her. She is at the castle. She is there." The words hissed out between Elden's lips as he sagged against Arden.

Pulling the horse to a prancing stop, Arden reached back and felt the side of the man's throat. Thank the gods there was a steady beat. This one must have the heart of a stag. Getting off the horse, he remounted and rearranged Elden's body on the saddle in front of him. His horse danced sideways and Arden, busy trying to settle the swooning man, gave a vicious tug at the reins. The horse stepped sideways once more then settled down. Arden kicked his mount into a trot. The jarring would not help Elden's ankle, but at least unconscious he would not feel the pain. Arden clucked again and the horse increased its speed. He hadn't liked the way the man had said with such conviction that Rowan was in the castle. Elden had spoken with a different voice when he had said those words. Arden didn't need to be told that the voice was the one the man used when speaking of his visions. So, she was there, truly. It was the full moon. He gave his horse another kick and the beast leapt through the forest.

***

"Where is Lady Lochalsh?"

The maid gave a squeal and jumped at the sound of Colin's voice. "I dinna know, Laird Lochalsh."

"She has dressed and gone out?" Colin saw the lass bat her eyes and look wildly around the room. She was frightened out of her wits. Taking a deep breath, he slowly walked over to her, fixing a smile on his face. "I would like to know where she is."

The gentle voice did its work and the maid relaxed. "She dressed then said she was going for a moonlight ride."

"Now?"

The girl cringed again under the harsh question but nodded her head yes. Colin paused then went to the window looking out, searching the fields around the castle lit by the moon's glow. Spinning on his heel he quickly left the room and headed to the stables.

"Did you saddle a mount for Lady Lochalsh?"

The stable hand jumped a mile at the harsh voice. Backing up against the wall he answered, "Nae Laird. I dinna saddle a mount for the Lady Lochalsh."

"She did nae go out for a ride?"

"Nae, Laird. Not that I know of. If she has gone out, it was on foot." The man's words trailed off and Colin caught the sound of muttering.

"What is that you said?"

"Nothing, Laird. I was just talking to myself."

"Say the words to me."

The man looked at Colin and swallowed hard. "I said that hopefully she is nae angry with me."

"Explain yourself." The man shrank before the words. Colin, seeing this, took a deep breath and tried to calm himself. Steadying his voice, he again spoke. "Tell me."

The man looked up at the laird and spoke the truth. "It is about Ewan."

"The man with the little head?"

"Aye, Laird. I heard that somehow, he angered Lady Lochalsh, and he hasn't been seen since."

Colin nodded for the man to continue.

"That's all I know."

"You have heard nothing about a lass?" Puzzled, the stable hand shook his head. "No."

Colin turned abruptly away and stalked across the courtyard, the new information adding to his anger. Gwynneth's trusted manservant was missing. Her old nurse was dead. Pausing beside the steps to the castle, Colin lowered his head and tried to clear his thoughts. Had Gwynneth and Silobah been arguing about the disappearance of Ewan? But how could that have made Gwynneth angry enough to push her old nurse out of the window, if indeed she had? Deep in thought, he slowly climbed the stone steps.

***

Gwynneth opened the door to the tower room and glanced about. The light of the full moon showed the room undisturbed. Smiling, she closed the door and hurried to the privy. Rowan had not moved. Good. She needed the witch unconscious for what she must do. Grabbing her under the arms, Gwynneth pulled Rowan into the room and stood over her, looking down. There was no question that this was a stubborn one. She would never give in. She would never cast the spell. But her strength was good.

She had survived hitting her head on the stones. It was a sure sign of her power, the power that lived in her blood. The power that Gwynneth wanted. And because the witch would not do as she asked, Gwynneth would take her power for herself. It was simple.

Walking to the window, she looked out at the full moon and gave a smile. Holding the bowl in one hand, and the knife in the other, she reached out her arms toward the shining sliver disc in the sky and smiled. Tonight, it would finally happen. Tonight, the laird would finally come to her bed. She would have his child and soon after, his death and her revenge. Her mother's journal was not wrong. Look at how she had enslaved her husband, Lord Stannard, for years. She gave a slight bow to the moon and turned back to the table.

***

Arden pushed his horse harder. The beast plunged through the night woods and Arden fought to keep Elden from falling to the ground. Rowan was at the castle. It was a full moon. Colin would take his time with questions. Would take his time getting the facts, planning his battle, when Arden knew there was no such time to be had. No time at all.

***

Gwynneth set the bowl and knife on the table. From the pocket of her gown, she withdrew a small packet of her mother's that had been carefully preserved. The journal writings said that a pinch or two would give overwhelming strength for a small period of time. Gwynneth smiled and, emptying the entire contents into her hand, licked the bitter herbs until her palm was clean. Reaching again into the gown's pocket, she withdrew a small bottle. Lifting it to her lips, she drank the tincture of lowberry that would ready her mind and help her do what she must. Now her body, surging with energy, and her mind, opened to her senses, were both prepared.

Taking up the striking stone she lit the candle. Not too much light. She didn't want to draw attention to the window and besides, the moon gave plenty of light on its own. Moving over to Rowan, Gwynneth held the candle as she knelt. Setting the candle down with care, she took the witch's hair in her hands and pulled her head back. Sliding the candle over, she examined Rowan's throat. A small pulse pumped near its base, strong and steady.

Gwynneth smiled and gently lowered Rowan's head back to the floor. It was time to begin. Picking up the candle, she rose, she placed it on the table then removed her gown, tossing it carelessly aside. Holding the candle, she walked to the window, stark naked. Lifting the candle, her body thrumming and trembling with power, she willed the candle's light to join the sacred light of the enormous full moon.

***

Arden cleared the woods and saw the castle looming in the distance. It was dark, foreboding, and he urged his horse faster. The beast tried to dance sideways, snorting in protest, but Arden dug in his heels and the horse jumped, then settled down into a gallop.

The jolt slammed Elden awake. "I canna feel her. Something is nae right."

Arden let the man talk but kept his attention on controlling the horse. It would do no good to listen to Elden now. Arden knew all he needed to know. Rowan was in the castle and Lady Lochalsh was completely mad and the laird was unaware. He concentrated on the castle hoping to make the distance disappear.

"Look." Elden's tone had changed and again he was speaking with that other voice.

A shiver went up Arden's spine at the tone. "Look."

Arden tried to ride and search the outline of the castle at the same time, following Elden's pointing finger. The bottom floor windows shown with lights, that was to be expected. His eyes continued to search the darkness. A tiny pinprick of light appeared high up on one of the walls. Squinting even as he forced his horse forward, Arden kept his gaze on the wall of the castle. A cloud covered the moon for a moment and the tiny light became a bit brighter. The cloud passed and the moonlight outlined the tower where the light had been. The tower that hadn't been used in years.

"Up there," Elden's voice echoed Arden's last thoughts and the man gave a shudder. Slamming his heels into the horse they raced to the castle.

***

Gwynneth lowered her hands and turned her back to the window. It was done. She had supplicated the full moon, chanted the correct words to the gods. All was ready. She walked to the table as if in a trance. Pausing by its side, she felt the power surge through her once again. She could pull the moon down from its very heaven to do her bidding if she wanted. Tensing her arms to still the power's surge, she picked up the knife and lifted it into the air. The moonlight flickered on the shining blade and for a moment she was mesmerized. Standing quietly, she ran her finger up and down the edge. A thought tickled the back of her mind and she wondered if she had forgotten something. Shaking the idea from her head, she knelt on the floor and moved the bowl close to Rowan. Slowly she turned the handle of the knife over and over in her hand. Putting her other hand once again in the witch's hair, she pulled Rowan's head back, exposing her throat. Using the hand that held the knife she edged the bowl over to the precise position. Looking down at the witch, Gwynneth put the point of the knife at the correct spot, the sharp tip gently poking into the tender skin. Lifting her head, Gwynneth suddenly remembered.

The song. That's what had been tugging at her mind. She had forgotten to chant the song that would turn the flowing blood into magic. Still holding Rowan's head with the knife pressing into her neck, Gwynneth began to softly sing in a thin, clear voice.

***

Colin walked into the great hall noting the silence. Where was Gwynneth? Not in her room and not out riding, according to the stable hand. Restless and remembering the man's uneasiness, Colin headed back to the stables to press for more answers.

"Get the laird!" The words pierced the night. Startled, Colin ran the last few steps to the stables and saw a black shape flying through the castle gates. It was Arden with Elden clasped in front of him.

Savagely yanking on the reins Arden stopped the heaving horse. "Here. Colin. Get him down. You, over there. Get this horse." Arden was yelling at the laird and the stable boy at the same time. Colin ran across the courtyard to Arden's side and began pulling Elden from the horse. As the man collapsed on the ground Colin started to kneel down when Arden grabbed his arm.

"Nae. Listen to me. The tower. We must go!"

Colin jerked his arm away. "Is he dead?"

Arden cried out, "He's fine. It's Rowan! We must go!"

Colin jumped up at the words. Arden grabbed his arm again and together they ran across the courtyard and up the steps to the great hall. Arden's words came out in gasps.

"She is in the tower. She is here. Gwynneth is mad. Madder than death." Arden panted as they raced across the hall. He tried to catch his breath and speak at the same time. "Gwynneth has her. Make nae mistake. Rowan is with her in the tower."

Colin planted his feet and jerked Arden to a stop.

"I've searched the tower. She's not there!"

Arden grasped his friend by both shoulders and spoke quickly, harshly. "Elden says she is. Elden saw it." Uncaring if the laird heard or understood, Arden quickly spun on his heel and ran through the hall toward the tower stairs.

***

The song was finished. Gwynneth smiled to herself. Finally. The moment she had been thirsting for. The power she had always wanted skyrocketed through her. Power from the moon, the ritual, and the herbs. She smiled, feeling the extraordinary force pulse through her veins. The moon shone its strong life-giving beam through the window, the flickering candle gave just the right amount of light and the cool breeze from the tall window gently swirled around her naked body. Gwynneth looked down at Rowan's face and paused for a moment, a strange thought flickering through her mind. If you looked at the witch in this light with her head turned just this way, she seemed somehow familiar. She pushed the distracting thought away.

Still on her knees, she checked the bowl's position. Savoring the vast power soaring within her, she again began to press the point of the blade into Rowan's tender skin. The first cut was small, barely a scratch. Drops of bright red blood beaded up on the witch's neck and Gwynneth watched them, fascinated by the way they sparkled and danced. She closed her eyes and thanked her gods that they were giving her the blood of the witch. Her hand tightened on the knife as she sat quietly, savoring the peace and silence, basking in the anticipation.

"This way." Colin veered to the right past Arden. Gaining the stairs, they lunged up the stone steps in powerful leaps, feet racing, breath rasping, hearts thundering in their chests. Up and up and up again until suddenly the wooden door appeared before them. Colin paused for one second, gathered his strength and crashed through it.

The laird jerked to a stop. Arden slammed into his back throwing them both off balance. As they fought to stay upright, Gwynneth slowly opened her eyes, seeing nothing, her gaze as feral as a rabid fox. The room was as silent as death except for their breathing. The men stood stunned by the scene. As if in a trance and completely unaware of their existence, Gwynneth remained kneeling and naked beside Rowan, pressing the knife against her throat. Both men saw the blade and knew that one movement from them and Rowan's life's blood would spill out of her body and onto the floor.

Arden looked at Colin. The man's face was hard as stone. Their eyes moved over Rowan taking in her battered body. Colin watched the gentle rise and fall of her chest. Drugged. She had to be or else she would be fighting with the rage of a wolf. He shifted his eyes back to Gwynneth trying to think of what to say to make her put down the knife.

"Gwynneth." He said her name softly and her eyes regained their focus for a moment then returned to a blank gaze. He tried again. "Gwynneth."

Her head turned and slowly she became aware of his presence. Her eyes fastened on him. Colin didn't like what he saw. Her eyes glittered. A tiny smile tugged at the corners of her mouth. Colin shut his eyes for a moment then opened them.

"Put down the knife."

Silence. Colin started to take a step forward and Gwynneth's hand jerked, pressing the knife a bit harder against Rowan's throat. A few bright beads of blood joined the others. Arden tugged on the back of Colin's tunic urging him to stop. Again, the strange small smile from Gwynneth.

Arden took a breath and stepped from behind Colin. Gwynneth whipped her head to the side to see him better. He stopped.

She spoke, "Yes. You stop. And now you go." She nodded toward the door, keeping her eyes on the laird's friend and the knife at Rowan's throat. Slowly Arden began to back up. He had no intention of leaving the room and every intention of grabbing the knife from this raving mad bitch and using it on her. He continued to take small steps backwards.

"Gwynneth." Colin snatched her attention away from his friend, "You do not want to do this."

Her eyes fastened onto Colin's. "Oh, but my laird, this is exactly what I want to do."

Underneath the sound of her voice Colin heard scraping noises from the stairwell. Elden? Of course. But how was he climbing those stone steps when only moments ago he had been lying half-conscious on the ground? Colin pushed the thought away and tried to concentrate. He raised his voice to cover the noise.

"Gwynneth. Give me the knife. You are not yourself."

Her voice came back at him, stronger now and filled with venom. "Do not waste your words on me. Why should I do your bidding? Your people killed my parents and seized this castle. It is my castle. It belonged to my parents. And now I will take it back by birthright. The birthright of the child you will give me. My father's blood will rule Lochalsh. And you, you will matter no more."

She turned her gaze away from Colin and looked down at her witch. Using the flat side of the knife she smeared the drops of blood over Rowan's throat. Arden tensed at the movement, but Colin put his hand behind his back, urging stillness. There was silence. The scraping in the stairwell had stopped. No noise, no movement, only the four of them. Rowan as still as death, Gwynneth ablaze in her madness, Colin poised to leap forward and Arden ready to kill.

A massive voice suddenly thundered through the room. "Use that knife and be damned to hell!" Colin and Arden jumped and, whirling around, saw Elden leaning heavily against the door. His yellow eyes were filled with a stunning and fierce light. Arden gave a shudder at the thought of the man's pain. How in the name of all gods had he gotten up those steps?

Colin shifted his eyes rapidly between Gwynneth and Elden, waiting. Arden kept his eyes on the knife. Slowly, Elden limped into the tower room, each step flashing fire through his body, but seemingly unaware of the pain. His eyes were firmly locked on Gwynneth, pinning her motionless. He moved past the two men. They might have been made of air. This had nothing to do with them. Nothing. It was between Elden and the madwoman; between Elden and the English builders of Lochalsh; the witch hunters. The murderers of his mother.

Dragging his injured foot, he neared Gwynneth. She sat poised; her naked flesh gleaming in the moonlight; one hand holding the knife to Rowan's throat and the other hand held in front of her, palm out, warning him to keep away. She knew no fear. The power flashed through her body.

Elden advanced, his yellow eyes flashing. "I willna keep away. I have come for you, Gwynneth."

Gwynneth stayed where she was, transfixed by his eyes. Ready to leap, to kill. Her muscles trembled, waiting.

Elden moved forward slowly. "You canna kill her. You canna have her blood."

Gwynneth shook her head as if denying his words. "You are wrong. I can. I must." She gathered herself and threatened him. "If you come any closer the knife goes in," she paused and once again smiled the strange smile, "but the knife goes in anyway."

Elden held his ground. In his seer's voice he spoke, "I know your mother wrote things in that journal of hers. But it dinna say everything you need to know. There is something about your witch that Lady Stannard never dared to put down on paper."

"You lie."

Elden took a step closer. Colin and Arden tensed. Gwynneth pressed the point of the knife harder into Rowan's throat and a thin trickle of blood ran down her neck. Colin began to move forward.

"Stay," hissed Elden.

Gwynneth smiled, her eyes not leaving Elden. "Yes, stay back my laird. You can come closer when it is time. I am not ready for you yet."

"You will be ready for no one but the devil."

Gwynneth's eyes widened at the power in Elden's voice and the smile began to fade from her face.

"Listen to me well, My Lady. The lass you have at the point of your knife is your sister."

Gwynneth began to laugh, rocking slightly back and forth. "Again, you lie."

The powerful voice continued and she stilled.

"Nae. I say the truth to save your mortal soul. I am the son of the highland witch and these things I know. Did your mother write in her journal that the witch was got with child by your father?"

Gwynneth looked stunned. Elden continued, "Aye, I was here when it happened. Your father raped the witch. And then your mother hid her. If the bairn had been a boy, she would have taken it as her own to rule, but the babe was a lass. The witch was badly torn from the birth. Your mother finished the task of her dying. Silobah took the bairn away. I followed and saved her. I raised her and now she is lying on the floor with your knife against her throat."

Gwynneth looked wildly at Elden and he nodded his head, keeping his eyes locked on hers, willing her to understand.

"You will go to hell, Gwynneth, to be with the very demons you wish to call forth and control. Your hate and thirst for revenge has led you to kill your sister."

Gwynneth sat completely still for a moment, only her eyes moving, darting back and forth from the knife to Elden, trying to make sense of his words. She looked down at Rowan. The angle of the unconscious girl's profile told its own true tale.

The herbs surged through her muscles. With a cry she sprang up and leapt at Elden, her knife raised high in the air. Arden jumped as she did, pushing Elden aside and cutting off Colin's own attack. Grabbing her upraised arm, he bent it sharply back. Howling, she whipped her head to the side and bit him, her teeth tearing his wrist to the bone. Blood spurted. Instinctively he dropped her arm and bent to his wrist.

In an instant, rising up on her toes, she swung the knife in an arc at Arden's back. Colin leapt to grab her, as did Elden, and they crashed together. Colin whirled aside to gain balance as Elden slammed into Gwynneth. They hit the stone floor, stunned. Power surging through her, Gwynneth again leapt to her feet and, holding the knife high, focused on Colin who was positioned for a frontal attack.

Years of battle and hardened muscles were no match for Gwynneth, no matter the herbs. Leaping over Elden and dodging the knife, he seized her wrists and yanked her arms high above her head. Imprisoning her wrists with one hand, he freed the other and began struggling to grab her around the waist. Elden, still stunned on the floor shook his head trying to clear it. Arden clamped his torn skin against the bare bones of his wrist watching Colin hold the bitch as she writhed and kicked. He wanted another go at her. In a fog, Elden saw two figures silhouetted against the window, struggling. He shook his head. He saw the gleam of her knife. Rolling his body sideways, he slammed into their ankles.

Shrieking, Gwynneth staggered backwards as Colin tripped, crashing through the table, momentarily winded. Elden saw her standing there, the knife still in her hand. Taking a deep breath, gathering the very last of his strength, he called on the spirit of his mother. She had helped him climb those steps. She would help him now. Forcefully, he rolled again towards Gwynneth. His body collided with her ankles and she stumbled, lurching back even farther, abruptly teetering on the edge of the window.

Off balance, her back to the sky, she dropped the knife and threw her arms wide, each hand grasping a window edge. For seconds she hung on, her eyes frantic with anger, her breath rasping. Elden watched her cling to the stones, a cross outlined by the moon's indifferent glow. Slowly, he reached out and grasped her fallen knife. For a moment, time stood still as he struggled with the need to kill and the need to save.

Seeing this in his eyes, Gwynneth slyly pulled one hand from the window edge and reached out with a pitiful gesture. The movement shifted her weight. Her other hand tightened on the stones. Her feet scrambled desperately for purchase. The floor offered no hold. Her outheld hand jerked back to grab the window edge. It missed. Her other hand weakened. Eyes wild in disbelief and contempt, Gwynneth fell into the night.

Chapter 27

SUNLIGHT PRICKED ROWAN'S eyelids. Shifting in the bed, she tried to turn her head from the light and felt the cloth around her throat. With a strangled scream she sat up, her fingers tearing at the binding. Colin, jolted from sleep, jumped to his feet in time to see Rowan leap from the bed and begin a mad dash to the door. Moving quickly, he stepped to the side and hooked his arm out, grabbing her by the waist.

Air whooshed out of her and she turned, hitting him. Raising his other arm, he grabbed her flailing hand. Flinging her head to the side she tried to bite him. He arched his body out of the way and her teeth met only air.

"Stop it. Stop now. You are safe. She is dead."

Rowan paused for a moment. It wasn't the words that caught her attention; it was the voice. Tense, her body on alert, she slowly twisted up and looked at the man holding her. Her next breath caught in her throat. It was the man from the woods. The one who had pulled her from the stream. The one who had protected her through the night. The one who called himself Arden. Her breath released into a deep exhale and she relaxed her body.

Feeling her go limp, Colin released her. Immediately she remembered. She was in the castle. Gwynneth! Like a hare she jumped away, leapt up on the bed and frantically looked around the room for escape, poised again for flight. For a moment Colin was astonished at her swift action. Then he was just as astonished at the picture she painted standing on the bed, completely naked, her long red hair flowing around her.

Rowan stood panting, her hand going to her throat. No. It was not a rope. It was a bandage. Her fingers worked it loose, then rubbed her neck feeling the long cuts crusted over with dried blood. Letting her eyes leave the man, she gave a fast glance around the room. Aye, she was still at the castle. Where was Lady Lochalsh? How high from the ground was that window on the other side of the room? It appeared unbarred. The man stood silent, watching.

Colin finally cleared his throat and spoke. "She is dead. If you are looking for Lady Lochalsh, she is dead."

Rowan looked at the laird and something in his eyes made her glance down at herself. She was naked. Appalled, she whipped down and grabbed the bedcover. Keeping her eyes fastened on the man Arden, she carefully wound the cloth around herself, leaving plenty of room for her legs to move.

"She is dead." Colin repeated patiently.

"Then what am I still doing here?"

Colin gave a smile. Direct as always. No coy questions. He replied in kind, "You are here to get well. You are still in the castle, but you are safe."

Narrowing her eyes at him she wondered why a mere hunter would have charge of her. And why anything this man thought or said should make any difference. "Just how do you know that I am safe?"

"Because Laird Lochalsh said that you are to be protected."

"Och. And I suppose you know the laird personally?"

"You could say that aye."

Rowan's eyebrows rushed together in a frown at his arrogance. It was just like the night they spent in the woods. She felt as much at a disadvantage now as she had then. Without warning, the burst of energy that had taken her from sleep to flight, deserted her. Shivering, she tried to control her legs but they gave way and she landed in the center of the bed with a thud. Colin moved to her side, reaching out to help. She slapped his hand away.

"Get away from me. Dinna touch me."

Her words were cold, haughty and the laird drew back, frowning. Rowan saw the look and smiled to herself. The great hunter was not used to being spoken to like that, was he? Well, if he thought that she was going to cower at the sight of him, just because he was her jailer, he was wrong. "So, I am a prisoner here?"

"Nae. You are here until you can heal."

Rowan's hands went again to her throat. A hazy memory came to her and she shuddered and swallowed hard. She shook her head, concentrating on the memory. At once everything unfolded like a flower in spring; Silobah's beating, her fall from the window, Gwynneth. She swallowed again and tried to control her shaking. Her eyes began to water. Fiercely she wiped a tear away. She wouldn't cry in front of this man. She refused to show weakness.

Colin watched her struggle, well aware of the power of memories. He had occasionally felt the same after battle. Memories were often stronger than the real event. Without thinking, he reached out his hand to smooth the hair on her head.

Rearing back at his touch, Rowan yelled, "Take your hands off me! Dinna you dare touch me!" Scrambling backwards to the other side of the bed, she threw the words at him while moving out of his reach.

"So, the laird wants me protected? So, the laird wants me to heal? Well, the laird can go to hell for all I care. I want to get out of here. Now. You can go and tell the laird exactly that."

A voice from the other side of the room took her breath away. "You just did."

From her crouch on the bed, she looked up. Elden stood in the doorway. Rapturous, she leapt off the bed to greet him, tightening the bedcover as she ran. Elden held up his hand and she jerked to a stop.

"Rowan, I know you were brought up in the wild, but do you nae think you could at least act like a civilized human being to the laird?" He nodded in Colin's direction.

She gave him a confused look. The laird? "Nae. This is no laird. He is the hunter, Arden. The one who has too many hands and eyes."

Elden shook his head. "No. Arden is the name of the laird's friend. The man in this room is Colin of Dunrobin, Laird of Lochalsh."

Rowan's mouth popped open. She looked at Elden and he nodded his head, eyes smiling. Turning back to the bed, she sat down, carefully arranging the bedcover. Her eyes suddenly narrowed to slits. Jumping up she faced Colin, her hands balled into fists. He had lied. He had let her think he was a mere hunter. She thought back to the night they had spent together and her cheeks went red. And this morning! He had continued the ruse, knowing well that she had no idea who he was. He had baited her and enjoyed it!

"You! The great hunter! You canna," her words were cut off as Elden walked forward, reached out, and grabbed her up into a hug.

"Rowan. I dinna think to find you alive last night."

Rowan looked into her brother's face, all thoughts of the laird vanishing. She kissed his cheek then snuggled deeply into his arms. As she did so, Elden staggered and Rowan pulled back looking down at his foot.

"What happened?"

"Nothing of great importance. You know how I am in the woods."

"You can barely stand."

"It dinna matter last night." Colin spoke up. His words were followed by silence. From the safety of Elden's arms Rowan turned her head and glowered at him. Tilting his head to the side, Elden peered around Rowan and gave the laird a look.

Colin began to move toward the door. "I am going now. You will let me know if you need anything?" He smiled at Elden.

"And you will do me the kindness of letting me help you when you decide to leave this time?"

Elden smiled in return, then turned his attention to Rowan. Colin closed the door softly behind him.

***

"She is going to be all right?" The question brought Colin up from his thoughts. Arden stood in front of him, his hands on his hips, his wrist heavily bandaged, his eyes questioning. Colin nodded his head then turned his eyes back to the fireplace. Arden walked to the opposite chair and sat heavily, truly not expecting an answer. He knew that Colin needed the time to absorb the events of last night. The gods knew he did himself. He rubbed his eyes, sleepily. How any of them had slept, after what they had been through was a mystery to him. Surely Rowan did so because she was still drugged.

What Arden didn't know, was that in his sleeplessness, Colin had paced the hall outside of Rowan's door until he had given up the battle and entered the room to persuade Elden that he needed his rest. He had pressed his case that he, Colin, was trustworthy enough to watch the lass through the night. After helping Elden to his room, Colin had returned to sit beside Rowan, watching the rise and fall of her chest, listening for anything that would indicate pain, hoping she dreamed at ease. All night he had sat thus, ready to tend to her needs.

While he sat, he dozed with dreams of his own. Dreams of taking her in his arms, running his hands down that long white body and twining his fingers in her curling red hair. He had awakened with a snort and a realization that dreams were one thing but reality was another. Looking over at her still form in the bed he knew that any such dreams must not include taming her. She was wildly independent and would tolerate no reins. It was part of her attraction, this fierceness and determination. Yes, he wanted her strong and free, but he also wanted her for his own. How could he place his claim on her when likely she would balk at his slightest advance? He thought sadly of poor Silobah. The old one would no doubt have given him a love charm. As thoughts of charms and prophecies flashed through his mind, he smiled. Perhaps his promise to Robert the Bruce to marry the daughter of Lord Stannard would come to his aid. After all, that is indeed what he would be doing if he could make Rowan his.

Abruptly he left his musings and returned to the present, finally answering Arden's question. "She is fine."

Arden looked up to see a smile on the laird's face. "You spoke with her?"

Colin looked at his friend and raised an eyebrow. "Spoken with wouldna be the words I would choose. Yelled, commanded, directed, threatened. Aye. Speak? Nae."

Arden watched his friend carefully. It seemed that any traces of sadness at Gwynneth's death were gone. "So, it is as easy as that?"

Colin's face changed. His jaw tightened. His words had a strangled sound to them as if he were dragging them up into the light. "I know what you are referring to and it is nae easy as that. I know it was partly my fault. Dinna think I havena blamed myself. I could have done things differently, aye. I could have faced things straight on instead of avoiding them. But no matter what I could have done, you know as well as I that Gwynneth was Gwynneth. I dinna think I could have changed her."

Arden heard the words of self-blame and nodded to himself, Colin was taking his share, as he should. Acknowledging that the past could not be changed and wanting to ease his friend's burden, Arden began speaking of other things.

"Do you think it came from her mother, this madness?"

Colin shrugged his shoulders, "That I dinna know. But I think it likely, partly by blood and partly by teaching."

"It could also be part of the prophecy of True Thomas. Remember, Lord Stannard destroyed the old grove and built the castle on its remains. And it is his blood that ran in Gwynneth's veins."

"Aye," Colin said, "but prophecy can only happen when the soul is willing."

"That sings true."

Colin looked at Arden and continued. "Gwynneth's willingness and the dark prophecy combined were powerful indeed, but at least now the Stannard name and blood are gone. It is time for castle Lochalsh to live free of hate and vengeance."

Arden nodded and spoke, "But Stannard blood remains on this earth in the girl Rowan. Can the castle and land truly be free unless she helps with the cleansing?"

Colin shook his head. "Only Briac will know, but it seems to reason that this would be so."

Arden nodded his head and spoke. "Briac, then."

Colin agreed, "Briac indeed. Send word for him to attend us. We need him here to set the old gods at peace and set the future for Lochalsh." He paused then continued, "and while you do that, I am going to set plans of my own."

Arden rose from his chair and looked down at his friend. "You sound as if you are preparing to go into battle."

Colin looked up and laughed. "My friend, you dinna know how truly you speak."

***

Elden finished recounting the tale. "And Silobah told you that you are Fiona's daughter, and Gwynneth's half-sister. Now you know all of it."

"All but who the laird is." Rowan's voice was wry and Elden gave a shout of laughter. It felt good to laugh. Laughter after tears was always a welcome release and the gods knew there had been tears enough.

He continued to speak as she pulled the long leine over her head. "How was I to know you would wake before I could come speak with you? The first thing I was going to say this morning was that the hunter who found you in the woods was the laird, but he beat me to it."

Rowan blushed at his words, recalling her thoughts about that night. She settled her garments, then frowned as the leine swished the floor. As sure a trap for the foot if ever there was one. Gathering the material in one hand, she walked to the window and looked out toward the forest. She longed for the peace of the woods.

"What are you looking at?"

"The forest. I want to go back."

"Back to what?"

Rowan turned and gave Elden a sad look. "Back home. Back to what we had. Back before this happened."

Elden watched the emotions play over her face. He understood what she wanted as clearly as he understood that it could never happen. Too much had changed, too much had been revealed. It was not the old path they could return to; it was a new path they would have to carve out. "We canna return, Rowan."

"Aye," she acknowledged tiredly, "I know that even you canna turn back time. But can we at least go back to the highlands?"

"Our home is burned. We have nothing but the clothes on our backs."

"But surely the laird would give us a horse and food after all that has happened. And there is the clan."

Elden nodded his head, "Aye but you know the clan has never felt easy with us. And by the time tales of what has happened reach their ears, the stories will have you as an enchantress and me as possessing the dark arts. No, it is not to the clan that we can go. And Rowan," he paused to look her straight in the eye, "you know well that things have changed."

"Then, perhaps not go to the clan, but we can build another croft."

His voice sharpened. "You know of what I speak. Get your head out of the forest and use your mind. I speak of other things. Our path has changed. You are now the daughter of the English Lord Stannard. You are heir to the dark prophecy that rose when the old grove was destroyed. You share a sire with Gwynneth and you share the blood that helped a curse fall on this castle and its land." He took a breath and tried to soften his words. "We must look for a new path."

Rowan folded her arms protectively over her chest. "We can think of a new path just as well in the highlands as here."

Elden matched her tone, "You mean you can hide from all of this just as well in the highlands."

"Actually, I'd rather neither of you went to the highlands They jumped as Colin walked into the room.

Rowan looked at him, her face hardening. "I will do as I wish."

Elden shook his head at her rudeness. Aye, he didn't expect her to treat Colin like a laird. Rowan would never treat anyone like a laird, but neither did he condone her rudeness. His words were sharp. "Rowan, this man saved my life and yours. Dinna be so rude."

Rowan whirled around and the words flashed out of her mouth in a torrent of hot anger. "And should I be pleasant to him? This man who allowed his lady to hunt us down like rabbits in the woods? This laird whose men burned our home. This ruler who could not even rule his own lady but let her prey on the weak and the helpless. I should be pleasant to him?" she paused panting for breath as if she had run a long distance, "I think not my good brother. You may find it in your heart to treat him as your laird. I see only an ordinary man and a weak and undecided one at that."

She turned her back on both of them and stared determinedly out of the window. Elden started to speak but Colin held up his hand for silence. Elden let his eyes travel from Colin to Rowan. So, the fates would have it settled this way. He had played his part and now it was time to let the gods have their turn. Quietly he took a deep breath and made his way to the door, closing it firmly behind him.

Rowan continued staring out of the window. "It wasna more than he deserved. Did your laird leave the room with his tail between his legs?"

A firm hand came down on her shoulder and she felt herself roughly turned around. "No, he did nae leave the room with his tail between his legs."

Rowan gave a strangled gasp. Looking up into Colin's eyes she struggled against his grip. Her words were low and harsh, "You let go of me. You get away from me. Now."

Looking down at her, he saw the lass in the woods, angry, strong, and defiant. But he also heard desperation in her voice, the fear and panic that lurked under the unforgiving tone. He released his grip and answered her anger. "If you would, will you nae give me the chance to explain myself?"

Rowan turned and faced the window, desperately longing to fly out of the opening and into the woods, away from all that had happened, all that she now knew.

He watched her. She had every right to hate him, every right to want to turn her back on him, on her heritage, and run to the highlands. But he couldn't let that happen. He could not bear the thought of sending her off knowing he would never see her again.

Rowan spoke to the open window. "Why should I listen?"

Colin could not think of one single reason except he did not want her out of his sight, and he did not think that would be something she would happily hear at the moment. He kept silent.

Looking down into the courtyard, Rowan saw Elden sitting on a bench, his foot being examined by a man and wondered if that was the real Arden. Was he a healer? Her brother certainly needed one. Silobah. Rowan shut her eyes in sadness.

Seeing her soften, Colin began. "I need you to listen because there are things between us that we need to set right."

Rowan opened her eyes, turned, and gave him a look.

He continued. "I was so involved with my own anger that I gladly ignored Gwynneth and any signs of her falling into madness."

"Anger?" Her words sharpened. "Were you hunted and had your home burned? Were you captured and almost killed? No?" She gave him a hard look. "What had you to be angry at?"

Colin paused. She was right. But he would never keep her if he did not explain. He pushed ahead. "Yes, Robert the Bruce gave me the lands and title as a reward for my part in the victory. But he also ordered me to marry Gwynneth to seal our dominance over this part of the land."

"So, you did. And that proved to be such a hardship?" She knew that it had been so. She knew well that he had been forced into a union with a madwoman. But the need to leave all that had happened behind and return to the forest drove her words.

Colin took a deep breath. "Not a hardship to obey Robert the Bruce. It was an honor to do so. But the marriage was doomed from the start with Gwynneth's hatred for the Scots and her belief that her parents were purposely murdered. Anger comes easily when the one you married hates you to the very marrow of your bones."

Rowan had no response. She had felt Gwynneth's hatred herself. She thought back to this man protecting her through the night in the woods and trying to send her back to the highlands.

She thought of him sitting guard in her bedroom as she recovered. Surely no man such as that should incur such hatred from a wife.

Colin plunged ahead. "I will admit that once I recognized her hate, instead of trying to change her heart or mind, I chose the easier way, the wrong way. I turned my back and ignored her. I was often gone, and when here I distanced myself by training my men and hunting. Those who Gwynneth injured turned to Silobah, and the old one forbade them to speak of it. Indeed, they knew it wise to keep quiet." He frowned remembering the stable boy begging that Gwynneth not be told his words.

"And so, you let her do what she would."

"And so, I let her do as she would, not knowing the whole truth of it."

Silence filled the room for a few moments and then he broke it. "As for her hunting you and Elden, I knew nothing until the deed was done."

Rowan thought back to her mad ride through the woods and Arden, no, Colin pulling her from the stream. Once more, she smelled the wood smoke. The image of Colin carrying her when she could not walk, rose in her mind.

"You wanted me to be safe and away in the highlands."

Colin wisely kept silent.

"I would like to go there now."

"And I would like you to stay."

There it was. Out in the open. Said and unable to be taken back. Rowan stood completely still, turning her eyes to look out of the window, across the courtyard, and into the forest.

Seeing her look of longing, Colin backed away to give her space. "I am sorry to have taken so much of your time. You need to rest. I will send your brother to attend you." He raised his hand to touch her, but wisely dropped it to his side instead. Quickly, and before she could demand a horse to ride away, he left the room.

***

Rowan stirred as the door opened. After Colin left, she had slept the day away, succumbing to the lingering effects of Gwynneth's herbs and days of unrelenting fear. But now she sat straight up in the bed, casting a wary eye on the man approaching her, holding a tray. "Where is my brother?"

"I sent him to an early bed with a draught for his ankle. It still pains him greatly."

Rowan gathered her legs beneath her and pulled the bedclothes closer. "You do not look like a wise woman."

The big man leaned his heavy head back and laughed out loud, "Nae I do not. And I'm no serving wench either." Smiling, he placed the tray of food on the small table beside the fire. "You'll have the food here or do I bring it to you?"

"No. I'll come." She slid out of the bed and swayed on her feet.

He walked over to steady her. Ignoring his hand, she weaved her way to the chair. He grinned to himself and leaned his back against the fireplace. He imagined his friend trying to put a leash on this one. He spoke. "The laird had me bring this food."

Rowan gave him a sideways look, "That would be Laird Colin? The one who told me his name was Arden?"

"Och, aye. And I told him that I was not to be insulted thus."

Rowan gave him a swift look as she settled in the chair. "Isn't he your laird?"

"He is my friend first, and a good and loyal one at that."

"But not so good at handling his castle and lady."

"I dinna say he was perfect, only that he was a good man."

Silence settled as Rowan picked at the food. Pausing for a moment, she leaned back and looked quietly into the fire, remembering that other fire. The one beside which Arden, no, Colin she reminded herself, had kept her safe and then let her go free. A frown crossed her face and she spoke to Arden. "You say he is a good man."

"Och, aye." He kept silent and did what he was very good at, waiting.

Rowan began her argument. "Then why did he not work to change his wife?"

Calmly Arden replied, "I said he was a good man, not one who can work miracles."

Rowan stared at him stonily and began to speak but Arden interrupted. "Remember Lass, you are here, well and alive."

Rowan sat back, blinking, then gathered her ammunition. "Yes, alive but just barely."

He moved away from the fireplace and sat in a chair on the other side of the table. He held her eyes and spoke. "You canna fault him for what he dinna know."

Seeing her look, he held up his hand for silence then continued, "Any more than he can fault you for what you did not know."

She looked up at him in astonishment and he calmly continued. "Aye, you did not, could not have known that you shared blood with Gwynneth. And he did not know the depth of Gwynneth's madness. No one knew these things except Silobah and she kept her secrets well hidden from us all." Settling himself back into the chair, he looked at the fire. "I'm nae saying he does na have a way to go into becoming a full-on man, but I am saying he is a good man with a true and solid heart."

The fire crackled and Arden continued. "I'm also saying that now that you both know these secrets what are you going to do with them?"

Rowan looked a question at him and he answered.

"You have Stannard blood. The same blood that destroyed the old grove and began the curse. This curse killed your mother and almost killed you. Are you going to stay and help cleanse the land and this castle, or are you going to run back to those highlands of yours and hide?" He stayed quiet, perfectly happy to wait.

"I have to get home."

"Why?"

Rowan frowned at the fire. "I'm safe there," she paused gathering her words "and free."

Arden broke in, "You were not safe in the forest, Gwynneth's men hunted you down and burned your home. And how can you be free if you lock yourself away in the high forest hiding from what you know must be done?"

Rowan gave a tiny shudder remembering growing up, knowing deep in her hidden heart that her mother had abandoned her. The knowledge had made her determined to let the high forest hide and protect her. But the highlands had done neither. And her mother had not abandoned her. In fact, she had died giving her life. What was there to hide from anymore? And shouldn't she honor her mother and her sacrifice by helping to remove the curse? Surely this hated Stannard blood has some useful purpose.

Turning from the fire, she looked thoughtfully at the quiet man. "You would have me stay, then?"

"Nae lass, I would have you want to stay. There is a difference."

Rowan thought of Elden resting and healing, thought of the burned croft, thought with heartache of Silobah, of her mother. No. No one could truly foretell the future. One dealt with what one had, what one gained through living. What she had gained had come with a terrible price, but the earth under her feet felt more solid, sweeter, and life suddenly seemed increasingly filled with promise.

Taking a deep breath, she gave a nod to the fire. And then a smile tilted the corner of her mouth. "Tell our good laird that I will consider staying on one condition."

Arden turned and gave her a look. "And what is that?"

"I will have that black war-horse he rides."

Arden exploded with laughter. This lass would only give in so much and would reveal her feelings to no one. But she had made up her mind to stay. This he could see in the set of her chin. And she was determined to do so on her own terms, this he could see by the gleam in her eyes.

Colin's prized war-horse. That would send him spinning in fury. The lass would certainly demand this bargain and he could hardly wait. Colin would be convinced he could handle her, and she would be convinced she could handle that stallion. Pausing, he looked into her steady eyes. Aye. Indeed, she most likely would handle both.

Printed in Poland
by Amazon Fulfillment
Poland Sp. z o.o., Wrocław

37301487R00152